CW01433068

FINDING LOVE AT THE MAGICAL CURIOSITY SHOP

JAIMIE ADMANS

B
Boldwood

First published in Great Britain in 2025 by Boldwood Books Ltd.

Copyright © Jaimie Admans, 2025

Cover Design by Alexandra Allden

Cover Images: Shutterstock

The moral right of Jaimie Admans to be identified as the author of this work has been asserted in accordance with the Copyright, Designs and Patents Act 1988.

All rights reserved. No part of this book may be reproduced in any form or by any electronic or mechanical means, including information storage and retrieval systems, without written permission from the author, except for the use of brief quotations in a book review. This book is a work of fiction and, except in the case of historical fact, any resemblance to actual persons, living or dead, is purely coincidental.

Every effort has been made to obtain the necessary permissions with reference to copyright material, both illustrative and quoted. We apologise for any omissions in this respect and will be pleased to make the appropriate acknowledgements in any future edition.

A CIP catalogue record for this book is available from the British Library.

Paperback ISBN 978-1-80483-888-4

Large Print ISBN 978-1-80483-891-4

Hardback ISBN 978-1-80483-892-1

Ebook ISBN 978-1-80483-890-7

Kindle ISBN 978-1-80483-889-1

Audio CD ISBN 978-1-80483-897-6

MP3 CD ISBN 978-1-80483-896-9

Digital audio download ISBN 978-1-80483-894-5

This book is printed on certified sustainable paper. Boldwood Books is dedicated to putting sustainability at the heart of our business. For more information please visit https://www.boldwoodbooks.com/about-us/sustainability/

Boldwood Books Ltd, 23 Bowerdean Street, London, SW6 3TN

www.boldwoodbooks.com

For Nancy Landry.
You were so much more than just my best friend's mum. You were an honorary mum to me as well, a ray of light, warmth, caring, and kindness, and the world got a little bit darker when we lost you. You are loved and missed, forever.

1

There are two types of people in the world – people who appreciate the value of *stuff*, and minimalists. I'm the former. An unfortunate number of my customers are the latter.

'Oh my God, this place is ah-maze-zing!'

I hadn't heard a customer come in, and I shriek in surprise at the unexpected voice behind me. I was on my hands and knees, trying to grapple a butterfly-shaped side table into a space in the window display after a customer had ransacked it, and I push myself onto my feet and pop out from behind a canvas painting of a fox dressed up like a Tudor king. My movement dislodges a bucket containing stems of dried flowers, and they go crashing down. The giant sunflower hits the floor with such force that the flowerhead explodes, sending seeds skittering noisily across the shop.

The customer is a young girl, probably teenage-ish, and her hands are clasped over her mouth to cover a gasp as she spins on the spot, looking around in awe as her eyes flit from the rainbow mosaic horse's head on the wall, to the drapes of vintage fabrics hanging from the ceiling, to the vast array of unusual ornaments and oddities that cover every available surface.

Now *that* is the reaction I want my customers to have. Maybe business would be better if more of them did.

The girl's eyes flick from me to the scattered sunflower seeds still pinging across the floor. 'Sorry, I didn't mean to make you jump.'

'It's okay, I should know my way around without bumping into things by now.' I wave towards the rest of the shop, slightly perturbed by a young girl coming in alone. Most of my customers are antique collectors and curiosity hunters, and the only youngsters I usually see are bored ones, being dragged along by parents and complaining all the way. 'Feel free to look around while I clear this up.'

She glances at the door behind her, almost like she's waiting for someone to come after her.

I grab the dustpan and brush from behind the counter and start sweeping, trying to keep a furtive eye on my visitor because there's something off about this, I'm sure of it.

'I'll help.' She crouches down and starts gathering the dried sunflower seeds with her hands, and I can't help noticing that she's sort of backing behind a display table, and she keeps glancing at the window, almost like she's trying to hide.

'Are you waiting for someone?'

'No.' She says it quickly and when I continue looking at her expectantly, she huffs with a typical teenage eye roll. 'Just my dad. He's *sooo* boring, he'd hate a place like this. He said I could come in on my own. He doesn't mind.'

There's something in her tone that makes me wonder if that's the whole truth, but before I can work out what to do about it, the door suddenly flies open with such force that it nearly tears off its hinges and a man rushes in. 'Have you seen a— *ow!*'

He's in such a flap that he doesn't see my hanging birdcage candle holders and crashes smack-bang into one, and I cringe as the sound of metal connecting with his very handsome face reverberates through the shop.

He lets out a yelp and a hand flies up to his forehead at the point of impact. His eyes scan the shop and fall on my young visitor. 'Ava! Thank God! Don't you *ever* do that again! You can't just disappear like that! I didn't know where you were.'

I *knew* she wasn't telling the whole truth there, and underneath the hand he's still holding to his injured forehead, her dad looks so flustered and panicked that he must have been racing around Ever After Street, frantically searching for her.

'We were watching the carousel and I turned around and you were gone!'

'I didn't want to go on the carousel! It's for babies!'

'You can't sneak off like that! I thought something had happened to you! And *you!*' He turns to me. 'Why are you harbouring a young girl on her own? You must've known she'd run off!'

'Me? How would I know something like that?' I feel myself bristling instantly. 'She told me you'd said she could come in by herself.'

'Oh, she did, did she?' He goes to raise an eyebrow and then winces when it obviously hurts the head injury.

'I don't want to hang out with you!' Ava gets to her feet and folds her arms. 'You're boring! And this place is *sooo* cool!'

'This place is a hellhole! *Who* leaves hanging things right in the doorway?'

'Oi! That's my shop you're talking about! And it's not *in* the doorway, it's to the side of the doorway – *you* weren't looking where you were going.'

'I panicked, okay?' He twists around to glance back at the

doorway and the birdcage candle holders *beside* it. 'I thought my daughter had been kidnapped! I didn't know if I was ever going to find her again! Anything could've happened!'

He puts a hand on his chest, forcing himself to take deep, calming breaths as he looks around. 'And now I see she's been swallowed up by the local junk shop, so I was right to be concerned.'

'It's a curiosity shop. It's not junk, they're curiosities, see?' I resist the urge to poke my tongue out at him. He's not the first customer who doesn't understand the concept of a curiosity shop, he undoubtedly won't be the last.

'Dad, shut up! It's a Treasure Trove!'

'The clue is in the name. Treasure wouldn't be treasure if you didn't have to hunt for it.' I point to the sign behind the counter where, admittedly a little bit obscured by all the other things hanging on the wall, The Mermaid's Treasure Trove shop sign is displayed, and I trill a line I've said to many customers who complain about the... well, they call it clutter, I call it beloved items just waiting for their new owner to find them and give them the home they deserve.

'Just ignore him, he was raised by wolves,' Ava says to me and then shoots an angry glance at her father. 'Unpolite ones!'

'It's *im*polite,' he corrects her, still grimacing underneath the hand held across his forehead.

'Wolves that are sticklers for grammar, apparently.' I try to ease the tension I can sense between them. I should probably keep my mouth shut, but anyone who calls my shop a hellhole deserves everything he gets. 'And actually, both are correct. The word started off as "unpolite" but that spelling has become obsolete over time and "impolite" has become the more accepted usage, but that doesn't make it wrong.'

She gives me a look that suggests she's about to burst with joy, and *he* gives me a look that suggests he'd quite like to roast me into a pile of ashes on the spot with his strikingly blue eyes.

'You are the coolest person ever! And this is the coolest shop ever! And look at your hair! I *love* your hair!' She comes over and picks up a lock of my long red hair. 'Oh my God, Dad, look at this. Someone put colour in their hair and no one died!' She tucks the lock back into place and turns back to me. 'No one died, right? When you went to the salon and had colour put in your hair? Nothing bad happened?'

Right now, my cheeks are arguably redder than my Ariel-red hair. I've never been considered cool before and I'm *really* not used to strangers touching my hair without permission. 'I, er, don't go to a salon, I do it at home over my bathtub.'

'And nothing catastrophic happens afterwards? No natural disasters? The world doesn't end? No police? No serial killers?'

'Er, no.' I feel awkward because I've clearly got myself into the middle of an ongoing father-daughter argument.

'Well, this random stranger is in her forties. When you're—'

'I'm thirty-eight!' I snap indignantly.

The man sighs before reluctantly correcting himself. 'Well, this random stranger is in her *late* thirties. When *you* are thirty-eight, Ava, you can do what you want with your hair. Until then, *nope.*'

She rolls her eyes and huffs. 'At least not everyone's got a stick up their bum like you, Dad!'

'You're way too young to be talking like that!' He shakes his head in despair. 'Where do you even learn these things?'

I stifle a giggle as she stomps off into the other half of the shop without answering. It used to be a storage room, but when my father ran the place, he got the doorway widened so we could expand the shop space, and the staff area upstairs became a storage area instead. Back then, it was just me and him, and the house is within walking distance, we didn't need a staff area, and now it's just me, I'd rather use the space we do have for my beloved objects.

'Sorry about that. And the age thing. I didn't mean to insult you.' The father's eyes flick in the direction his daughter went. 'Blame my tired eyes rather than your wrinkles. Not that you have wrinkles. Or not that I've noticed if you do.' He makes a noise of frustration and scrubs a hand over his face, pulling my eyes to the way his fingers catch on the dark stubble covering his jaw. 'I'm going to stop talking now. Sorry.'

When he takes his hand away from his forehead, I grimace at the sight of a bleeding cut and what will be an *angry* bruise tomorrow. 'Stay there, I'll get you something to clean that up.'

I race up the stairs, grab a cloth from the kitchen and soak it under the hot tap, and then run back down to find him hovering in the same place near the door. He takes the cloth from me and holds it to his head.

'Is it bad?' I step away to give him some space and accidentally back into a life-size resin model of a flamingo and steady it as it wobbles precariously.

'What, the gaping cut or the thumping headache?' He takes the cloth away and checks it for blood. 'I'll live, probably. Today has been stressful enough without the added head injury though, so thanks for that.'

It's totally sarcastic, and after how insulting he's been so far, no one would blame me for ignoring his earlier apology, but I'm intrigued by how utterly weary he sounds, and he's still got a slightly panicked look about him, like he hasn't quite recovered from Ava's disappearance yet. He keeps looking in the direction she went, like he's worried there might be a back entrance she can sneak out of and vanish again. 'Long day?'

He looks at his watch. 'Well, we left the house three hours

ago, and I feel like this afternoon has lasted for three months. I thought this would be the perfect father-daughter outing to kick off the summer holidays but, apparently...' He raises his voice to ensure his daughter overhears. '...Ever After Street is for *babies* and is *seriously uncool!*' His voice lowers again as he looks at me. 'So I've been told 24,601 times so far today, anyway. This is the first shop she hasn't wanted to leave immediately in case she gets spotted by someone she knows and is *sooo* embarrassed to be seen dead in somewhere *so babyish*. Maybe I'll get something right one day, but I won't hold my breath.'

'Teenager?' I ask.

'Thirteen. What gave it away? The sulking, the insults, or the tantrums in a public place?'

'I heard that!' Ava calls from the other side of the shop.

I often worry about the lack of customers, but with these two in here, it's probably a good thing there *isn't* anyone else to get in the middle of the tension between them.

'And *you* weren't interested in hearing *that*. My apologies, again.'

He's got the whole Prince Eric look going on – bright blue eyes and the darkest black hair, a straight nose with a wide tip, not unlike one of Flynn Rider's wanted posters. He's the kind of gorgeous that makes your mouth go dry, and makes you stand up straighter, self-consciously smooth your hair down, and suck your stomach in without even knowing why. He's highly unlikely to be single, and even if he was, I have no intention of trying to seduce him. My last relationship ensured I'd never be tempted to try to seduce anyone ever again, or let myself be seduced, in the unlikely event of anyone trying.

Even so, I can't help myself sneaking a quick peek at his ring finger. No wedding ring. Promising?

No, not promising. Mickey! What are you thinking? He's obviously struggling with summer holiday parenting and schools only broke up on Friday. Men with issues are even more off-limits than men without issues, and all men are no-goes for me for the rest of forever.

I watch him as his eyes wander around the shop, his lips pressed into a thin line that's becoming thinner with every object he takes in, like he's trying to figure out what to criticise first. Eventually he goes back to the hanging birdcage that nearly took him out just now. 'Why do you have a birdcage with no birds?'

'It's decorative. You can put candles in them. And a curiosity shop is hardly the place to keep birds in captivity, is it? They're Victorian, from the times when families used to capture wild songbirds and keep them in the house to sing to them.'

'Victorian birdcages would have been made of brass or wood. This is aluminium if I'm not mistaken. Cheap aluminium that will bend if you press it too hard.' He reaches up and does exactly that. 'Aluminium was discovered in 1825 and the difficulty in obtaining it made it rarer than gold in Victorian times. Believe me, they weren't building birdcages out of it. They're not Victorian, they're cut-price tat, most probably made in China.'

'They're a *throwback* to Victorian décor. I didn't mean they were actually Victorian. This is not an antiques shop. There's a *curious* mix of everything in here.'

'From the looks of it, there's not a *mix* of everything, there's simply *every* single thing that anyone's ever thrown out.' His hand shoots out and he rummages in a basket and pulls out a scrap of fabric and holds it up. 'Why do you have a basket of fabric pieces?'

'They're *old* fabric pieces. Scraps of fabric can be important to crafters or vintage collectors or people who remember things like curtains or bedding from their childhood and want to remi- nisce.' Even as I say it, I wonder why I'm defending myself. What

I stock in my shop has nothing to do with this judgemental stranger and I don't have to justify it to him or anyone else, despite how guilty I feel about the bloodied red mark blooming on his forehead.

He grunts and puts it down again. One hand is still dabbing at his forehead with the damp cloth, and he shoves the other one into a pocket of his smart trousers with a pin-sharp centre crease. Hopefully the spiky tone in my voice was enough to tip him off that his opinions are unwanted here.

A few minutes pass in awkward silence, interspersed only by gasps of joy and various iterations of 'ohmigod, I *love* it' and 'coolest thing *ever*', and I keep expecting him to follow his daughter through and have a look around, but he seems glued to the spot right inside the entrance. 'You can come in, you know. You don't have to loiter in the doorway.'

'I have a great fear of what else might fall on top of me. I've found a safe spot here, I'll stick to it, thanks.'

'You're blocking the door for other customers.'

He glances at the door behind him with a look that suggests other customers are about as likely as seeing Bigfoot toddle up the road carrying a handbag and twirling an umbrella. 'Well, if you're suddenly overwhelmed with a rush, I'll get out of the way. Or provide Search and Rescue support when they get lost inside, or first aid when something leaps forth and attacks them. You can barely move in here!'

'That's not true! You can move.' You can't move *much*, mind, but I'm not giving him the satisfaction of admitting that. All right, it's a tad overcrowded, but it's a charming hotch-potch of treasures. It's not supposed to be organised with military precision. It's intended to be a jumble where customers can unearth objects they'll love and cherish for the rest of their lives, but his words make me squirm uncomfortably. I worry my shop has reached the stage where it's too crowded, and hearing it said so blatantly does nothing but confirm my fears.

'You can't honestly believe all this has value. Given the quite odd disembodied half-mermaid statue outside, I thought it was going to be mermaid themed but there's no theme at all. It's like you opened the shop door and let every forgotten storage unit in Britain throw up in it.'

I want to laugh at his turn of phrase, but I stifle a snort behind my angry look. Who does he think he is? I want to tell him that this is a perfectly successful little business, full of treasures that I rescue from where they're unwanted, and I keep them safe until a new owner can find them and give them love again, but given the lack of customers lately, 'perfectly successful' might be pushing it a bit. Besides, I don't have to justify that to anyone, let alone some random man who thinks he knows best. 'Does it ever cross your mind that not everybody wants your opinion? I've been running this business for the past couple of years, and for decades before that with my father. What gives you the right to come in here and be so judgemental and derogatory?'

He goes to answer but ends up mouthing at the air when no sound comes out. He blinks at me, open-mouthed for a minute, and then goes to push a hand through his hair and accidentally clonks the hanging birdcage again, sending a metal clang ringing through the shop, and shakes his head, and I get the impression that it's more at himself than at me.

'You're right,' he says quietly. 'It's been a rough day and I'm taking my frustration out on you and lashing out at your shop. I'm sorry.'

'At least your daughter has better taste than you, and better manners when it comes to giving strangers their unfavourable opinions,' I mutter, secretly quite glad to see the look of shame that accompanies his apology.

He's an odd one. Opinionated but also, quite apologetic? That's not the first time he's said sorry in the past few minutes, and his face has reddened at being called out on his rudeness. He's the kind of man I should dislike, but he's also quick to apologise and there's something about him, a sadness or tiredness that makes it seem like there's no heat behind his words, plus it's really hard to dislike someone who looks like the real-life version of my first ever childhood crush, Prince Eric from *The Little Mermaid.*

'And it's not a weird disembodied half-mermaid statue. It was a full mermaid once – my dad bought it for me when I was a little girl. It's stood outside for decades, but it was looking a bit sorry for itself after years of wear and tear, so my dad cut it off at the waist, repainted it, and turned the tail upside down, so it looks like the mermaid is diving into the street.' I struggle to keep the emotion out of my voice because it was one of the last things he did before he died. He wanted to give my beloved statue a new lease of life when he knew that *he* wouldn't be around for much longer. 'No one insults my mermaid's tail.'

'Sorry, I didn't know it was so important.'

I've obviously failed at hiding the emotion it brings up, because he looks genuinely guilty, and I wish I hadn't bothered trying to explain. Why does it matter to me if he likes my shop or not?

He takes a tentative step further in and touches a hand to the side of his head, indicating the starfish clip in my hair. 'You're really committed to the role, with the hair and the T-shirt.' He runs a hand across his chest, meaning the slogan across my top.

It's not a uniform as such, but I collect T-shirts with mermaids on them and I've amassed quite a collection of pun slogan tops, and today's one is blue with waves and a mermaid's tail diving into them, and the words 'Nice to sea you'. 'I love mermaids. I wanted this place to feel just like Ariel's underwater cave of wonders but on dry land.'

If he was going to say something disapproving in response, he doesn't get a chance because a shout comes from the other side of the shop. 'Oh my God, I *love* it! I *have* to have it!'

There are footsteps as Ava comes barrelling back into the main shop with an ornament tucked under her arm. It's a skeleton in an elegant sitting position with a huge pair of colourful butterfly wings on its back. I've been calling it a dead fairy and I knew someone would love it one day.

'This is the best thing I've ever seen!' she squeals. 'It's going to look incredible in my Instagram photos! All my friends are going to love it!'

'Ava... Not everything is about social media.' When she turns and glares at her father, he trails off and pinches the bridge of his nose, and I feel a bit sorry for him. Despite his harshness, he seems out of his depth, and that look crosses his face again – the one that suggests he's secretly wishing for someone to rescue him.

'I want to buy literally everything.' She puts the butterfly-winged skeleton on the counter and I hurry back over to serve her. 'This place is so cool.'

'Thank you.' I blush as I say it. It's been a while since my shop was complimented like that. It used to be cool, but it doesn't feel cool these days, not even to me. It feels cluttered, and if I'm honest, maybe a bit stifling? I used to love spending the days in here when my dad ran it, but now...

'You have the best taste. And I love your starfish clip. And, oh my God, you're even wearing Ursula's necklace.' Personal space is not an issue for her as she reaches over the counter and lifts the large gold-painted shell that's hanging on a cord around my neck, an exact replica of the necklace the Sea Witch uses to capture Ariel's voice. 'That's so awesome.'

'Thanks. My best friend, Lissa, runs the Colours of the Wind museum and she had it made for me as a birthday present. If you're staying on Ever After Street for long, you should go there. It's the coolest place.'

Ava nods excitedly.

'Maybe next time,' her father mutters, sounding like there might be an icy blizzard in hell before there's a next time.

The tension between them is palpable and I try to ease it. 'Right, one dead fairy coming up. I have a box somewhere.'

Ava laughs at my description and I can feel her eyes on me as I crouch down to root around behind the counter. Most things I sell don't come boxed, but I keep a selection of boxes that are likely to fit certain items, and bubble wrap for fragile things, and it's all in a heap under the counter shelves and I can never find anything when I want it.

'Is that a mermaid on your arm?'

Ava has spotted my tattoo and I stand back up and lift my sleeve, revealing the outline of a mermaid sitting on a rock. We can only see her back and her long hair as she looks out into the distance, and most of her is hidden under the sleeve of my T-shirt, but her tail wraps around my elbow.

'That's so cool.' Her fingers reach out and brush over the scales of the mermaid's tail. 'I want a tattoo but Dad won't let me.'

I laugh out loud and then glance at her dad. 'I don't think me and your dad would agree on many things, but he might have a point with that one. Maybe one day, eh?'

'Why doesn't it have any colour when you're so colourful?'

I blush again because I haven't felt colourful for a while now, but my cheeks go so red that they definitely qualify.

'I couldn't decide what colour I wanted it. I was going to go for a green tail and red hair, but she wasn't meant to *be* Ariel, so then I thought of a blue tail and black hair, but... I was going to go back when I'd decided but I never did. What colour would you choose?'

'*All* the colours! A rainbow mermaid! Something bright like you.'

My cheeks burn as I blush even harder than I ever knew it was possible *to* blush. 'Do you want to colour it in for me?'

'She's thirteen, she's not a tattoo artist.' Her father sounds exasperated.

'I know, but I meant... Look, I found these a few weeks ago.' I crouch down again and root around underneath the counter, wondering where the heck I put the pack of pens in question and how things manage to go walkabouts in this shop as soon as I take my eyes off them.

'Here they are— argh!' I stand up to thrust them in the air victoriously and let out a scream of surprise. The father has finally stepped into the shop, and now he's leaning so far over the counter to see the disorganisation behind it that I nearly collided with him. He jumps backwards and holds his elegantly fine jaw like I've punched him in the face with the pens, even though I'm certain I would've felt it if I'd made contact with *that* stubble, and my shop has surely caused him enough injury for one day.

I put them down on the counter with a satisfied nod, and he peers at them. 'You shouldn't put ink on your skin. I have enough problems without strangers in shops teaching my daughter that it's okay to draw on her skin with Sharpies.'

'They're not Sharpies, they're tattoo pens. They're completely safe for skin – you use them to test out designs and placement for tattoos before getting anything final done. They wipe straight off.'

His raised eyebrow has 'disbelieving' written all over it, so I add, 'Look, I'll prove it.'

I draw a star on the back of my left hand, shake it for a few seconds to let it dry, then clumsily tip water out of my bottle and wipe it away with a tissue. It fades slightly but leaves a definite star-shaped stain. I hide my hand behind my back. 'Well, it'll come off with a bit of soap.'

'Can I, Dad?' Ava is already selecting her colour choices from the pen pack.

'Only if…' He looks bewildered as he holds a hand out towards me, asking me to fill in my name.

'Oh, Mickey. I'm Mickey.'

'Only if Mickey doesn't mind,' he finishes.

'It would be an honour to see someone else's vision for my plain tattoo.' I rest my elbow on the counter and stretch my arm out so she can reach the entirety of the mermaid.

Her hand clamps around my arm to hold me in place. 'Mickey like the mouse?'

I laugh because it's not the first time I've heard something similar. 'Mickey as in short for Michaela, but no one's called me that since the headmaster in primary school when I helped the class hamster make a bid for freedom.'

She giggles. 'I'm Ava.'

The dad doesn't offer to introduce himself, so while she colours my arm like a colouring book, I look at him expectantly until he relents with a reluctant grunt.

'Ren.'

'Ren?' I raise an eyebrow. 'Is Stimpy nearby?'

For the first time since they came in, his mouth turns from a thin line into a smile, and it's a thing of beauty. 'You must be a nineties kid with exquisite taste in childhood cartoons.'

'They don't make TV like they did when we were growing up,' I say, because I assume he's roughly a year or two older than me. 'Is Ren short for something?'

'No.' His huff suggests that it *is* but he's not about to enlighten me.

'Dad's name is Brennan,' Ava says without looking up from her work.

'Dad's name is only Brennan when he's in very severe trouble with your grandmother,' he clarifies.

She looks up at me. 'He's in very severe trouble with Grandma *all* the time.'

I glance up at him and meet his eyes. 'That I can believe.'

It's almost like he wants to smile again, but he looks away instead, taking another moment to cast his nit-picky eyes around my shop. 'Okay, I get that there are weird things in here, but why on earth is there a jar of forks on the counter?' He takes a step closer so he can pull one out and hold it up to the light. 'And why are they all bent and twisted?'

I go to answer, but Ava gets in before me. 'Dad! They're not forks, they're dinglehoppers!'

I grin. 'Exactly. You know how Ariel thinks a fork is called a dinglehopper and it's for brushing her hair, and then she goes to dinner with Prince Eric and sits there combing her hair with one? I get a lot of old mismatched cutlery collections that are useless for selling, so why not make the most of them with a quirky touch? A bit of heat from a hot air gun, and I can curl the tines to make them a little bit different. Some people think it's weird, some people get it.' I nod to him and then to Ava in turn – the former and the latter. 'They're free. You can take one if you want.'

He looks at the jar like he'd rather stick a bent fork up his own nostrils, but Ava stops colouring to carefully select one. Her brown hair is in a side plait, and she uses the dinglehopper to brush through the ends and then hands it to her dad to hold for her. 'Thank you so much!'

'Yeah, we'll be sure to treasure it forever,' Ren mutters. I have no doubt that, if it was up to him, he'd be looking for the nearest bin as soon as they get out the door.

Eventually Ava steps back from the masterpiece on my arm, where my mermaid tattoo has now got her tail scales neatly coloured in every shade of the rainbow, and purple streaks amongst her black tendrils of hair, and it's such a bright explosion of colour that I'll be sad to wash it off in the shower tonight.

'Best fun ever! Can I take a photo?'

'Only if you take one for me too.' I get my phone out and hand it to her and she makes an effort to get the perfect angle.

I tidy the pens back into the packet, and Ava moves the skeleton to the middle of the counter again, and I go back to hunting for a box under the counter, and when I stand back up again, one clutched in victory, she's opened a purse and started counting money out onto the counter. There's a five-pound note, a two-pound coin, and I can see the panic on her face as she desperately roots through her purse, counting out small change. She looks towards her dad like she's about to ask him for the extra money, and I decide to save her the trouble. 'You know what, I'll take a fiver for it.'

She gasps. 'Will you really?'

'Sure.' It was priced at £10, but I'd rather things go to someone who really loves them, no matter what they can afford. 'I don't own anything in this shop – I'm just keeping it safe until it can find love again with a new owner, and this dead fairy has definitely just found her new owner.'

'Oh my God, thank you *so* much, you're the best!' She looks so delighted that she might be about to vault over the counter and hug me, and I can't help smiling at how happy it's made her. *This* is how I want customers to feel when they find a treasure they can't live without.

Ren's look of disdain suggests he thinks otherwise. I meet

Ava's eyes and roll mine in solidarity as I fit it into the box and poke polystyrene packing in around it. 'Maybe your mum will like it.'

His lack of wedding ring has piqued my interest and, when I see an opportunity to work it into the conversation, I can't stop myself pushing for more info...

'I don't have a mum.'

...and regret it immediately.

'Ava! That's categorically untrue. Just because your mother's not here right now—'

'Mum left.' She interrupts him to explain to me, and then turns back to him. 'Why do we have to pretend she didn't? I used to have a mum, now I don't. Now she's swanning around in Italy with her new boyfriend and she's forgotten we exist because all you do is read and drink tea!'

I cringe internally at the oversharing, but he cringes visibly. He turns to me with his hands held up. 'Sorry, Ava hasn't learned that we don't share personal matters with people in shops yet.'

'It's not personal, it's fact. What am I supposed to say when someone mentions her like that? "Oh yeah, I'm sure she'll love it, except she hasn't bothered answering a text message in over a year and couldn't care less if we were alive or dead?" If I pretend everything's fine, you'll have a go at me for lying!'

'Ava!' He pinches the bridge of his nose again, looking like he's trying and failing to stave off a headache. 'Mickey doesn't care. She doesn't know us. We don't know her. This isn't a conversation to have with a stranger.'

'I care.' I bite my lip, feeling stuck between the metaphorical rock and hard place. He's right, of course, whatever's going on in their family is nothing to do with me, but Ava clearly needs someone to talk to, and I recognise her need for someone, *anyone*, to know what she's going through. 'I like hearing stories. Every object in my shop has one, and so does every person. Everyone deserves to have their story heard. And I'm sorry,' I say to Ava. 'It was presumptuous of me to mention your mum. I know all too well what it's like to grow up with people assuming you have one, and how awkward it is to have to explain that your family isn't like other families and to feel different and out-of-place.'

'You don't have a mum?'

'My mum died when I was five. I grew up with my dad who was trying his best too. I'm sure there are many, many...' I glance at Ren and give him a half-smile to let him know I'm joking. Well, half-joking. '...*many* things to insult your father about, but is drinking tea really one of them? Would he be a better person if he drank lemonade instead?'

'At least it might fizz him up a bit!'

We both giggle, and Ren is trying not to laugh too. 'Oi! I think tea-drinking is a gene that every Brit has but it lies dormant until you hit your twenties and then you suddenly realise there's nothing better than a cuppa.' His blue eyes flick up to me under thick black eyelashes. 'And the reading is for work. I'm a history teacher and I take my students' books home with me for marking.'

A history teacher? Colour me surprised, although that explains the knowledge of aluminium and Victorian times. 'You're way too—' Hot. Gorgeous. Um... I've got myself into hot water with this unfinishable sentence. 'Young!'

A spark of imagination strikes at last, but I'm certain they both know what I was really thinking. 'You're way too *young* to be a history teacher. When I was in school, my history teacher was so decrepit, the entire class joked that he taught history because he'd been alive since the 1700s. He used to drone on and on about various battles. Sometimes he'd go quiet and someone would have to poke him to double-check he hadn't died mid-lesson.'

Ava giggles and Ren gives me a grateful nod, like he realises I'm trying to ease the atmosphere. 'I'm sure your customers don't usually overshare this much.'

'Oh, you'd be surprised. I know *everything* there is to know about Mrs Moreno's bunion trouble, her wait for a hip replacement, and her cat's urinary incontinence problems. There's oversharing and there's *over*sharing.'

Ava giggles again and Ren tries to suppress a smile. I can see the tension in his shoulders physically ease under his blue jacket, and it gives me a warm glow inside to have given them a moment of light relief. It didn't seem like they were having the best afternoon. This is exactly why I like trying to engage with strangers who come in. *Everyone* has a story. Everyone is going through something, and most people are all too happy to talk about it, and I love hearing stories.

'What's the story behind the skeleton fairy?' Ava's hand rubs over the box as I wait for the ancient till to finish printing the receipt.

'I think she was waiting for a boy she loved. It's the way her hand is reaching out towards someone. Maybe he was a fairy prince, promised to someone else, but he swore that he was going to be true to himself and come to her, but ultimately he was too much of a coward, and she died waiting because she never gave up on love.'

'Awwwww.' Ava's looking around like she wants to know the stories behind more objects. 'How about those plates?'

She points to a display of a dinner set, the key pieces shown off in a glass-fronted cabinet, the rest boxed up underneath. They're a beautiful pearlised white plate with delicate red roses and green stems around the edges. 'I got them from an auction. I like to think they belonged to a young married couple. Maybe they got them as a wedding present. I can picture them sitting down to their first meal together as husband and wife, or maybe this was the good china that they only got out on special occasions. Maybe this was saved for the meals when both sets of in-laws came over. Maybe one disapproved of the other, but the only thing they could agree on was how pretty the china was.'

Ava looks enthralled, but Ren looks confused. 'But what make are they? Are they a sought-after brand? How old are they? Are they in good condition? Are they valuable?'

'I don't know. I'm not running an antiques shop here. I think they meant something to someone once and they will do again one day, they're just waiting for their new owner to find them.'

'And, meanwhile, gathering dust and taking up a huge amount of space you could use to display something that might actually sell or clear some of this clutter.'

'Dad! You can't call it clutter! It's a collection, like Ariel's!'

'Ariel had a cave full of junk, and so does Mickey. The only difference is that Mickey thinks other people want to see hers, whereas Ariel had the decency to keep hers private. Disposophobia is what it's called – the fear of getting rid of things.'

Ouch. I recoil like an insect has stung me. I square my shoulders and try to look unbothered, even though he's hit a nerve. 'Well, it's a good thing it has absolutely nothing to do with you then, isn't it? Why *are* you so interested in how I run my shop anyway?'

'I'm not, I...' He seems stumped for a moment, like he's just realising how his opinions are coming across, and then he waves around the cloth he was still holding to his forehead. 'If there was less clutter, there'd be fewer head injuries. My interest is solely from a health and safety perspective.'

Ava gives him a death glare and then turns back to me. 'Just ignore him. He doesn't mean it.'

'It's okay. He was raised by wolves, right?' I try to cover it with a carefree grin, but that comment *hurt*. It shouldn't. His opinions shouldn't be relevant to me, but the lack of customers lately has made me wonder if he isn't the only one who thinks this, but he's the only one both brave enough and rude enough to say it out loud. He's also unwittingly confirmed one of my underlying fears – that there's too much clutter in here and, one day, a customer could get hurt.

'Some people will always be too uninspired to believe in the magic of things, and will never understand how wonderful it is to find an item that feels like it was meant to be yours, or to look at something and be transported into another world.'

I think he can hear the wobble in my voice because that look of guilt crosses his face again, and he goes to say something but stops himself before any words come out.

'We're all puzzle pieces. Parts of us are scattered across the world, and every so often, someone will find one of their missing pieces and it's a joy to witness. That's what my dad wanted when he started this shop and that's what I want with my collection.' I'm fighting to keep my voice calm, but they can definitely hear the internal struggle.

One man's disparaging opinion is no different to every other person's disparaging opinion. Usually I can shrug those off, but there's something about Ren, a sharpness combined with a softness that makes me wish he was one of the ones who got it.

'Well, this is the best shop I've ever been in.'

'Thank you.' I try to cling onto Ava's words, while he shoves a hand through his product-filled hair awkwardly, knocking one foot against the other, like he still wants to say something.

'We should go.'

'I don't want to go,' Ava replies.

'I think Mickey's about to evict us,' he says with the guilty look again.

'*You*, maybe.' I frown at him. 'Ava can stay as long as she likes.' She gives him a 'so there' look.

He edges towards the door, keeping a watchful eye as if other items of my stock are about to leap out and attack him. 'Well, as the adult in charge of today's activities, we've got about ten minutes of paid parking left before we get a fine, so *now*, please.'

Ava huffs like a typical teenager, complete with an 'it's not fair' eye roll, and picks up the box with her skeleton ornament in it. 'Thanks for everything! We're totally coming back soon!'

He holds the door open to ensure she goes through it without being distracted by anything else, and once she's safely outside and taking a photo of the mermaid's tail statue, he turns back to me. 'And thanks for looking after her when she'd run off. At least when they're toddlers you can put them in reins, but people frown on that when they're teenagers and you're just expected to be able to keep track of them... a glaringly impossible task.'

I appreciate the difference between what he said at first and now he's calmed down. 'No problem. And I'm sorry about the...' I point to my own forehead and grimace. 'I *will* move the birdcages. I didn't mean for that to happen.'

'It's okay. Not much harm done. I'm sorry about the teenage drama and the oversharing and the...' He waves a hand in the general direction of my stock, probably meaning being so forthright with his unfavourable opinions. 'Maybe we'll see you again. If you're not crushed to death by an avalanche of dinner plates, that is.'

'Hah hah!' I call even though he's already closed the door, just to let him know how utterly hilarious his quips are. It's highly unlikely that an avalanche of plates would actually kill me. A serious maiming, perhaps, but death is unlikely.

Despite it only being 3 p.m. when they leave, they're the last customers of the day. I wanted a string of visitors to metaphorically prove Ren wrong, but it isn't to be. I tidy the displays outside, hoping to encourage people in, but no one comes, despite there being plenty of activity on Ever After Street.

We're a little shopping street in the foothills of a castle in the Wye Valley. Every shop is themed after a different fairytale, like me with *The Little Mermaid*, the Neverland Sweet Shop next door, or Marnie, a few doors up the street, who runs the Tale As Old As Time bookshop. As it's the school holidays, there are a lot of parents and children running around. The old music of the carousel turning fills my ears and I stand and watch children shouting joyfully with their arms flung out as their wooden horses glide up and down, filling the clearing at the bottom of the steps up to Lissa's museum, full of fairytale artefacts and wishing wells and magical fountains, and I wonder again what I'm doing wrong. Every shop on the street seems to be busy, except mine.

After another couple of hours of staring at the door, willing it to open and hordes of treasure-hunting customers to pour in, I give up and flip the shell-shaped sign over to 'closed'.

I leave the starfish hair clip and Ursula's shell necklace on the counter, because they're part of my costume for work, not really me, and I walk home with Ren's words ringing in my ears. I tell myself it's because it sticks in your mind when you meet someone so rude, but I can't help dwelling on it. Dwelling on how anyone can have so much nerve, I try to tell myself, but the dwelling isn't on that, not really.

I purchase more stock than I sell, and the money my dad left to keep the business going is dwindling. Fast. Customers are few and far between, even when the rest of the street is busy – a fact I've been trying to ignore, but Ren has hit a nerve. My shop does nothing to encourage people to come in. In fact, there's a good chance that so much clutter actively encourages them to stay out. And I keep replaying the sound of my Victorian-style hanging birdcages clattering into his face today. Every time I'm in the shop, I'm constantly bumping into things and knocking things over. I've wondered if a customer could get hurt one day, and now that day has come, and it feels like I *have* to do something about it. I just don't know what. There's so much stuff that it's debilitating, and I haven't got a clue how to make the shop like it was when my dad ran it again.

At home, the house is surprisingly empty. A few ornaments that I've fallen in love with over the years. Some of my dad's most-loved things. There's a tiny framed photograph of my mum, partially obscured by the double-exposure of an old film camera, and now it's been joined by a photo of my dad, smiling before he got ill, and I talk to them like they're really in the room.

I spend most of my time at work, because in the shop, I can pretend to be someone else. The items in my shop let me escape and live in someone else's shoes for a while. I can imagine where every item has been, who it belonged to and how that person came to own it, the romance of the people in their lives and the stories behind who gave it to them and what it signified.

So much of our lives and our loves centre around objects. My fingers rub over the necklace that I wear all the time, *under* my slogan top and Ursula shell necklace. A small, nine-carat gold mermaid's tail on a delicate chain. The one thing of my mum's that remains. That's all I have to remember her by, apart from a few clothes in the wardrobe upstairs, things that Dad recognised but I was too young to remember. That's why I run the shop the way I do – because we know what it's like to be parted from sentimental items and if I can help someone else to find things that might matter to them, then that's what I want to do.

But Ren's got to me. I keep thinking about him. I hope I never have to see him again, and also, kind of hope... they might come back one day. He might have been harsh, opinionated, and unfair, but there was obviously a lot going on beneath the surface, so much tension between them, and they both seemed so unhappy. My instinct has always been to dig into people's stories, and I can't help thinking about his soft eyes and acerbic grin, and Ava's hopeful optimism, like most kids at that transitional age – wanting to both grow up and also cling onto the belief in Disney castles, princes, and fairytale endings, and even though I *know* fairytale endings don't happen in real life, I want there to be people in the world who still believe they do, and I've always wanted my shop to be part of that.

2

The following morning, I wedge the door open with a seashell-shaped doorstop to encourage customers inside. It's a lovely July day, sunny but with a breeze that prevents us moving into hot-and-sticky territory, as I tidy up the tables that I display things on outside for customers to rummage through in the hopes that it might pique people's curiosity enough for them to step through the door. There are tables displaying baskets of smaller goods, and half barrels and wooden crates holding other things, and some artificial plants to spruce things up, pink trees and planters full of plastic lavender.

I swipe a hand across my forehead and lean on the blue mermaid's tail statue for a minute. My shop has an old-fashioned Dickensian feel to it. There are window boxes under the two upstairs windows with yellow petunias tumbling down that I really must remember to water. I can't help wondering what my dad would make of the shop now. He was more into antiques than I am. He used to laugh at me making up stories about every item in his shop and sometimes he'd know their real history and counter my fairytale fantasies with boring old reality.

That's why I'm doing the Philip Teasdale Antiques Fair at the Ever After Street castle at the end of August. My dad loved nothing more than antiques fairs, and he put forward the idea of holding one in the grounds of the castle on the hill at the end of the street. He didn't live long enough to see it come to fruition, but Witt, the owner of the castle, has been kind enough to name it after him, and give me a prime spot for my stall.

I just need to choose my most spectacular pieces to display there, and it could be the difference between days as bustling as they used to be and days as quiet as recent ones. There will be write-ups in trade publications and the whole thing is being filmed and broadcast on local news channels. It's a *huge* deal, and my dad would've embraced the opportunity with open arms, but I've let my doubts creep in.

What do I know about antiques? I deal in 'things people might like' whereas my dad was more into bargain purchases that sold for high-value prices and gave the business much-needed financial boosts. Yesterday, *my* financial boosts amounted to a £30 footstool that a woman bought in the morning, and the winged skeleton I sold to Ava. No business can survive on that.

But if I can display stock that's a talking point, that gets people interested, I could be featured on the TV spot that goes out to millions of households. The Mermaid's Treasure Trove would be front-and-centre in front of many pairs of eyes that have never heard of it before, both casual shoppers and antiques trade insiders, and I could make my dad proud of what I've done with his shop. I just need to find a few special items with *perfect* stories to tell, and maybe business will be booming again.

As I go back in, my hand trails across the basket of fabric scraps and I think of Ren's words yesterday. *Are* they pointless? When I put them out, I thought they were cute and quirky and would be a hit with crafters, but no one's had a look in there in... I rack my brain but I can't think of a time when anyone's *ever* been interested in the basket of fabric scraps. There's even a cobweb around the basket handle.

Impulsively, I take the basket and dump it in the bin behind the counter, and then quickly rescue the basket and just tip the fabric scraps into the bin instead. Something else can be displayed in the basket, minus the cobweb, but Ren might've had a point about the fabric scraps. He might've had a point about more than one thing yesterday.

Even with the door wedged open, the morning is quiet. Mrs Moreno pops in on her way home from the doctors to tell me about her latest consultation in the ongoing 'is it gout or a bunion?' saga, and a few people peek in, take a few steps and look for a pathway through. Others are braver and come in, look around like they're scared to touch anything, and quickly leave. One woman accidentally bumps into a stand of vintage postcards and sends them flying across the shop, and as I scramble around on my hands and knees to clear them up, Ren's words replay in my head. It *is* too cluttered in here, I know it is, and I'm relying on the antiques fair to turn things around by bringing me a flock of customers who *like* hunting for treasures in amongst clutter, but it's starting to feel like that won't be enough. Business is failing. Sales are down, and it's starting to feel like it would take a miracle to improve things, not just an antiques fair.

Perhaps tellingly, a man comes in and buys the rose-edged dinner set. I'd priced it at £50, but he haggles to get it for a tenner below asking price, and seeing as it's my only sale of the day, I agree. I tell him about my theory behind it as I carefully pack the displayed pieces into the box, but he pays no attention to my heartfelt tales.

By midday, I'm leaning on the counter, willing a load of customers to come loping in or accept that it's time to shut the door for five minutes and run across the road to grab a sandwich for lunch from the Alice-themed Wonderland Teapot opposite.

'Hiiiiiiiiiiiiiii!'

I look up at the sound of a very enthusiastic greeting and grin as Ava bounces in the open door.

'Hiiiiii!' I squeak back, easily matching her enthusiasm. She made me feel good yesterday – it's always nice to meet someone who understands where you're coming from, especially when you're not even sure if *you* do any more, and while I hoped I might see her again sometime, I didn't expect it would be the very next day.

I shouldn't, but I can't help looking beyond her to where Ren is standing outside, and I suddenly feel all of a flutter at the sight of him.

'Hello.' I give him a much more solemn nod and sensible-adult type greeting as he hovers in the doorway, holding a Wonderland Teapot-branded box and cup.

He nods in response, but he's obviously not moving fast enough for Ava's liking because she marches back over to the door, takes the box and cup out of his hands, and plonks them on the counter in front of me. 'We got you these! Dad wanted to apologise for being the rudest man on the planet.'

I stand upright in surprise. I wasn't expecting that. I open the box and find a red velvet cupcake inside. 'Oh, my favourite! How did you know?'

'When Dad went up to pay, we were talking about what you might like, and the lady in there overheard your name and said red velvet was your favourite, and tea with vanilla milk.' She nudges the cup towards me too.

I'm so touched, it's a struggle not to well up. What a kind and thoughtful thing to do. 'That's Cleo, she opened last spring and it's been my favourite place on the street since.'

'It's awesome in there! The Mad Hatter did a trick with a rose! He threw it in the air and made it vanish, and then heart-shaped confetti rained down all over us, and then he clicked his fingers and it reappeared again!' She shoves a hand into her pocket and pulls out a handful of heart-shaped confetti made from playing cards and scatters it all over the counter.

I can't help smiling at her excitement. 'That's Bram. Did you love his blue hair?'

'Coolest man ever!'

'Well, you read my mind, I was *just* thinking of running over there to grab some lunch.' I let my eyes flick to Ren again. 'Thank you both.'

'Thought you might not let me back in without some sort of peace offering,' he says, despite the fact he's still hovering in the doorway and he hasn't *come* in.

'I would have.' I don't have enough customers to be turning any away, even the disparaging ones, but I'm not about to tell him that. 'But it was a nice touch. Thank you.'

I smile at him as he finally takes a step inside, looking around warily for the hanging birdcage candle holder, which I've moved to one side of the window, safely tucked away where it can't cause any further harm. 'Thought there might be glaciers in hell before you came back here.'

'I'm weak in the face of being badgered relentlessly all night. I had to accept that we were coming back today or give up a night's sleep because she kept on and on. Apparently I was rude to you yesterday and owe you an apology.'

'You *were* rude, but you're entitled to your opinions, and as far as an apology goes, tea and cake more than covers it.' I hold my cup up like I'm making a toast before taking another sip.

'No. I went too far, and I *am* sorry. It wasn't just Ava's badgering. I felt bad too.'

That apologeticness again. I didn't expect him to give me another thought after yesterday, other than every time he looked in the mirror and saw the cut on his forehead, which is covered up with a couple of butterfly stitch plasters today. I certainly didn't expect him to show up with tea and a cupcake, but it's nice that he did, even if it was mainly Ava's idea.

He doesn't seem like a man of many words, and I'm surprised when he continues. 'I keep doing this thing where I know I shouldn't say something but it comes out anyway. I don't know what's wrong with me, but you didn't deserve to be on the receiving end of it.'

It's a curious confession, an odd thing to admit to a stranger, and yet he sounds humble and serious, so I decide to challenge him a little. 'So what you *really* think is that my shop is charming and quirky and full of treasures untold?'

'No, of course not, I think it's an indoor junkyard, but it would be rude of me to say that.'

I burst into laughter, and he clamps a hand over his mouth and his blue eyes widen as he realises he *did* just say that.

He looks at me in horror for a moment, but slowly, slowly, the lines at the edges of his eyes crinkle up like he's trying not to smile, and he starts laughing too. 'See? I'm a lost cause.'

Again, I should probably be annoyed, but his laughter fills the shop and I realise it's the most I've laughed in ages, and we're both standing there giggling for no real reason.

Ava looks between us like we've both lost the plot. 'Dad thinks you're pretty.'

'I *don't* think you're pretty. I mean, no, wait, you are, of course you are, in an ethereal "creature of the deep" sort of way, with the Ariel hair and the sea-flower.' He touches the side of his head, indicating my hair clip of choice for today – a billowing flower made of blue net and glitter-edged petals. 'Sorry, this has got horribly convoluted. What I was trying to say is Ava was talking about you on the way home yesterday, and I started singing that "Hey Mickey" song, and she didn't get it because she's too young to know it. It wasn't *me* talking, it was the lyrics.' He hums a few lines of 'Hey Mickey' by Toni Basil, and abruptly stops. 'From the look on your face, I'm guessing you've had creeps quoting that song at you all your life?'

'I *have* had creeps quoting that song at me all my life.'

'At least I had the self-awareness to stop?'

'True.' I can't help giggling again because I've gone all flittery inside. Despite the insults, he just called me ethereal. That's such a lovely word and a really, really nice way to describe someone. No one's ever called me anything that complimentary before. Although, by 'creature of the deep' he could have meant mermaidy, or he could have meant that I bear a striking resemblance to a giant squid or a humpback whale. 'Creature of the deep' is open to interpretation.

'And he thinks you're *fine*.' Ava's eyebrows are waggling.

'Ava! It was a song lyric! I *don't* think she's fine.' He looks at me with both hands held up in surrender and a grimace on his astoundingly red face. He looks *so* embarrassed that I almost feel sorry for him.

'Do you have children?' he asks me.

I shake my head.

'Don't. Ever. They will twist everything they hear to humiliate you as much as possible in every way they can conceivably think of. Way more trouble than they're worth.' He gives Ava a pointed but joking look and she grins back at him, clearly loving every moment of winding him up.

'Have you got a boyfriend?' she questions me.

'No.'

'Girlfriend?'

'No.'

'Ava!' Ren chastises her.

'I'm just asking. Mickey doesn't mind, she's cool.'

Cool. I don't think I've ever been cool before. 'I don't mind. I have nothing to hide. All right, so I'm thirty-eight and single again after many disappointing years with my ex-fiancé. I'm not interested in getting into another relationship, ever. I spend way more time with my shop than I ever would with any man and we're very happy together. Is there anything else you'd like to know?'

'Nope, that's it, thanks!' She's already started wandering around the shop, picking up things and putting them down again like she doesn't know what to look at first. 'Dad says I can get one thing today, but it has to be something sensible and practical.'

'That sounds like a very "dad" thing to say. Mine would've said the same.'

She glances over like she wants to question me further, but she gets distracted by going to look at a bejewelled ornament of a melting ice lolly.

'Sorry about that.' Ren takes another tentative step into the shop, looking around for any stock with a thirst for blood. 'I'm trying to teach her that you can't just say the first thing that pops into your head to complete strangers but...'

'But *you* say the first thing that pops into *your* head to complete strangers, so how is she ever going to learn from that?'

'Touché.' He gives me a sarcastic smirk that quickly turns soft. 'And that was really nice of you yesterday to knock money off the skeleton. It made her day. Thanks for doing that.'

'My pleasure. There's nothing better than watching someone find something that feels like it's always belonged to them. It's not about the money.'

'That's a terrible way to—' He cuts himself off before finishing the sentence, and I appreciate him not making it into something derogatory. Maybe there's hope for him yet.

Until he ruins it by saying, 'I'm sure you appreciate me not adding "to run a business" onto the end of that.'

I laugh. 'Yes, very considerate of you.'

We can hear Ava wandering around in the other half of the shop, and he still hovers awkwardly, looking around without actually moving. He looks at the empty spot where the fabric scraps basket was earlier. He must notice it's gone, and this time, I appreciate him *not* saying anything about it.

'How's the head today?' I touch my fingers to my own forehead, trying not to think about how dark the bruising looks around the edges of the butterfly strip plasters.

'Bruised. It's fine as long as I don't touch it, turn my head too fast, or move my face even a millimetre.'

'I really am sorry about that. I kept thinking about you all night. I didn't mean for that to happen, and if there's anything I can do to make it up—'

He holds up a hand to stop my rambling. 'It's fine. I was so worried about Ava that looking where I was going wasn't on my mind. Don't worry about it.'

I appreciate the reassurance because he struck me as the type of person who'd sue the living daylights out of me, given half a chance. 'You can come in, you know. I moved any stock likely to attack unsuspecting customers. You might even find something you like.'

'I don't like anything.'

'What, in my shop or in general?'

He laughs, a completely fake, indulgent little chuckle, and I feel goosebumps prickle my shoulders. He doesn't specifically *say* anything in general, but I have no doubt that's what he means. He'd lowered his voice so Ava doesn't overhear, and I get the sense that *this* is a rare glimpse underneath his sarcasm and bluntness, and I feel my breath catch as a desire to help, to do *something*, overwhelms me.

For someone so outspoken, he seems incredibly shy and unsure of himself, and there's something magnetic about him. I *should* despise him, and yet, I was *hoping* to see him again, and now, I'm desperate to know what that means. He's obviously gone through something with the divorce he mentioned yesterday, and the absent ex-wife that Ava blames him for, and now he doesn't seem like he's having the easiest time with single parenting. There's a hard set to his mouth and the way he holds his shoulders at a pointed angle that gives me a sense of someone barely holding it together.

Like he knows I'm trying to stop myself asking questions, he starts wandering around and examining some of the things on display. 'Why is there a...' He picks up a diving helmet that's been repurposed so the faceplate now holds a clock and then puts it back down again and shakes his head. 'I'm actually not going to ask. I'd rather not know.'

'Just because *you* don't like something doesn't mean someone else won't think it's fabulous.'

He ignores me as he continues to look around. 'It's like a fever dream in here, like that time they brought out mint chocolate flavour Pringles or Jeremy Clarkson was voted Britain's sexiest man.'

It makes me laugh again, even though being compared to mint chocolate flavour crisps or Jeremy Clarkson is definitely *not* a compliment.

'Some of this furniture could actually be quite decent. This is oak, and it looks reasonably old.' He crouches down at a wooden dresser and pulls the decorative cloth covering it aside and rubs at the wood with his thumb. 'Shame about these marks.'

'They give it character.'

He runs that cynical raised eyebrow over it. 'Someone's cat used it as a scratching post, more like.'

'No! There's something deliberate in those marks. Maybe it was in a young boy's bedroom. Maybe he had a crush on the girl next door and he would watch her from the window and he put a mark on it every time she waved to him...'

'So stalkerish *and* fictional, good to know. Where do you get these ideas from? This is a once-expensive cabinet that someone's let their cat go to town on. Nothing more. Seriously detrimental to the value for you though. Antique?'

I shrug. 'No idea.'

'Well, you *should* have an idea! You *should* know the exact value of the things you're selling. You're running a business here!'

'I'm glad you know so much about my business, Mr History Teacher. I didn't realise my homework assignment on antiques was due in today, Mr...?'

He rolls his eyes at my sarcasm. 'Montague. But I go by Ren to anyone over the age of sixteen.'

'Montague? *That's* your surname?'

He nods, and I put a hand on my chest and recite Shakespeare. 'Oh Romeo, Romeo, wherefore art thou, Romeo?'

'Oh, that's clever, I've *never* heard that one before.' His laugh is both sarcastic and good-natured.

'That's pretty cool to share a surname with the greatest romantic hero of our time.'

'Greatest romantic idiot of our time! Note to men everywhere: check your beloved is *actually* dead before drinking poison to quell your heartbreak. It rarely ends well.'

Ren Montague. I repeat the name in my head, feeling like a kid of Ava's age, scribbling the name of my school crush all over my maths exercise book rather than doing any work. Maybe a clue as to why I'm so bad at business now.

It's impossible not to watch him as he continues looking around. Thick black hair, parted at one side and pulled over in a way that would be soft and touchable if it wasn't held stiff with hair product. Smart black trousers and a plain T-shirt with a jacket over it that looks too warm for this time of year. Someone sensible who likes to be prepared for all eventualities, perhaps? Probably the type who never leaves home without an umbrella, even in the middle of summer.

'Why is there half a dragon fruit?'

For a moment, I think he's found some abandoned food a customer has left behind, and then I realise what he's looking at. 'Oh! It's a side table. Isn't it amazing?'

'Amazing?' He echoes like I'm using the word in the wrong context.

'Oh, come on. You've never seen anything like that before in your life.'

It's an entire table, designed so the base is the scaly, almost pineapple-like pink skin, and the tabletop is the white pulp specked with black seeds. It's made of resin and hand-painted to perfection. It looks exactly like someone has cut a huge plastic dragon fruit in half and kept it as furniture. 'One day, someone is going to come in and say, "Ah, this is it! Exactly the thing that I've needed all my life without ever knowing I needed it," and instantly realise they can't live without it.'

He picks up the price tag and draws in a breath. 'For fifty quid, I think we *might* just get by without it.'

'If anything, I've underpriced it. It's made lovingly by hand. Maybe a devoted husband made it for his wife who really loves dragon fruit. What a romantic, one-of-a-kind gift!'

'I don't think *anyone* likes dragon fruit enough to desire a table made in its likeness. No wonder she threw it out, and if your story is anywhere near true, then it probably took place not long before divorcing her husband for his terrible gift-giving choices. Probably the first case of its kind where "side table" is cited on the divorce papers.'

I giggle, and he stares at me for a moment, and then he starts laughing too. 'I want to say that's the weirdest thing I've ever seen, but I *know* there are weirder things lurking in here, and this shop is an endless parade of weird things that will continue surprising me.'

'I like weird things. Plenty of other people like weird things too, otherwise I wouldn't still be in business.'

'Some people *are* weird things.' His blue eyes meet mine and he stops laughing and looks away quickly. I don't think he meant it as an insult, but it didn't come across as a compliment either.

Before things have a chance to get awkward, Ava squeals, 'Ooh, this is it! This is what I want!'

She comes back, carrying a wooden chest that's clearly very old and looks like it was made by hand from sea-battered drift-wood. It's always even smelled of the ocean, and it's decorated with a selection of shells, pearls, and painted ropes, and has got a padlock on it in the shape of a hand-carved anchor. You can imagine Ariel herself keeping treasures from the human world inside it.

Ava looks like she's staggering under the weight, and plonks it down on the counter, panting for breath. 'It's soooo beautiful!'

Ren comes over to examine it and eventually gives a nod of approval. 'That's not bad actually.'

He lifts the lid and pulls open the two drawers with wooden starfish handles at the bottom, checking it over for flaws before he checks the price tag. 'It's heavy and well-made, and you can store things in it. And not *too* extortionate. Okay, we'll take it.'

'I love it! And it will always remind me of Mickey with the shells!'

'Good choice,' I say, blushing that she wants to be reminded of me as I put the price into the till. 'I loved it so much when I saw it, I nearly kept it for myself, but I knew it would find someone who'd love it even more than I did.'

Ava catches sight of my mermaid tattoo and reaches over to touch my arm. 'You didn't wash it off.'

I glance down at the colours on my arm. 'Full disclosure, I kept my arm out of the shower last night because I liked it so much.'

'Awww! I can always come and colour it again for you! Can't I, Dad?' She pointedly cuts off the 'no' that was about to come out of Ren's mouth before he has a chance to form a single letter.

'You're welcome here anytime.' I grin at her and then at Ren. 'Him, on the other hand...'

'Let me guess, only if I bring tea and cake and pay for my daughter's purchases?' He gives me a sarcastic smile and holds a twenty-pound note out, and when I go to take it, the tips of my fingers brush against his. I hadn't realised my hands were cold, but his are warm and the heat makes me jump like static electricity has sparked between us. I look up into his blue eyes and blink for a few moments in silence as a flushy, blushy, feeling of bubbling warmth floods my body.

Suddenly the money is dangling limply in my fingers as he yanks his hand back and shakes it, like the touch has burnt him, and it takes me far too long to pull myself together.

'Works for me,' I say shakily, in response to the question he asked... hours ago? In reality, it was only moments, but it feels like an era has passed.

What am I doing, feeling sparks? There should be no sparks, no sparkles, no fluttery feelings with *anyone*. Especially someone who doesn't get me at all, and is clearly off-limits. Very, very off-limits.

All relationships begin with sparks and then fade into nine years of building a life together that ultimately goes nowhere and leaves you feeling like a needy, clingy basket case. Been there, done that, got the uncomfortable T-shirt.

I wait for the till to print his receipt, because he's definitely the kind of man who *always* keeps the receipt, and slap it down on the counter and push it towards him, because I'm not risking a repeat of handing anything else to him again, ever.

'Yes, right. Thank you for the interesting showcase of the world's strangest items. We'll, er…'

'I want to come back tomorrow!'

'Let's see if we've got time in our busy schedules, eh?' He gives Ava a tight grin, and looks like he's hurriedly trying to come up with a vast itinerary of other summer holiday activities to fill their time rather than coming back here.

'This is ridiculously heavy. Way heavier than it should be.' He grunts as he picks the wooden crate up and shakes it around in his arms. 'And there's something banging around inside it. I'm not paying full price for something that's defective.'

'I've checked it over, Ren. It's in perfect condition. Maybe *you're* defective!'

'Maybe I am.' He pulls both the drawers out from the bottom, and when he lifts it again to give it another shake, there's *still* something clonking around inside.

He puts it down again and reaches in, and there's a hollow clunk as his knuckles knock against the base, and Ava bends down so she can look through the spaces where the drawers were. 'There's something in there.'

'This is a false bottom.' Ren tries to prise open the inner base of the chest as Ava reaches a hand in through the drawer hole and pushes upwards, and there's a creaking noise of swollen wood being moved for the first time in a *very* long time, and the base separates from what I thought was a solidly wooden chest.

We all peer in, and hidden inside the bottom of the chest is a book. A very, very, very old book. The scent of aged paper and the ever-present smell of the sea that accompanies this chest fills the shop, stronger than ever after being shut away for so long.

'What have we here?' Ren lifts the huge book from its hiding place.

A tingle goes down my spine. This is the stuff I live for. A hidden compartment! An ancient book! That smell! I *knew* there was something special about this chest, but I couldn't figure out what it was. I should've known it was hiding a secret of epic proportions. 'Be careful with that! Place it gently on the counter and back away slowly.'

Everyone who deals with old things *dreams* of finding a secret like this. This is the holy grail of things I've always wanted to happen in my shop, and now it actually has, and my heart is thrumming with the possibility of what we're going to find inside, the endless secrets it could hold, and—

'Why would I do that? I've just paid for it. It's mine.'

'It is not!' I gasp in indignation. 'It wasn't included in the price. I didn't know it was there.'

'That isn't my fault. It's up to you to correctly appraise your items. I've purchased the chest and all contents. It belongs to us.'

I wish I had some tea left to throw all over him because he deserves a hot drink straight to the face at the moment, and I'm positively *livid* at his nerve. So livid that, without thinking, I reach over and grab the book from his hands. 'I'll refund your money right now.'

Now it's his turn to gasp in indignation. 'I don't want a refund. I want what I've paid for.'

I can't believe I didn't even know it was there. I remember the feeling of something clonking when I marked it up, but when I didn't see anything, I put it down to a quirk of the old wood. I never noticed that the base of the chest was higher than it should have been. And now this... I curse myself again. Was I too busy making up fantasy stories about the chest to accurately assess it? I imagined a little girl, painting shells she'd gathered from the beach to decorate it with, excited to keep her most special things inside. How could I have got so caught up in fantasy that I missed something so important?

'Well, you're getting one.' I turn to the till and the momentary lapse of concentration gives him an opportunity to snatch it back. 'Be careful! You'll rip it, it's old!'

He holds it with one hand and runs the other one over the aged leather cover. 'We don't even know what it is yet. It could be some old bat's recipe book for all we know. Why are we fighting over it?'

'It's special! We both *know* that. And it's not bloody yours!' I hold my hand out for it, like I'm honestly expecting this ornery, cantankerous man to return it so easily. He knows it might be valuable and is hell-bent on securing it for himself.

He looks down at the book like he's considering it for a moment, but before he has a chance, Ava takes it firmly from his hands.

'Finders keepers! I was the first to spot it, and I want...' She glances between us and then hands the book back to me. 'I want Mickey to have it. She knows about fairytale stuff and old things.'

'I have two history degrees! I know a fair bit about "old things" too. She thinks some bloke made half a dragon fruit into a table for his wife!'

I ignore him and clutch the book to my chest, turning around so he can't grab it again, but instead, he steps away. It seems like Ava's words have taken the wind out of his sails. I place it on the counter and brush my top down like I've been in a physical fight. 'Thank you,' I say to her. 'Do you want to see what's inside?'

She squeals and nods enthusiastically and I beckon her to come in behind the counter with me and then glance at Ren, who at least has the decency to look marginally guilty.

I feel like I should have white cotton gloves on as I open the cover a millimetre at a time, terrified that the spine is going to crack or the pages are going to fall out and scatter across the shop. It's seriously *old*. The pages are brittle, the edges frayed, almost like they could've got wet and dried out again many moons ago. There's a bookmark made of plaited wool, with shells hand-tied onto the ends of it, and the cover is so soft and well-worn that it feels like the leather might rub away under my fingertips.

'Whatever this is, someone loved it very much.' My voice is a whisper because it feels like speaking at a normal volume would be somehow disrespectful to the book.

Out of the corner of my eye, I can see Ren creeping closer again, trying to feign disinterest but peering over anyway.

The writing on the first page is exquisite. The kind of hand-writing you just don't see in this day and age. Ink blotches from a dip pen and inkwell, and calligraphy-like looped letters of faded wording. 'Sixteenth of January 1899,' I murmur aloud and glance at Ava. 'It's a diary!'

'Should we read it?' she asks. 'Diaries are private and whoever wrote it didn't want it found.'

She's got a point, but if this *is* a hidden diary from 1899, there's no *way* we're not reading it, and my eyes have already picked out the first line and to say I'm intrigued is an understatement. 'Well, whoever it belonged to will be long gone by now, and maybe they'd like to think of their legacy living on and their words being read by strangers over a century later...'

'It could have historical value,' Ren says, and despite his earlier attempt at stealing it, I give him a grateful smile for justifying my nosiness, and he takes that as a cue to come closer until he's standing on the other side of the counter again, reading the book upside down, and some parts of his stiff dark hair break free from their product and fall forwards.

'And maybe we were meant to find it?' I suggest. 'I mean, it made itself known just at that moment. Maybe it wanted to be found and it thought we were the right people...'

'I *did* feel like this chest was meant for me as soon as I saw it. So you think it's okay? We're not going to get in any trouble?'

'I think it's fine,' I say, feeling a swell of pride that she turned to me for reassurance like I'm an authority on old things. 'I think we'd be doing the author a disservice if we didn't.'

She nods like that's all she needed to hear, and I'm touched by how thoughtful she is. I deal with old things for a living, and it wouldn't even have crossed my mind to question the morals behind reading someone else's diary, at least, not when it belongs to a stranger from so long ago.

I start reading the first entry aloud.

16 January 1899

There's an unconscious man on my beach. Both of these things are my fault – the fact he's unconscious and the fact he's on my beach.

I thought he was dead at first, but he's not. He struggled as I pulled him from the water, and now, I see his chest moving. The ship he was on is lost to the waves, there is no trace that it ever existed, and the other shipmate is also missing. I couldn't save him. The current was too strong as it pulled the ship beneath it. The other man was still on board, but this one was thrown clear. He was slipping under the water. I probably should have let the evidence of my crime die with him, but I could not watch a human life ending when I was able to stop it.

If anyone asks, they will know it's my fault. They will hunt me down, like they do with all of my kind.

'My kind...' I echo, glancing between Ren and Ava. 'What odd wording.'

His leg is broken. It lies at the wrong angle on the sand. I have seen doctors treating broken legs before. I know it must be set, but I have no equipment here and no knowledge of how to use it. There is wood from the shipwreck and there is rope. I will do it now, while he is still unconscious. His arm is bleeding too. There is so much blood. But I don't know if I can make it up the beach. My fins don't manage well on land.

'Fins?'

'Oh, you have got to be kidding me,' Ren mutters. 'Come on, seriously?'

'This sounds like it's being written by a...' I glance around the shop like it's too ludicrous a notion to speak aloud. 'It couldn't be, could it?'

'A mermaid?' Ava says, looking like she's expecting us to laugh at the suggestion.

'Or some other kind of sea creature? A selkie, maybe? Or a—'

'Great white shark, perhaps?' Ren mutters sarcastically. 'Well-renowned for their ability to hold pens and jot down intimate thoughts.'

'Read more.' Ava nudges me excitedly, ignoring his cynicism.

The wind is still howling and the rain is lashing down. I crawled up the beach. I caressed the broken leg, wishing I had legs just like his. Maybe I would be normal if I could walk like a human can? I pushed a plank of wood from the ship against it and tied it with rope, but it wasn't tight enough, so I used my teeth to tear strips from his wet shirt and fastened the wood against his leg.

He doesn't wake up, but he cries out in his sleep. His teeth grind together. He thrashes against the sand. Does he dream like sea creatures do? Is he dreaming to take himself away from the pain, as I do?

I stroke his hair away from his face. I murmur words but, as usual, no sound comes out. I cannot speak, I don't know why I thought this night would be any different.

I've never been alone with a human like this before. Not one so handsome, anyway. He is... delightful. The way his hair falls across his forehead, covering some of the marks and cuts that I caused. There is blood dripping onto the sand. I make a compress out of seaweed and hold it to the worst wound. There are the black marks of bruises rising on his arms. They are my fault too.

I want to stay, but I know he will be in pain. He will be angry and scared. And I cannot soothe him. I will do nothing but make him angrier, or scare him further. He will not be accustomed to seeing a creature such as I.

I had no warning about his ship coming. It came from nowhere, as did the storm that came across the Atlantic, and now it moves onwards to the east, battering the mainland as it hits the edge of the British Isles, passing across my island like it was never there.

The sun will be up soon. Will he awaken with the sunrise? But then... he will see me. He will know what I am. He will know I am the creature who lured him to his doom. I must go. I must not come back.

'You're not seriously suggesting...' Ren says as the diary entry ends.

'I don't know what else to make of it,' I say slowly. 'I mean, obviously she *couldn't* be... could she?'

'What if she is?' Ava looks at me hopefully.

I feel a little flutter in my chest as my heart fights against my head. Obviously this *isn't* the diary of a real mermaid. Mermaids don't exist, that we know of. But maybe... What if we *don't* know? What if this is somehow proof that they really do exist or at least, they did in 1899?

Ren recognises the war playing out behind my eyes. 'Mermaids aren't real.'

'You don't know that. There's a big ocean out there, with vast depths that have never been explored. Maybe they did exist in 1899 and people didn't have the technology to find them back then. No one knows what could be out there.'

'I'd venture it's not bloody mermaids. And this is way too much of a coincidence. A mermaid-themed shop, run by someone who loves mermaids, and we find this in a seashell-covered mermaid's chest...'

'Maybe it was meant to end up here?' Ava suggests.

'Yes! Exactly that! That's the whole point of my shop – people find things they were meant to find. Who better to find this than us?' I glance at Ava. Me and her, maybe, but probably not him. He doesn't seem like the type for believing in mermaids – he doesn't seem like the type for believing in *anything*.

He rolls his eyes, but still keeps reading upside down across the counter as we read the next entry.

17 January 1899

The sea is calm this morning. I hide on my sandbank. I lie in the water and only peer up occasionally. This sandbank caused his ship to run aground last night. They say all sandbanks were raised from the seabed by mermaids, and what am I, if not a mermaid?

I give Ren a 'so there' look, and barely refrain from poking my tongue out at him.

I should not be here. I was going to leave my island until he is not here, but I do not know how he will not be here. He cannot leave my beach. There is no way off without a ship, and there is no trace of his, only some broken wood drifting on the water.
He still hasn't woken up, but he is restless now, reaching for the surface of consciousness. His body is shaking. Shivering. The sea is my protector – I do not feel the cold from it, but I am not like him. I know where there are blankets. I must get them for him, but I cannot risk being seen. I will go now, before he wakes.

There's a break in the entry, and then she continues.

He is unlike any human I've seen before. He is young, like me. Most of the ones I've seen are old. They want to study me. They push me and prod me and sting me with needles. Others, they want to put me in a cage and charge an admission fee so other humans can come and look at me, for I am something not seen in the human world before.

I go nearer than I should. I sit beside him on the beach. I cover him with a thick blanket. I check his wounds under the seaweed compresses. They are worse this morning, the bruising is darkening, but the blood has dried. I think this is a good sign.

I have signalled for help, but help has not come. I will try again later, but my signals are unlikely to be seen. Help will not arrive until summer. I am alone until then. I try to speak to him again, but my voice does not come. I sing a song my mother tried to teach me, a song to bring peace to sailors, but no words come out. My voice is missing, a flawed and worthless part of me, something that sets me aside from both humans and other merkind. All I wish, just once, is for someone to understand me.

Ava puts her hand on her heart like it's tugging on her heart-strings. 'Why can't she speak?'

'Maybe she's made a deal with a Sea Witch?' Ren's sarcastic suggestion earns him a scathing look from both of us.

'We need to read more.' Ava nudges me. 'I can't wait to find out what happens when he wakes up!'

'Before we get any further *swept away* in this fantasy, why don't we fact check this?' Ren puts his hand on the book, preventing me from turning the page, while also looking pleased with himself for the pun. 'If you're *sure* this isn't some kind of ploy? Something you've planted for publicity?'

'No! I've never seen it before! But publicity... This would be amazing to take to the antiques fair at the end of August. If we could find out more about it... find out if she really was a mermaid... This is the kind of thing that could be the difference between making my business or breaking it. Can you imagine being able to go on the local news with real, true-life evidence of a mermaid's existence?' My mind is flooded with possibilities. This is what I've always dreamed of finding. This is *why* I love old, unwanted things so much, and why I was always so fascinated by the treasures my dad rescued. Every item has a story behind it, and I've always thought that, one day, one of those stories would be truly magnificent. And this is it. This is the most special thing I've ever found.

I need to do something spectacular for the antiques fair. I need to get people talking about The Mermaid's Treasure Trove like my dad would've done. What better way than being the only person in the universe with genuine evidence found in *my* shop? People the world over would hear about it. Customers would travel for miles for a chance of uncovering a rare treasure right here. Maybe some of these items would sell and give me half a chance of paying the bills next year...

I feel like I've fallen out of love with my shop lately, and this has instantly reminded me of exactly how much I love this shop and the things I sell. I used to think this place was magical, but all that has faded since my dad died. This is a perfect way to recapture the magic and remind myself of what was always so special about my dad's magical curiosity shop. 'We have to find out who she was – *what* she really was.'

'Yes!' Ava agrees.

'This is bonkers. You do know that, right? Utterly bonkers.' Ren glances between us and clearly sees that we're both standing firm on this. 'Well, we have two very clear facts that can easily be verified – a shipwreck and a date. There are logs of these things. At least that would be a starting point of figuring out what this is. The other man on board has died – drowned, or been lost at sea. If it's real, there would be a record of that. Whoever she is, she has a beach of her own, and help isn't coming until summer, so she's somewhere alone for over six months, which is very strange. And she's been around medical care, so it sounds like she's met humans before, so presumably, they've also met her. You're trying to tell me that these doctors, and whoever else wanted to charge a fee... that they've encountered a mermaid and this isn't documented anywhere? No one thought to make a record of meeting such a magical creature?'

All right, that is rather a good point, admittedly. *Surely* we would know if mermaids were keeping diaries in the previous century. There would certainly be some documentation about it if humans had ever had contact with an actual mermaid, but I don't see the harm in considering the magic of possibilities that this book could unlock.

'This is clearly old, genuinely old,' he continues. 'But being old doesn't mean it was written by a mermaid. It hasn't been under the sea. Ink from an inkwell is not watertight. If this had ever had so much as a sniff of water, the ink would've dispersed beyond recognition. I know it doesn't fit your whimsical fairytale narrative, but this is someone's flight of fantasy. It's the beginning of a novel. That's why it's hidden – not because it's a diary but because the writer didn't want anyone to know she was writing a novel. Times were different then, women weren't always allowed to have ambitions like they are now.'

'But that would make it special too. Even if it's not a mermaid, wouldn't it be wonderful to have the first draft of a forbidden novel from so long ago?'

'Is there anything you don't put a positive spin on?' He looks from me to Ava. 'And I don't want *you* getting excited and getting your hopes up that this is something fantastical, because it will only lead to disappointment, so let's do some digging before we carry on reading it as a work of fiction and nothing more. I'm in if you both are.'

'I'm definitely in,' I say happily. 'Where do we find records of shipwrecks?'

'The library will have access to archives. If not, a librarian should be able to direct us to the right place. I'll look into it tomorr—'

He yelps when Ava stamps on his foot and he looks down at her, seeming to understand what she means without a word being spoken and then looks back to me. 'If it makes you happy, maybe we could all go... We *should* all go, seeing as we seem to be in this together.'

'I'm up for it,' I say, because despite only meeting them twice, I'm not sure how much I trust Ren to be completely upfront when he so blatantly doesn't *want* this to be anything special, no matter whether it is or not. 'I can close up for a bit anytime and come meet you. It'll be fun. I'm *positive* that we'll find a log of a shipwreck on that exact date.'

'Positivity only leads to disappointment.' He sounds downbeat as he goes to slide the book off the counter and take it, but Ava stops him.

'No! Let Mickey keep it, she'll look after it. She understands the importance of it.'

'*I* understand the importance of it, as a work of fiction, *not* as the diary of something that doesn't exist.'

'Well, with that cynical attitude...' I mutter, although I'm intrigued too. He might be harsh and abrupt and standoffish, but his words speak of someone who's been hurt and disappointed and is trying to make sure it never happens again, and the memory of that tingle earlier hasn't gone away. The thought of getting to see them again, even just for a library visit, sends butterflies swirling through me, and I'm not sure if it's the idea of

proving him wrong or simply the idea of spending more time
with him.

I shake my head at myself. It's nothing to do with *him*. We
have evidence of a *real* mermaid writing a diary here, and it
should be pretty easy to prove whether the things mentioned in it
really happened, and *that's* what I'm excited about, obviously.

'Do you promise not to read any more without me?'

'I promise.' I smile at how much Ava sounds like a little girl
again, and at the sparkle in her eyes that I used to get when I
watched Disney films about princesses and handsome princes,
and believed that was what life would be like when I was older,
and for a moment, that's taken over the part of her that's
desperate to appear grown up and be treated like an adult. 'I
won't touch it again until we can all read it. If *we* want to.' I direct
the last part of the sentence at Ren, who gives me a sarcastic smile
in response.

We arrange to meet on Saturday outside the library in town,
and he picks up the now-empty wooden chest and hovers in the
doorway for a moment as they leave, and looks back at me with a
lingering smile that makes me feel even more excited than the
possibility of uncovering evidence that mermaids are real.

3

'Cleo said a handsome man and his daughter bought you tea and cake from The Wonderland Teapot.'

There are many good things about working on Ever After Street – everyone knowing your business before you do is *not* one of them, even if that person is your best friend.

'I think it was more the daughter's idea and not the handsome man's.' I explain to Lissa about the past couple of days and meeting Ren and Ava, and the book we've found.

'And now you're going to the library with them?' She waggles her eyebrows like she's trying to turn it into something suggestive, because the most important fact of my explanation is the involvement of a handsome man and not the potential evidence of mermaids existing. 'That sounds like a date. A very weird date with a teenager tagging along.'

'Ten a.m. on 26 July is the *only* part that makes it a date. He is astoundingly off-limits. I think he's probably a nice guy deep down, but he's obviously been hurt and seems determined to make sure it never happens again. He's so prickly that he may as well be wearing a coat of angry hedgehogs. And he doesn't get the theory behind a curiosity shop and clearly thinks that if there are worse places on earth, he's yet to find them.'

'Right, where does he live? I'll go round there right now and punch him in the nose. No one insults my best friend and her shop, no matter how handsome they are.'

I can't help giggling even though I love her for her protectiveness. 'Luckily I have no idea where he lives and no desire for my best friend to commit acts of physical violence on my behalf.'

'Maybe he's just never met anyone like you before.'

'I assure you, he never wants to again either.' I shrug it off even though I know she was trying to give me a compliment. The less said about Ren and his opinions of me, the better.

'Can I see the book? This is the sort of thing that should be displayed at Colours of the Wind.'

Lissa's fairytale museum is the most incredible place. She has recreations of items from fairytales, displayed like true, real artefacts. Even the most grown-up of hearts could go in there and come out feeling like a child again. Children get to dress up as princes and princesses and literally walk in Cinderella's glass slippers or spin silk on Sleeping Beauty's spinning wheel. It's the most magical place on the street.

'How has it taken you *this* long to ask about the book?' I grumble as I get it out for her. 'You can only read up to the bookmark. We can't go any further than that, I promised Ava.'

'Aww, how sweet. She's got you wrapped around her little finger already.'

'I like her. She reminds me of myself at that age. Caught between the peer pressure to appear grown up and the desire to still be a little girl and believe in magic, and *he* is... I don't know what he is, but he's not conducive to believing in magic. And he's struggling. He seems both angry and completely lost.'

'You've learnt a lot about them in a couple of short visits.' She waggles those eyebrows again.

'It's nothing compared to what I know about Mrs Moreno's cat's bladder issues.' I gloss over it because Ren and Ava have both intrigued me like no other customers ever have, so I change the subject instead and go back to the book. 'What do you think?'

'I don't know, Mick, it's both exciting and too unreal to even consider. All I know is that you must text me updates when you read more or, even better, text me when they're here and I'll come over and meet him. There's no point in working across the street from your best friend if you're not going to let me come over and assess any potential dates.'

'Not a date! And speaking of dates, I'm going to take it to the antiques fair at the castle next month, at least, I am if we can find out more about it before then.'

She squeals. 'You're definitely going to do it then?'

Lissa's had a front row seat to my back-and-forth with my own self-doubt over the antiques fair and trying to live up to my dad. 'I needed something spectacular to stand out, and this is *spectacular*. It could really turn things around for me. A *real* mermaid's diary would get everyone talking, and hopefully, everyone *buying* some of this junk.'

'Junk?'

Lissa's never heard me refer to my stock as junk before, I don't think I ever *have* referred to it that way before, but Ren's words have made me focus on the doubts that I've been trying to ignore, and I keep looking at my shop through someone else's eyes, and what I see no longer feels as magical as it used to feel. It doesn't feel like a shop filled with possibilities, it feels like a shop filled with clutter, where a customer has genuinely been hurt because of it, and *I'm* filled with the feeling that I have to do something or it's not going to survive for much longer.

I'm not ready to try to explain any of that, not even to Liss, and I'm saved from having to when an older couple come in the door.

They look around and glance at each other with a clear look of trepidation on their faces.

'Hi! Can I help you find anything specific?' I say brightly. It's lunchtime and there have only been a few customers so far today, less than a handful of trinkets have sold, but every new person through the door brings the potential for a life-changing sale.

The woman peers at the carpeted floor like dust bunnies are creeping out of the corners, ready to attack her at any given moment, and the man clears this throat. 'We're Clarice Cliff collectors and someone online recommended this place as a source of rare finds. Have you got any?'

'Yes!' I say excitedly. I got some from a vintage fayre ages ago, and although no one's given them a second glance yet, I *knew* they'd be a good investment someday. 'The question is... where did I put them? Bear with me just a mo.'

Dammit, *where* did I put them? I look around the shop cluelessly. There was a whole box full of the colourful ceramics – they *were* over there, but I moved them to make room for something, and then I put them in the second room, and then something else was put in front of them... Panic rises as the memory of when I last saw the Clarice Cliff collection remains out of reach. There had been no interest, and stuff gets pushed aside in favour of new things that might attract more attention, and then it just disappears into the black hole that my shop is surely standing on top of, which is probably the most rational explanation for things disappearing at the precise moment I want them.

'Won't be a tick, I know they're here somewhere.' I flee to the second room of the shop, and stand there looking around, hoping they'll magically hurl themselves at my feet, in the least breakable way possible. Come on, Mickey, *think*. They were down there... no, *there*, and then they... I look around with my finger hanging limply in mid-air like it might magically lead me in the right direction. Oh! Didn't I move them over there and then put a display table in front of them? Yes, I did, I'm sure of it. I pull things aside and dive under the table, letting out an 'ouch!' as I bang both my knee and my head at the same time, and then scramble further in. Everything is at least three things deep in this place, and the things that haven't attracted much interest get left at the back.

My crawling around knocks the table leg, and that knocks something else, and there's an almighty crash as a well-loved life-size nutcracker topples and goes careening into a crate of vintage books that was precariously balanced on a shelf. The books go tumbling downwards and one of them somersaults straight into a display of candle holders, which sends them crashing to the floor where they smash into smithereens, and displaced book pages finish the gymnastic display by fluttering down around the mess.

It's like a life-size game of Mousetrap, where you knock one thing and create a domino effect, but I finally spot the box I'm looking for and yank it out, sending everything around it wobbling too. 'Got it!'

'They've gone, Mick,' Lissa calls out.

Oh, brilliant. I grumble to myself as I clamber out and avoid looking at the surrounding debris and how big the clean-up operation will be this time.

'Did they say anything?' I step over the broken china and poke my head back into the main shop.

She grimaces. 'They muttered something about "chaos" and clicked their tongues a lot. Don't worry about them. They just didn't get it.'

I appreciate her being so nice and trying to save me from the worst of customers' opinions, but as I stand there and survey the damage from trying to find *one* thing, I can't help wondering how many more times I'm going to have to use that excuse. How many more times are customers going to ask for something that I know I have, I just don't know *where*?

Every time I look at that dragon fruit table, I wonder who the heck would buy it. What was *I* thinking in buying it? And how long will it take for another idiot like me to come along and think it's fantastic?

I've always thought that the sentimentality behind my stock is what sold the items, but I've just missed what could have been an easy sale if I focused less on stories and more on organisation, and it makes me wonder again how I ever let things get this bad, and how much longer things can go on like this.

4

I've always loved libraries. The smell of all those books, pages that have been turned and read and loved by so many pairs of hands, and offered so many hours of escape to voracious readers, like me when I was little and looking for a way to lose myself after my mum died.

It's Saturday morning and I'm early because I figure Ren is the kind of man who is *always* punctual and I don't need to add 'perpetually late' to his list of reasons for disliking me, and sure enough, he and Ava are waiting in the library car park and he's looking at his watch, even though we weren't due to meet for ten minutes yet.

Ava squeals and runs over to give me a hug. 'Have you brought it with you?'

'Of course.' I wasn't expecting the hug and I pat her back awkwardly, and then tap the bag over my shoulder, which holds the book, wrapped in a blanket to ensure it doesn't get damaged.

'I can't wait! We're going to prove that his ship went down and a mermaid saved his life!'

'We don't know that,' Ren says cautiously. 'We have no idea

how this ends. The mystery man could die from his injuries in the next entry, and it's very unlikely that there really was a shipwreck at all. Don't get your hopes up, okay?'

I can't help noticing that's the second time he's said something similar to her, and I'm torn between appreciating his overly-cautious-parent approach and wanting to tell her to throw caution to the wind and believe in the impossible.

He turns to me. 'Hello.'

'Hi.' Why am I blushing after just one word? The simplest word, at that. Why has my pace quickened as I follow Ava back to the sensible-looking car he's standing next to?

He gives me a nod. 'I almost didn't recognise you without your costume.'

I touch my hair self-consciously. It's tied up in a messy knot at the back of my head, and there's no flower hair clip or shell necklace. I'm wearing jeans and a batwing top, and didn't bother to plaster on the blue and green glittery eye make-up that I usually wear as a mask. 'It's not a costume. It's a...' I struggle for the right word. It's not a costume, is it? It's just a way of embracing the shop's theme.

'Shield.' He finishes the sentence for me. 'I know. I get it.'

Is it a shield? I've never thought of it in that way before, but now he says it, I realise that I do put things on like armour when I go to work. When my dad was ill, it was *hard* running the shop, telling myself that I was temporarily looking after it for him while he recovered when I knew, deep down, that he never would. I plastered on sparkly make-up, used a brighter shade of hair dye, and amassed a collection of hair flowers, like becoming someone bright and mermaidy created a gap between the woman running the shop and the woman falling apart inside while her father was dying.

I tilt my head to the side and study Ren for a moment because it makes me think of the hurt behind his eyes and wonder about the apologies behind his ruthless words. Are they a shield of sorts too? Maybe he really does get it.

He looks exactly the same as he has on the other days. Black single-pleat trousers, a tightly buttoned shirt, and a navy jacket over the top, despite the fact it's a warm summer's day and a jacket really isn't necessary. Black hair stuck fast with product and a look on his face that wordlessly says, 'What am I doing here?'

'Shall we?' He eschews the need for small talk and gestures towards the library, and when we all walk over, he holds the door open and lets me and Ava go through first.

I stop to inhale the bookish smell, but the library is quiet and the librarian comes straight over. Ren asks her what information they hold about shipwrecks, and we wait while she looks it up.

'There are national archives of wreck reports from 1876 to 1988. I can give you access through one of our computers and you're welcome to browse for as long as you like.' She leads us over to row of computers along the end wall of the library, leans over to put a password into one and navigate to the correct archives, and then briefly explains the search function and the information we'll need to enter, and leaves us to it.

Ren takes the main seat in front of the monitor, and Ava and I pull up a chair on either side of him, leaning close to see the screen over his shoulder, and I catch the scent of his aromatic aftershave, spicy and close to his skin, and it makes me glad I'm already sitting down.

'Right, shipwrecks on the sixteenth of January 1899.' He rubs his hands together and puts the date into the search engine.

No results.

I feel my stomach sink.

He puts in 17 January as well, but there's still nothing. Search parameters for the whole month of January also bring up nothing.

I can feel disappointment biting at my toes. I *really* thought this was going to be real. 'Try February. Maybe the shipwreck would've been logged on the day it was found rather than the day it actually sank. Rescuers would have no way of knowing what day it went down, would they? They'd log it for the day it was discovered.'

He enters search dates for the month of February and it still brings up no results.

I sigh. 'It might not have been found for *months*. It sounds like they're somewhere remote and she said help wasn't coming until the summer. Maybe they weren't found until then. Add March. Actually, let's go through the results until summer and see if that brings anything up.'

He glances at me and then changes the search end date to August. 'I will happily sit here and browse every shipwreck in the nineteenth century if you want. We are not going to find something that never happened.'

'Well, if that's your attitude...'

'My attitude has no bearing on whether this ship ever existed.' He holds a hand out towards the screen and gives me a 'see?' look when the results *still* turn up empty.

I lean over him and change the end date until the January of the following year. Still nothing. As it turns out, 1899 was a remarkably shipwreckless year for the British seas.

'What if it never *was* found?' I can feel hope deserting me and clutch at a straw. 'What if she really did cause this wreck and covered it up somehow? If the ship disappeared beneath the waves and there was no trace of it, maybe when they were rescued, they never told anyone, or—'

'Or the sailor died of his injuries so there was no reason *to* tell...'

'No!' I glare at him. 'Maybe he had amnesia and didn't remember the accident or where he'd come from...'

'Because that's realistic.' He rolls his extraordinarily blue eyes with a bemused half-smile on his face, but he's clearly having none of my optimistic possibilities.

I go over and ask the librarian. 'Would there be reports about ships that were lost at sea? If a wreck was never discovered, it wouldn't be logged as a shipwreck, would it?'

She gives me a curious look because we haven't explained anything about *why* we're after all this info on shipwrecks, but I don't elaborate, because this seems like something we need more info about before we openly tell strangers what we've found.

'There are Missing Vessels books that cover a substantial period between 1874 and 1954, they've recently been made available online.' She leans over her computer at the front desk and then writes down a website address for me, and I go back over, victoriously waving around the bit of paper.

Ren reads what she's written down. 'This won't help us. We have no idea what the ship was called, where it came from, where it was going to, or where it went missing. At this point, reading these won't help. It'd be like looking for a needle in a haystack that's bursting with needles.'

Oh. Damn him and his sensible attitude. Why did he have to have a point? I'm doggedly determined not to give up though. He shifts aside and I pull my chair across to the computer and find a Missing Vessels book that covers most of 1899. There are a load of entries. Ships that were reported missing during that year. I print some pages off, in case it might help later, but Ren is right. There's entry after entry of ships that never made it back to port, but *our* missing ship could be any one of them, or it could not be on here at all.

'Let's read more of the diary!' Ava suggests. 'Maybe that will give us more clues?'

The library is thankfully quiet, and there's a table behind us and we all scoot our chairs over to it. I heft the book out of my bag and Ava turns excitedly to the bookmarked page.

19 January 1899

He's sitting up on the beach. The blanket I covered him with is around his shoulders now, but it's wet with the rain. He hasn't tried to move yet.

He keeps shouting out a name – a man's name. John. I wonder if it is the name of the other man aboard the ship. Does he think that he survived too? Does he think that the other man is responsible for his rescue?

I stay hidden, but I am unable to stop watching him. I should swim back beneath the waves, but it's like I am held here by an unseen force. Try as I might, I cannot leave him.

He's looking for me. At least, he's looking for the person he must realise has helped him, because he assumes I am a person.

'Hello?' he shouts to the sea. 'Is there someone out there?'

Shouting takes his strength from him, and when he recovers, he shouts again. 'Where am I? Where are you? I know there's someone out there!'

At first, I go to reply. I do that, sometimes. I forget that my voice is missing. For just a moment, I feel normal, like someone will speak to me and I'll be able to speak in return. A normal conversation. Something that so many people take for granted without ever knowing how fortunate they are.

'Maybe they've gone for help.' He says it to himself, not realising that I am hiding in the waves, listening. 'That's good. I need help.'

Something thrums in my chest. Help. He does need help. He keeps holding his head, like the wounds are paining him, and every time he looks down at his leg, his face turns a pale colour and he looks unbearably ill.

Water. Food. He will die without them. There are supplies here, but only enough for myself, and they must last until summer. I will have to share them with him, or he will die and my efforts in saving him will be for nothing.

I cannot let him see me. I will wait until he is asleep again, and then take him water.

'John,' Ren says. 'That's one of the most common names from that era. If only we had a surname, we could cross-reference it with databases of people lost at sea, but it would be hopeless without.'

'I thought you didn't believe in this.'

'I don't. But you two do, and I always enjoy an opportunity to prove myself right.' He sounds jokey rather than serious, but the best way to prove him wrong is to read more of the diary.

20 January 1899

He knows I am here.

It was night and he was asleep so I took him some water, I was going to put the cup on the sand beside him, but I couldn't stop looking at him. I stayed too long. I touched his hair, brushed it away from the wounds on his forehead. My hair was wet and the seawater dripped onto his face and woke him.

He reached out and grabbed me. I tried to scream. I dived back to the safety of the ocean, but it was too late. He has seen me.

He sat up instantly. Now, he peers into the darkness in front of him, but I have swum away. I am hiding on the sandbank again, around the shoreline from where he saw me.

'Come back!' he cries out. 'Who are you? Where are you?'

He tries to stand, presumably to chase me, to catch me, but he is unable to because of his injuries. He slumps back onto the sand with a howl of pain. 'Please come back!'

I feel his pain inside of me. I wish I could make it better, but I cannot. People think mermaids have magical powers, but they are mistaken. I am more powerless than any human. I cannot speak for myself, and therefore, I have no value to anyone. I am a creature of no worth and life is better for everyone when I am exiled here, and not on the mainland with them. He will only be disappointed if he sees who I really am.

I put my hand on my heart and glance at Ava. 'This is heart-wrenching. How could anyone feel like that?'

'And she was a mermaid.' Ava looks like she's feeling the same emotions as I am. 'The most special creature of all. How could anyone not value her? How could anyone's life be better without her?'

I assume Ren is going to say something disparaging, but he nods to the book, wordlessly telling me to read on, because he's trying and failing not to get invested in this.

21 January 1899

He knows that I am hiding on the sandbank. Since daylight, he has been watching the water's surface, studying it, searching for the creature he saw last night.

I should have gone, but I stayed. When his eyes moved my way, I went to slip under the water, but my reactions were too slow, like they were on the night of the shipwreck, and he saw me. He has not tried to walk, but he has dragged himself closer to me. He is on the edge of the sand now, the water is lapping at his broken leg.

He speaks to me, even though I am underwater and his words are dulled through the waves. He has a voice unlike any I've ever heard before.

An accent is what they call it. The men who brought me here, they had accents too. They told me they were Welsh accents as they laughed and joked and invented callous names for me, but his is unlike theirs.

'Welsh!' I bang my hand down on the table excitedly. 'The men who took her there were Welsh! This helps! They're somewhere in Wales.'

'Yes, it should be easy to narrow down the 1,680 miles of Welsh coastline. Good work, we've almost found them. And being Welsh is just an assumption, Welsh people can exist outside of Wales, you know.'

I narrow my eyes at Ren's sarcasm, but again, he isn't wrong. But it's our only clue so far, even if it is a *bit* on the vague side.

His accent is soft, lilting and melodious. I feel like falling asleep every time he speaks because his voice is so soothing. Sometimes I drift off and imagine that I can speak too, that we can engage in a conversation, that I could be normal for just a moment.

He tells me he is from across the sea. Ireland. He tries to point towards the borders of his land, but it is too foggy to see so far. I have never been to Ireland. I have never been anywhere but here.

He asks if I was the one who rescued him. He asks if I know the fate of his friend aboard the ship. He doesn't realise that I cannot answer his questions, even though I know the answers.

He starts to cry. I have never seen a man cry before and my arms ache with the desire to slip them around him, like I have so often wished someone would do for me when I am upset. Like my mother used to do when I was little.

Afterwards, he is shaking, and his voice is unsteady when he speaks. He apologises to the water, even though I have not surfaced. Maybe he can sense that I am still here, still listening.

'I'm sorry,' he says. 'I am in agony. I am lost. I am alone. I don't know if John is alive or dead. Please do not think me weak. If I am going to die here, please do not let me die alone.'

It tears apart something inside my heart. I can feel my resolve breaking. I want to reassure him that he will be well, that help will come, but I do not know that. Help may not come. He may not be well. The thought takes my breath away with the force of how desperately I want him to be well. I must do everything in my power to save him.

'Awwww!' Ava and I say the same thing at the same moment, and I continue onto the next entry without waiting to ask.

27 January 1899

'I just want to talk to you. I mean you no harm. You must be the one who has helped me – so you know what a state I'm in, and you know that I'd be unable to harm a crab, should one

happen along. Show yourself, please. I only want to know what you know. I want to thank you for what you have done for me.'

For days now, he has been talking to me. I have taken him food and water at night, and I am almost positive that he is just pretending to sleep, but he has not tried again to catch me. Maybe he is trying to show me he can be trusted, and I feel the tendrils of goodness in me reaching out towards him. He asks for nothing except my company.

I want to sit beside him on the sand, but when he sees me fully, when he sees me for the monster I am, he will know that there is only one creature responsible for his predicament, and for the death of his friend. He will blame me for luring him to his doom, like mermaids are rumoured to have done to sailors for so long.

I have always been scared. I have lived a small life, afraid of what I am and what people will think of me, but now, I can feel the pull to be bold stirring inside of me. To show myself fully, as I am. To give him the company he asks for.

To be brave...

Ava has got hearts in her eyes and the look of someone with a major crush on a new book boyfriend. 'This is amaaaaazing. It's soooo romantic!'

We're about to read another entry when we're interrupted by the librarian coming over to politely let us know that they close at lunchtime on Saturdays, and my desperation to find out what happens next is cut short as we have to leave.

'Of course, we might know more if Mickey knew where this came from...' Ren says as I slip the bookmark into the old book and close it gently.

'I know where it came from.' I slide it back into my bag and pad the blanket around it. 'It was a house clearance, I'm almost positive.'

'Yes, but *which* house? *Where* was this house? If we knew that, we might have a hope in hell of tracing someone who knows something about it. What other items came with it? Was there anything else of oceanic origin? Any papers? Any photos? Any *thing* that might give *any* clue as to the legitimacy of this?'

'I don't know,' I admit, annoyed with him for being right again, and with myself for not keeping on top of things like this. Because he *is* right. The one thing that would help more than anything would be knowing where this came from and if there were any other related items that might be connected to it in the same lot, and *I* should know that, but I don't. Because when new stock arrives, I push aside sensible things like paperwork and organisation and get lost in imagining the stories behind it, and now it seems like we've found a truth that might just be stranger than fiction, and I've failed in the one thing I could have done to help uncover the reality behind it. I've always known I should be more business-minded and stay on top of things like paperwork and record-keeping, and I always feared it would come back to bite me in the backside, and now it has, big time.

5

'We should come back to your shop and go through every single thing to see if there's anything else from the same house clearance,' Ava says as the three of us walk along the road after being kicked out of the library. It's a warm summer's day and she's suggested we walk through town to the park, get ice cream, and read more diary entries.

'Or you're just nosy and want to know what's lurking in Mickey's shop so you can persuade me to buy it all for you.' Ren goes to ruffle her hair but she ducks out of his reach with a scolding, 'Daaa-aad!' like he's the most embarrassing human on the planet.

I can't help smiling. I didn't intend to go anywhere else with them, but none of us knew the library would be closing before midday, and the lure of reading more of the mystery mermaid's diary is impossible to refuse. Given the lack of customers lately, this seems more important than opening the shop today. If we can prove that evidence of a mermaid existing has been found in *my* shop, it would lead to a *huge* increase in customers. And honestly, this unplanned diversion is not the worst way I've ever spent a Saturday morning. I glance at Ren. Not the worst way at all.

Suddenly Ava gasps and lets out a wail under her breath, and her eyes shoot to a group of girls on the other side of the street, carrying paper bags with various shop names on them. 'My friends from school! Oh my God, I can't be seen dead with you! You're a teacher outside of school!'

'I'm also your father,' Ren protests as Ava grabs both our arms and hauls us down a side street in a flurry of panic.

'No one cares about that! Do you know how uncool it is to hang out with your history teacher in the summer holidays?' She shoves her dad until he crashes into me and we both get bundled into the recessed doorway of the nearest shop. 'Go away! Just go away! Not you, Mickey, you're awesome! I'm so sorry!' She glances back across the street to where the girls are gathered outside Claire's Accessories and then looks back at us, and I can see the dread on her face. 'Stay there! Don't come out!'

With one last panicked look, she backs away from us slowly, takes a deep breath and smooths her hair down, and then turns to run over the street and greet her friends. There's a lot of squealing and more air-kissing than you'd expect to see with fashionistas in Paris, never mind schoolgirls in Herefordshire.

I hadn't noticed Ren's height before, but at this proximity, I realise he's around six foot tall and I have to crane my neck to look up at him. I go to take a step away, but the small doorway doesn't allow for it.

He's got his arms up against his chest in a protective stance, and we've been shoved so closely together that they're also against my chest, and his aftershave is in my nose, but his eyes are still on the group of girls gathered across the street. 'Why do I feel like a naughty dog who's just been given a "sit and stay" command?'

'Oh, come on, you must remember being that age,' I say without taking my eyes off the gathering either. 'The worst thing you can *do* is anything that makes you stand out, and the worst thing you can *be* is different in any way. All you want when you're a young girl is to be exactly like every other young girl, so no one has any excuse to pick on you or single you out. A group of schoolfriends going Saturday-morning shopping on their own – she's not going to easily live down being spotted out with her history teacher.'

'Also her father.' He holds up a finger as if trying to make a point, and I jerk my head backwards when it nearly pokes me up the nose. 'She's way too young to be shopping on her own. *They're* way too young too, but their parents must be more laidback than I am.'

'I was shopping on my own at thirteen. My dad would park the car, go his own way and I'd go mine, and we'd meet back at the car park at the agreed time. And that was before the days of mobile phones, so at least she can get hold of you if she needs to.'

'Well, your dad was clearly more laidback than I am too. It seems like *everyone* is more laidback than I am.' It doesn't sound like he means it in a favourable way to himself.

'So you teach Ava's class?' I ask because I'd been wondering about that.

'I teach history to every year group from year seven to eleven, including hers.'

'Is that as awkward as it sounds?'

He looks down and blinks like he can't focus on me at such close proximity. 'Excruciating. She blanks me in every lesson, and I know the other kids tease her about being "teacher's pet" and say she's going to get a 100 per cent pass grade on every exam and an A-plus on every assignment, but I have to be objective. She hates me for not giving her an easy ride, but it doesn't help her in the long run to give her good marks on something she clearly hasn't understood. I just hope *she'll* see that one day.'

'She will.' Without thinking, I reach out and rub his arm because he sounds really unsure of himself, and I get the sense that Ava's aversion to being seen with him has upset him more than he's letting on.

I want to say something reassuring, but I don't know this man *or* Ava, and I'm only imagining the feelings playing out behind his blue, blue eyes.

The one thing I'm not imagining is the look of horror on his face as he peers down at my hand on his arm with a look fiery enough to scald me and I yank my hand back with such force that I clonk my elbow on the doorframe behind me. What the heck was I thinking in touching someone so standoffish?

The girls across the street are about to go into the shop and clearly assume Ava's going with them, and she throws a worried glance in our direction and then follows them inside.

Ren breathes a little sigh of relief and steps out of the doorway, and I think it's quite sweet that he stayed hidden for so long just to avoid embarrassing her.

'Do you want to go?' He's scuffing one sensible black loafer against the other and trying to avoid eye contact. 'If you need to get back to your shop, I can stay here and wait. I don't know if you've ever witnessed a group of thirteen-year-olds in Claire's Accessories before, but it's like the Tardis in there. They could be missing for hours.'

I think about it. I've been in Claire's Accessories while there are teen girls on the loose and there *is* a good chance they'll get lost in the space-time continuum and we won't see them again until late afternoon, but I'm also not ready for today to end yet. 'No, it's okay. It's nice to be out of work for a change. All I do is man the shop and go to auctions or car boot sales. I can't remember the last time I had a Saturday morning off.'

'I know that feeling.'

'You go to a lot of auctions and car boot sales?'

I meant it as a joke, but it goes straight over his head. 'No, I mean with work. Marking books, planning lessons, preparing materials... It feels like all I ever do is work – and embarrass everyone who knows me.'

I follow his gaze to the doors of Claire's Accessories again. 'Don't take it personally. Ava's thirteen. If you're not in a boyband, you're not cool. Are you now, or have you ever been, in a boyband?'

'I have not.' He laughs and gives me an appreciative look, like he knows I was trying to cheer him up. Awkwardness hangs in the air, only broken when a customer goes to come out of the doorway we're standing in and we both jump aside to let her pass, and then look up at the building itself.

It's a café, and inside there's floral bunting and fairy lights and quaint chairs and tables covered by dainty tablecloths, and glass display cases of delicious-looking cakes.

'Do you want a tea or something?' Ren sounds surprised, like he didn't intend the words to pop out but they did anyway. 'Or are you duty-bound to never buy a hot drink from anywhere other than the Wonderland-themed place?'

I can't help smiling on Cleo's behalf. She'll love knowing she's made an impression. 'Morally bound, not duty bound, but my morals are weak when it comes to tea, and have you seen that chocolate cake in the display case? Morals don't apply when it comes to chocolate cake.'

He looks at the cake I point out and then smiles a wide, unguarded smile that makes my stomach do a little flip. 'I could be tempted by that. Shall we?'

I go to walk in, but he stops me by reaching out and touching a tendril of my red hair that's escaped from my bun. 'You look really nice today.'

'Thanks, I think...' I feel like a statue, frozen to the spot, wondering if the doorway of this café is some sort of parallel universe or if we've suddenly stepped onto a different plane of existence where he says things like that.

He drops his hand quickly. 'Just in case you thought I didn't know how to say nice things. I've been practising. Ava *made* me practise.'

It makes me giggle as he pulls the door open and holds it for me to go through first and I get a little flutter at that chivalry, even though I'm quite capable of opening doors for myself.

Inside, the café is cosy and smells of brewing coffee, and the sound of other diners chattering fills the air. Ren and I both go up to the counter and order a cup of tea and a slice of chocolate cake each, but when I go to get my purse out, he stops me. 'Don't even think about it. This is on me.'

I thank him and take my cup and plate and make my way to a table near the window so Ava will see us when she comes back, but I can't help liking that gentlemanly vibe again. He seems older than he is, with values that come from a time before our own, but in a nice, respectful way.

I've already sat down when he comes over and takes the seat opposite me, and I find it nigh-on impossible to take my eyes off him. He's beautiful in an introverted and bookishly intelligent sort of way, but it's not just because he's nice looking, there's something more about him than that.

Thick dark hair that's neatly parted, but would probably be unkempt and tousled if it wasn't for the product holding it flat against his head, and I'd love to know what kind of clothes he wears when he's not wearing the officewear-style blue button-up shirt, the sensible black trousers, and the jacket that he *really* doesn't need on a sunny day like today.

Before I can overthink it, I blurt out something that's been haunting me since Wednesday. 'I'm sorry I called you defective the other day.'

'Don't worry about it. I *am* defective, and...'

I meet his eyes as his sentence grinds to a halt, and in that moment, I can *see* a much softer man underneath, someone with sad eyes who's clearly built a wall around himself and is working frantically to keep adding bricks to it.

'...and it's always enjoyable to have that pointed out by complete strangers, especially ones who are like quirky, energetic children's TV presenters.'

I don't think it was meant as a compliment but it makes me smile. 'Thanks.'

He smiles too, like it *wasn't* meant as a compliment but he doesn't mind me taking it as one, and then he takes a mouthful of his tea without checking the temperature first and lets out a yelp because it's clearly still at tongue-burning temperature.

He sinks down in his seat when other customers look in our direction at the sound, his cheeks blazing adorably red with embarrassment as he tries to hide behind his hand.

I take a forkful of gooey, glazed chocolate cake and let out such a moan of pleasure that I'm probably moments away from re-enacting the famous scene from *When Harry Met Sally*, which gives the other diners another reason to look over at us, and Ren dips his head further behind his hand in embarrassment. I'm used to people looking at my red hair and bright clothes and if they'd all tried the chocolate cake, they'd know where that moan of pleasure came from. I nod towards his cake. 'That's not as good as it looks, it's *way* better.'

He takes a forkful too and lets out a moan not unlike mine.

'Oh, that is unfairly good. So good that I don't even care if people are looking. I don't know about you, but I'm not leaving here without having another slice of that.'

He blows on his tea before taking another sip and lets out a long, overdue-sounding sigh. 'I have no idea when I last...' He looks at me, blinks a few times, and seemingly decides to be honest. '...let myself enjoy something. A simple pleasure with no pressure to do something else or be somewhere or just...' He sighs again and shakes his head, like he doesn't know what else to add to that, and I fight the urge to slide my hand over his where it's resting on the table and give his fingers a squeeze. Judging by the arm touch earlier, that would not be met with approval.

Another sip of tea makes his shoulders slump, like the pin-straight rod that seems to go through them has started to bend, and after another mouthful of cake, it feels like he's loosened up just a tad.

'Hey, speaking of seconds – can I ask you something? Do you think a crew of two is quite small for a ship?'

'I guess so...' he says slowly, like he's wondering where this is going.

'It's just I've been thinking...' I put down my fork and get out one of the pages from the Missing Vessels books that I printed in the library and run my finger down it. 'Look at these logs. Crew of sixteen. Crew of thirty. Crew of thirty-two. Crew of fourteen. But there were only two men on our mystery sailor's ship. What if we've got this wrong? What if she's describing it wrongly or if *all* vessels would seem like a ship to a mermaid? What if it wasn't a ship, but a small boat? It wouldn't be logged as a shipwreck, and the vessels logged as missing are generally much larger...'

'It's feasible, I suppose, although "feasible" is the wrong word for *anything* to do with mermaids or this diary being anything other than complete fiction. And it doesn't narrow down our chances of tracing the boat.' Ren gives me the same look I gave him earlier – annoyance because he knows I have a point – and then sighs, shoves another forkful of chocolate cake into his mouth, and gets out his phone. 'There's something in this cake that's making me take leave of my senses. Every time I look at you, I find myself believing that we're actually looking for a *real* ship that really existed.'

Lately I've been feeling so small and insignificant, like I just keep plugging away in the shop but no one ever notices and it never makes any difference, and the thought that *I* could make someone believe in anything – especially someone as cynical as him – makes something flicker inside me.

'Maybe we are.' I watch as he types a question on how to find historical small boat sinkings into Google, his eyes flick over the results page, and then he hands the phone to me.

'Consult regional newspaper archives from the area. Local authorities will have an archive of historical articles from their locality at the time of the sinking,' I read aloud and then look up at him again. 'So we just need to know *where* they are, and then we can go to the local council and ask for copies of newspaper reports from 1899 and that might give us some proof.' I hand his phone back and take another forkful of cake, trying not to think about the way he's watching me thoughtfully. 'What?'

'Nothing. Just... how can you be so positive? How can you really *believe* in this? With Ava, I get it, she's a child, she wants to believe in the fairytales she loved when she was little, that Prince Eric was on that boat and Ariel has just saved him from drowning, but you...'

'How can you think people ever grow out of that? The older I get, the *more* I wish fairytales were real and that magic and fairy dust solved real-life problems, and underdogs really would get happy endings. Something like this is a hint of possibility. It might be nothing, but it might be something really special too. It would be naive of us all to believe that what we know about the universe is all there *is* to know.'

He looks like he wants to protest, but another forkful of cake mellows him out enough to reluctantly mutter, 'Can't really argue with that point.'

'Hurrah. So far we've agreed on two things today – chocolate cake and that. Progress, right?'

He lets out a chuckle that slowly builds into a full-blown burst of laughter, and he shakes his head, but there's definite progress because it's in a fond, despairing way this time rather than a 'this woman is a lost cause' way. 'What's your story, anyway? You have all these stories for every item in your shop, but what about your own?'

'I'm the one thing in my shop that doesn't have a story.' I sound too abrupt because the thought of sharing it makes a prickly feeling break out across my skin. I'd rather make up a thousand stories than talk about my own, even once.

'I find that *very* hard to believe.' His blue eyes are intense and my face has heated up, but it's impossible to look away even though I find myself squirming under his watchful gaze, and I'm strangely tempted to spill out my entire life story in one cringeworthy fell swoop, despite my usual misgivings. If no one ever sees behind the bright and sunny mask, no one ever asks, and I've always preferred it that way. 'How long have you been in the curiosity shop business?'

'My dad opened The Mermaid's Treasure Trove nearly thirty years ago,' I tell him. 'He was one of the first businesses on Ever After Street. I've helped him out since I was really young. I lived away for a while with an ex, did a mind-numbingly boring corporate job that paid the bills and crushed my soul, and when the relationship ended, I came back home.'

'And your dad, he...?'

'Died, a couple of years ago now,' I finish the leading question for him. 'I took over while he was ill, and then the shop became mine when he passed.'

'I'm sorry.' His fingers twitch where his hand is resting on the table, and I wonder if he had to stop himself reaching out to touch my hand like I've had to do a couple of times so far today too. 'Wait, so the mermaid theme was your dad's doing? Not just your whimsical touch?'

'No, that was him. My mum loved mermaids and it was in her honour.' His questions have caught me off-guard because I wasn't expecting him to ask anything about me. He thinks I'm a younger, battier version of Auntie Wainwright from *Last of the Summer Wine*, I'm sure he's not really interested in my shop's origins and my parents' backstory.

'Is that why you're so determined this diary has to be real? You think it would... bring you closer to your parents?'

I reach inside the neck of my top and pull out Mum's tiny gold mermaid tail necklace and show him. 'She drowned when I was five, and afterwards, my dad told me that she'd turned into a mermaid and gone home to the sea, and even though I *knew* that wasn't what happened, it was a nice thought – a comforting thought. I grew up feeling as though she was still out there in the ocean somewhere. Every time we went to the beach, we picked up those conch shells that you can put to your ear and hear the ocean, and we'd both speak into them and then throw them back into the sea, and it was like a way of communicating with her.' I stop and take a deep, shaky breath. I've never shared that with anyone except Lissa, and my ex-boyfriend, before now and I don't know why it's suddenly popped out with this relative stranger who will definitely disapprove of something so whimsical. 'I still do it even now, and I really don't care if you think that's childish or silly or—'

'I think that's really nice,' he interrupts me quickly. 'Both my parents are gone too, so don't think I don't understand.'

I meet his eyes again, softer and kinder now than the usual suspicious apprehension that seems to cloud them, and I can *feel* how easy it would be to let my walls down and open up to him, and I blink and look away. Maybe there *is* something in this chocolate cake. I don't intend to ever let a man in again, especially one who clearly has a *lot* of baggage and past hurt. 'This is the only thing I still have of my mum's. I haven't taken it off since the day my dad found it again. She loved mermaids and she was convinced they really existed. Her whole life, she felt a pull to the ocean and thought she'd been a mermaid in a previous life or something. The diary being real would make her so happy.'

'Found it again?'

'It's how the shop came about...' I hesitate. 'Are you sure you want to hear this? You don't need to be polite or pretend to be interested. I prefer blunt, unsugarcoated honesty and you're good at that.'

He reaches out and covers my hand with his warm fingers, effectively ending my sentence. 'I want to hear it. I've never met anyone like you. There has to be some kind of superhero origin story and right now, I've never wanted to hear anything more. Tell me, please.'

His voice is so quiet but full of gentle steel, his accent perfectly polished, polite and sophisticated, like he's been taught how to speak properly, and it's impossible *not* to tell him.

'My mum died a hero. We were on holiday on the beach, it was the Easter holidays, right before lifeguard season began. There were these two little boys messing about on an inflatable dinghy, and there was a sudden... I don't know, a riptide or a current or something, and they were swept out to sea. I don't even know if I remember it or if I only remember what my dad told me and the newspaper cuttings my grandparents kept afterwards, but my mum was a strong swimmer, her childhood home was on the seafront and she'd swum in the ocean her whole life, and she went in after them. She thought... I don't know, I guess she didn't *think* at all, she just acted on instinct and tried to save them. And she did. She managed to get a rope to them so the others on the beach were able to pull them back in, but she didn't... she couldn't...' My voice is breaking and I'm focusing on the cup of tea in front of me rather than looking at him.

I don't realise how long it's been since I told this story. I don't meet many new people who I *want* to open up to, and everyone else in my life already knows what happened to my mum and don't bring it up for fear of upsetting me.

'The current was too strong. She disappeared. A kindly old man on the beach with his grandson offered to take me round the corner to get ice cream so I didn't have to witness what was about to happen when the coastguard arrived and pulled her body from the water. All I can remember is it was the worst ice cream I'd ever eaten because I *knew* something bad was happening and could hear all these sirens and the coastguard helicopter overhead, and this poor old man was trying to distract me by asking about school and things I liked, and we stayed there for hours, he got us chips and two more ice creams, and eventually my dad came, he had a policewoman with him, and we went back to the hotel we were staying at... and life was changed forever.'

There are tears streaming down my face, and when I realise, I swear under my breath, and grab a napkin from the table and turn away, trying to compose myself. I don't dig up these old traumas very often, but even so many years later, that day and the difficult years that followed it are back in sharp focus and it's impossible to pretend it hasn't made me emotional.

Ren's chair scrapes against the floor, and before I realise what's happening, he's crouched down beside my chair and leant up to put his arms around me. The hug is so unexpected, even more so because it's *him* that it's enough of a shock to stop my tears in their tracks. Probably like when people say being startled can stop a case of hiccups. He's quite possibly the *least* touchy-feely person I've ever met, and I didn't expect him to squeeze my hand like he did just now, never mind a proper hug like this.

His arms wrap around me and pull me close, his chin hooks over my shoulder, and my senses are instantly filled by the softness of his sensible shirt, the strength of the arms that hold me so tightly, and the scent of his hair product. The feeling of being held and the sense that he cared enough to push himself so far outside of his comfort zone just to console me makes me bite my lip and slip my arms around his shoulders and squeeze him back just as tight. I press my chin into his shoulder and turn my head slightly, so my cheek brushes against his dark hair, and I feel him let out a long exhale that makes his shoulders sag and his spine curve towards me, and we hold each other tightly for a few long minutes, oblivious to any potential looks from other diners. Between us, we've given them quite a spectacle today.

Eventually Ren grunts and pulls away. 'Sorry, pins and needles.' He gets up and stamps his feet a few times to get feeling back into his legs and then shuffles back to his chair and slumps down in it.

I watch him for a few moments, but he's focused intently on the pattern of the tablecloth rather than meeting my eyes.

'Sorry,' I say eventually. 'This is why no one should ever ask me about myself. I'm an embarrassment who should never be allowed out in public.'

'That's the first time I've hugged someone in years.'

'What?' I blink in surprise. 'Seriously? Not even Ava?'

'Ava's "too old" for hugs now. Hugs are "for *babies*" and if I try, she pushes me away with a "Don't be so embarrassing, Daa-ad!"' He mimics her young voice perfectly and I see a hint of someone who was once much more smiley and less uptight than he is now. 'And other than that, do I strike you as someone who welcomes hugs?'

Considering he's more bristly than a pincushion modelled after a porcupine... 'No, you don't.'

'No, I don't.'

It was probably intended to be a joke, but his voice takes on a downbeat tone that suggests it isn't something he's happy about.

This has got unexpectedly intense, and I try to use a lighter-hearted tone when I respond. 'Well, thank you for giving me your hug revirginity.'

'Hug revirginity,' he repeats, shaking his head in a bemused way as he looks at me, his smile getting significantly bigger with every passing second. 'I don't think you can use a phrase like that without chocolate. This calls for that second slice, yes?'

I nod because I'm never going to say no to cake, and he grins in response. 'Be right back.'

I let out a sigh as he goes back to the counter, like he knew I needed a minute to compose myself. I blow my nose and scrub a napkin over my face, and try not to think about how good that hug felt or what happens to make someone go for years without a hug. No wonder he's so grouchy.

I'm still lost in thought when another slice of chocolate cake is placed on the table in front of me, and Ren sits back down in the chair opposite. 'Okay, riddle me this. I don't understand how that led to the shop opening... but if you want to leave it there for today, rest assured that I *will* question you mercilessly about it on another day.'

It makes me smile again, and I realise I never got as far as the part about the shop's origins. 'Afterwards, my dad was *so* angry at my mum. He thought she'd done it unnecessarily. Yeah, she'd rescued those boys, but she didn't need to. They were screaming, panicking, but they were safe-ish, you know? They were on a dinghy, not *in* the water. The coastguard had been called. A lifeboat had been launched. They would likely have been okay, and he was so angry that she'd dived into dangerous water without thinking about the consequences. He thought she should have put her own safety and her own family first. She'd helped someone else's kids at the cost of ripping a hole through *our* family. He always said that you have to be selfish when you have kids. You have to do everything you can to ensure you're okay *for* them, and he was distraught, and grieving, and so, so, so angry at her for doing something so dangerous and impulsive, and paying the worst price. I stayed with my grandparents for about a week, and when I went home, he'd taken his frustration out on her belongings. It was like he'd tried to erase every hint of her from our lives. Photographs were torn up, wallpaper she'd chosen was ripped down, and he'd gathered up all her things and dumped them at charity shops.'

Ren looks horrified and I quickly defend my dad. 'He was lost in a haze of grief. He didn't know what he was doing. He didn't think about me, or her parents, wanting things to remember her by, he just acted out his rage when he didn't know what else to do with it. A couple of months later, he realised what he'd done, and he tried to get everything he'd thrown away back. He trawled the charity shops looking for things that hadn't been sold yet. He begged them for info about the customers who'd bought things, but nothing was traceable. No one at the shops knew there was anything different about *that* donation, and everything had been put out and sold as normal. He could barely remember the shops he'd taken boxes to, so he trawled every charity shop and second-hand shop in the area. He managed to find a few bits of clothing that he knew were hers, and this necklace.' I'm still holding the tiny gold mermaid's tail in my fingers and I show it to him again. 'By some miracle, it had fallen down the side of a workbench in the sorting room and only been found and put out that morning. He knew it was hers because it has this line where she bent it with her fingernail while she was sitting on the beachfront years earlier, waiting while he paced up and down, trying to build himself up to proposing, and after she'd bent her necklace, she got so annoyed at his dithering that she got up and proposed to him instead.'

Ren laughs. 'She sounds like a special person.'

'She was, I guess. I was too young to remember more than snapshots, but my dad filled my childhood with stories about her, the things she'd loved, things she'd done. He tried to make up for the photographs he'd ruined with mental images and tales of her escapades, and he never stopped searching charity shops. Every time we passed one, he went in and rooted through, but we never found anything else. But in all his searching, he realised something – that second-hand shops were *full* of treasures that someone had once loved. He came across so many things that had clearly meant something to someone once. He started buying things that he felt had a story behind them. A well-loved teddy bear. A dog-eared Judy Blume book with significant paragraphs highlighted. A battered doll from the 1950s.

'I don't know what he initially thought he was going to do with them, but he felt they deserved better than being thrown in a charity shop's "reduced price" basket. He feared that they'd ended up there by mistake and their owner might be frantically looking for them, like he was for Mum's things, and when he happened upon Ever After Street in its early days and saw an empty shop there, waiting for an owner, it was like something clicked into place for him, and he found a way of showcasing these wonderful treasures. His advertisements were on the basis of, "Are you looking for something you thought you'd never see again? You might be in luck!" and it struck a chord with people. He realised he was never going to get things back to their original owners, but he could sell them on to other people who saw the value in the history behind them as much as he did, who would look after them and give them the new home he thought they deserved.'

'That explains so much.' Ren's voice is soft and he sounds mesmerised by what I'm saying, and neither of us have even taken a forkful of our second cake slice yet.

For once, it doesn't sound like a bad thing, so I carry on. 'At first, the shop was just a little weekend side project, but pretty soon he was taking time off from his day job because customers couldn't get enough of his treasures. His shop was a living tribute to times gone by. Antiques but with a story behind them, a story that was more valuable than their monetary value, and customers appreciated that.'

'You're making me feel bad about my initial aversion now.' Ren's eyes flick down to the table and then back up to mine. 'Can we call it a misunderstanding and move on? I'm sorry I was so callous about your shop.'

I could accept his apology and call it a day. I *like* the fact he's willing to apologise and own his mistakes, and this is the perfect opportunity to prove that *I* know what I'm doing with my shop and he doesn't, but no matter how brutally his opinions were voiced, he had a point, and it feels wrong to pretend he didn't. 'No.'

I glance at him and a look of disappointment clouds his face, and I clarify my point. 'Because you were right, Ren. My shop *is* a hellhole. It's crowded and cluttered and anything of real value in there is lost beneath quirky nonsense items that I've made up a story behind rather than stocking things with actual stories, like my father did. I'm losing customers daily, and it's probably a matter of time until I actually lose one when someone wanders in and is never seen again or bumps into something and gets crushed by an avalanche of bric-a-brac. You were right, and you're the only person who's been honest with me since my dad died. He left some money in the business account, enough that I haven't had to worry about expenses for the past couple of years, but now it's running out, and it *matters* that I'm not earning much of an income. I need to change. Take it back to what it was years ago. I've been trying so hard to make him proud that I've lost sight of what he wanted to do in the first place.'

Ren's finger traces a floral pattern on the tablecloth as he thinks about it. 'Surely there's room for both *him* and *you*? Your shop is totally unique, and *you* are the strength behind that because you're totally unique too.'

Just when I thought I couldn't melt any more today. I don't know whether it was intended as a compliment, but that's the nicest, warmest thing to say, and it makes my heart glow inside my chest, almost as red as his cheeks are glowing.

'At the moment, both me *and* the shop are overcrowded and cluttered, and I think people are going to buy things like dragon fruit tables.'

He laughs, but I continue. 'I need to get rid of stuff. The trash that's wormed its way in, the stuff that no one is *ever* going to buy, and I need to be honest with myself. I need to admit that I've got too caught up in fantasy tales as a way of avoiding the reality of running my dad's shop without my dad. I need to admit that I still live in the hopes that, one day, something that belonged to my mum will cross my path, and the clutter is a misguided way of clinging on to both my parents, and maybe it's time to let it go and focus on the important things.'

'You're off to a good start. Admitting it,' he clarifies quickly. 'Not of decluttering. Yet.'

'I'm only admitting it to you. I haven't got as far as admitting it to myself yet.'

He smiles, that understanding smile of solidarity again. 'It's often easier to admit things to other people rather than to yourself.'

I never thought someone who was so harsh at first could be so emotionally intelligent, and it makes me think again about what Ava overshared on the first day, and what he's been through to make someone with so much inner sensitivity be so prickly on the outside.

'Do you want help?'

I would probably have been less surprised if he'd asked me to accompany him for lunch on the moon. 'From... you?'

'Yeah, why not? Someone sensible, practical, who doesn't believe in fairytales and knows enough about history to possibly recognise some truth behind the fantasies you concoct...'

I can feel an eyebrow rising. 'High opinion of yourself there.'

'The opposite, actually.' He pauses and I see that flicker of something in his eyes again. Shyness or lack of confidence or something. Whatever it is, I want to know more about it and what put it there. 'Seriously, Mickey. Next weekend. Ava's at her grand-parents' all day on Sunday – my ex's parents – and well, I *could* catch up on the housework, but helping you sounds like the more interesting option.'

Instinctively, I go to refuse, but I stop myself and think it over. On the one hand, this is a *terrible* idea. I will surely murder him within ten minutes, if we make it *that* long. On the other hand, he's the only person who's been honest about my shop in recent months, and a few of his barbs have hit closer to home than I would've liked. Who *else* would be a better choice? Lissa doesn't want to upset me and there's no one else I could ask for help, and honestly, I don't know where to start on my own and the thought of trying to throw things away feels overwhelmingly impossible. And I'm touched by his offer. He's objective, he's not sentimental, and he has no qualms about upsetting me. And after today, the idea of spending more time with him isn't an altogether bad one... 'You take your life in your hands.'

He grins, a wide smile that reaches his eyes and changes his sharp features into much softer ones. 'Duly noted.'

'I'm not a declutterer by nature.' Thank God he's not an English teacher, he'd probably have me arrested for butchery of that word. 'It's unlikely to end well for either of us.'

'Oh, are you not? I hadn't noticed.' His lips twitch like he's trying not to smile any wider than he's already smiling. 'Do you honestly think *any* person has *ever* walked into your shop and thought, "Ah, yes, now *this* is the lair of a minimalist!"'

The laugh that bursts out of me takes me by surprise. He's unintentionally much funnier than he realises, and there's something about his bluntness, how he says whatever pops into his head without second-guessing it, whether it's good or bad or kind or insulting, and for just a moment, the thrill of getting to know him better outshines the fear of any potential decluttering.

6

By the following Sunday morning, the thrill has been entirely subdued by the realisation that he's going to expect me to throw things out. This was a horrible, terrible, ill-fated idea, and I should just give up now and carry on as I am, hoping that something will work out if I just wish for it hard enough. Maybe I'll find a magic lamp and give it a rub and out will pop a genie to make things magically better? It worked for Aladdin, it *could* happen...

There's a knock on the shop door, and the sight of dark hair through the glass is only enough to quell my doubts for a few seconds before they set in again. This is the worst idea I've ever had. I don't know much about his life and thought processes, but I'm pretty sure it's one of the worst ideas he's ever had too.

When I open the door, Ren's standing there with a Wonderland Teapot-branded cake box in one hand and two steaming takeaway cups in a cardboard tray balanced in the other. 'Good morning.'

'Since when does The Wonderland Teapot open this early on a Sunday?' I say instead of any eloquent or traditional greeting.

'Since I used my charm and powers of persuasion?'

I raise an eyebrow, because although I think he can be quite charming, he keeps it well hidden. Very well hidden, sometimes.

'All right, I saw the Alice-looking woman and the bloke with blue hair in there and knocked, and she recognised me from the other day and said I could only come in if I was buying something for you.'

'It seems like all you do is buy me tea and cake.' I try not to think about Cleo's matchmaking ideas. She's got totally the wrong end of the stick there, so much so that she's chewing on the tree trunk itself.

'Tea and cake with the occasional insult thrown in?'

'And the occasional unexpected hug which balances it out,' I add.

His cheeks redden at the mention of the other day, and I hold the door open for him to come through. He pushes aside the bust of Michelangelo's David blowing a big pink bubble that's on the counter and makes space for the cake box. 'No red velvet today. The Alice-woman said they were testing out new flavours and I was only allowed to buy these lemon and hazelnut shortbread crumble cakes if you promised to give her your verdict next time you see her.'

'I will, although my verdict when it comes to cake is usually, "yay, cake". Thanks for this' I lock the door again, to make sure no customers mistakenly think we're open and wander in, and go over to take one of the cakes and the cup of tea he nudges towards me. 'And for *this*.' I duck my head to indicate the shop around me. 'You didn't have to volunteer for this. You're a brave man.'

'Ava's so jealous. When I told her where I was going today, I suddenly became "cool dad" and she made me promise not to be too hard on you and not to throw out anything "awesome".' He does the air quotes, and a thirteen-year-old's protectiveness of me warms something in my soul, and also, makes me worry that she has more experience with her father than I do, and knows *exactly* how brutal he's going to be with my carefully curated stock.

I can't help looking at him as he picks pieces off his cake and pops them into his mouth. His hair is still tamed with hair product, but he hasn't shaved today, turning his otherwise ordinary jawline into quite possibly the sexiest jawline on the planet, with a shadow of dark stubble that's *screaming* to have fingers rubbed over it. He's wearing a much more casual plain black T-shirt and navy jeans, and he looks preposterously gorgeous, all the way down to his mid-calf steel-toe-capped boots.

'Good footwear choice.'

'I figured this was the kind of place where many heavy objects are liable to crush me. Or I'll annoy you so much that you'll batter me to death with...' He looks around and picks up a silver-plated swordfish on a wooden stand, and jabs it outwards a few times like he's trying to fence with it. '...this rather strange fish ornament.'

'Nah. I mean, I'll consider it, but I like you too much to murder you.'

'Aww, just when I thought my life was a lost cause, someone likes me enough not to commit homicide. I must be doing something right.'

I nudge my shoulder against his and he smiles down at me, and I realise I wasn't exaggerating. I *do* like him, almost definitely enough to let him stay breathing. I like how self-deprecating he is. I like his sarcastic sense of humour, but it's not just that. I don't know how today is going to go, but he's offered help for nothing in return. Just out of the goodness of his heart, trying to help a virtual stranger, and he must know that this is not going to be an easy task, and that suggests he's a good guy under the spiky outer layer.

Like he can tell I'm not quite ready to start on the decluttering portion of the day, instead of pushing me, he wanders around, picking up things and putting them back down again, probably unaware of the disapproving noises he's making. 'Is this a whale-shaped butter dish?' He picks up an iridescent ceramic thing from a wooden bureau that's piled up with knick-knacks. 'Who would buy this?'

'Someone who likes whales. And butter, obviously.'

He puts it down and picks up an angelfish-shaped china plate with hand-painted detailing so it looks like a real angelfish. 'Don't tell me, a perfect item for the discerning customer who loves fish so much they can't bear to be parted from them long enough to eat from a normal plate?'

I sigh. 'All right, maybe I've got a bit carried away and bought too many ocean-related things to fit the shop theme, but someone will love them, one day.'

'You keep saying that,' he says gently. 'I'm privileged to have a better understanding of your collection now, but this is a retail establishment. Nothing flows, nothing makes sense. There are antiques here. There are probably valuable things here, but you don't focus on them. Instead, you keep hoping that the right person for the right item is going to come along and...' He turns the plate over and looks at the price sticker I've put on the under-side. '...save your business by spending a whole three pounds. Something's got to—'

'Change, I know.' I finish the sentence for him. I was going to defend my choices, to say that if *enough* people came along and purchased trinkets for small amounts then it would make a big difference, but I know what he's getting at. There are so *many* trinkets on that bureau that even if the ideal customer looking for a fish-shaped plate happened along, they'd struggle to find it. If things were displayed in a more sensible way, there would be a better chance of *anyone* buying them. 'From the moment you walked in, you have had *views* on my shop. Why are you so invested in this?'

'What, you mean apart from the new scar on my forehead and my desire to ensure your Victorian birdcages don't cause bodily harm to anyone else?' He thinks for a few moments before giving me a quietly serious answer. 'Because it's been a long time since I've seen anywhere that makes Ava so happy. She's struggling with confidence lately – with finding out who she is and being comfortable in her own skin, and there's something about this place that lets her be herself with reckless abandon. I'm not a "reckless abandon" type of person, but you are, and it's doing her good, and you're obviously struggling to keep things afloat. I can see ways that might help to stop it sinking, and I understand that feeling of treading water all too well, and Ava adores you. Why wouldn't I try to help?'

I nod, appreciating the boat metaphors *and* the honesty of his answer. He's not wrong, I *do* feel like I've been treading water for a while now, and I'm kind of grateful that he's the only person who's looked hard enough to see that.

'Oh, that's awesome. I love that.' He's picked up a mug shaped like a welly boot with a handle on the back. I came across it at a car boot sale and knew someone would love it one day.

'Wait, there's something you like? Are there flying pigs and three blue moons in the sky?' I joke, but I hear that 'knew someone would love it one day' line echoing in my head again. How many times have I said that? How much longer can I go on purchasing and hoping to resell things that I hope to find a buyer for one day? Judging by the business account balance – not long.

'You can joke but I'm going to buy that.'

'There's a cowboy boot one knocking around somewhere too.'

'This illustrates my point. Why are they not together? Organised. If someone comes in looking for a mug, point them to a shelf where *all* the mugs are.'

'But if someone comes in and goes over there but doesn't go over there, they might miss it.' I point my hands in opposite directions.

'If things were better organised, they *wouldn't* miss it.'

I go to spout a clever and witty comeback, but no words come out. He is frustratingly good at making points.

'Ava will love that one.' He spots the cowboy boot mug and comes back to put them both on the counter. 'There you go, two sales already today. Shall we make a start or are you leaving that tea until it's stone cold or just unpleasantly lukewarm?'

He's seen right through the diversion of nursing my cuppa then. I swallow the last of the offensively tepid drink and steel myself. I *have* to start somewhere, and the scene of the Clarice Cliff crash is the perfect place because I never did get around to tidying it up properly.

Ren follows me through to the second room of the shop and surveys the mess. 'Well, look at that, the junk has started self-ejecting already.'

He says it so totally deadpan that it makes me break out in a nervous giggle, and when he looks at me and grins, the nervous giggles turn into outright laughter, and he laughs too, making his bright eyes twinkle and crow's feet at the corners crinkle up, and I realise this isn't a bad thing.

He's practical, logical, and sensible, and brave enough to help me. It's *worth* putting in an effort too.

* * *

By lunchtime, my resolve about not killing him is weakening. Would a lifetime in prison and an orphaned thirteen-year-old on my conscience be worth it? This morning, I thought it wouldn't, but now, I'm wavering towards... maybe.

Ren's blocked off an area of the second room and is piling all the things to go to the tip into it, along with separate boxes for donations to charity shops, and another one for recycling.

'Why would anyone...?' It's an unfinished question that he's asked several hundred times so far today. The end of it is some variation of '...buy this... want this... be stupid enough to buy this *and* think other people would want it...' but he stopped adding those parts several hours ago, after I gave him a look that made him think he needed full body armour, not just steel-toe-capped boots.

'It's a curiosity shop. It's supposed to be full of weird things. Curiosities, some might say.'

'Yes, but why are they all fruit related? Seriously. This is a raspberry planter in the shape of an actual raspberry.'

'Yes, and imagine growing raspberries in it. Raspberry-inception. A never-ending circle of raspberries. An endless circle-of-raspberry-life.'

He looks like he's trying to hold it back, but eventually he bursts out laughing. 'Maybe you need a certain type of mindset to run a shop like this, and I clearly don't have it.'

He's trying to be kind, and I'm trying to embrace this, because I *know* he's right, and the more stuff he picks up and questions, the more I think about how my dad would never have bought something like it, and how much I've strayed from what he wanted his shop to be, and as much as I hate having to downsize, I appreciate Ren being the first person to make me realise that.

Ren picks up a little glass bottle and examines it. 'Why do you have a random inkwell from, at a guess, the 1860s?'

'Because it's adorable? Come on, can't you just imagine some lovelorn man, a Mr Darcy type in his frilly shirt and breeches, sitting at a table in the window, looking out over his country estate and penning letters of love to his beloved with his quill and ink from *that* little bottle?'

'Mickey, I hate to break it to you, but...' He comes over with the bottle turned upside down, reaches for my hand, and when I hold it out, he takes hold of my wrist and positions my fingers on the bottom of the bottle, so they're running over the embossed lettering that's stamped in the glass. His fingers hold mine in place for longer than strictly necessary. I'd seen the branding before and assumed it was the name of the manufacturers of the inkwell, but he seems to know otherwise.

'You know who these people were? They were the leading divorce solicitors of the late nineteenth century. In 1857, there was a landmark legislation that allowed people to obtain a divorce through the courts for the first time. It was expensive and a privilege given only to upper-class men. There were no equal rights for women. The only things likely to have been written by ink from *this* inkwell are the signing of divorce papers of a hoity-toity man who'd got fed up with his wife and wanted to get rid of her and leave her destitute. Love letters between Mr Darcy and Elizabeth Bennett, it was not.'

I yank my hand back like the empty inkwell has burnt me. Why did I invent a story about it rather than doing any actual research? That's a *horrible* history behind it, and I want to throw it out immediately. 'I don't even want to touch it. It's like a cursed object masquerading as something good.'

'Fear not.' He tosses it from one hand to the other, trying to hold back laughter at my reaction. 'I'm already cursed in that department, I'll put it in the box for recycling.'

When he comes back empty-handed, he bows and tips an imaginary hat in my direction, like he's expecting the welcome of a conquering hero, but I've got stuck on his joke about being cursed and I'm suddenly more desperate than ever to know more about his life.

'Why are they always about love?' he asks. 'Why is every story you invent connected to love and sweeping romantic gestures and unrealistic expectations?'

'Why shouldn't they be? Objects become symbols of love. Gifts. Tokens of appreciation or little ways of showing someone they're cared about. People love *things*. Sometimes things become a physical representation of feelings that don't have anywhere else to go.'

'These have been thrown out or sold on. They can't mean much any more.'

'You don't know that. Maybe they've been sold accidentally, or in a fit of rage, or maybe the person has died and their family hasn't known the significance, or the things have been lost or stolen. There are multiple possibilities as to why much-loved objects can end up straying far from home...' I'm thinking of my dad and how he reacted after my mum's death. I've always hoped that if anyone else was in a similar situation, desperately looking for something they'd lost, *my* shop would be the place they'd find it. 'Why are you looking at me like that?'

It takes him a while to answer. 'Because from what you said on the second day we came in, you're single and it didn't sound like you'd been particularly happy in that side of your life. How can you believe that all this trash is enchantment and magic and fairytales when you *know* that love *doesn't* conquer all, and probably just makes us more miserable than we were to begin with?'

'Because it gives me something to hope for. At our cores, we all go through life hoping to find life-changing, world-shaking love. We never really outgrow the idea of over-romanticised Disney movie happily-ever-afters. On some level, everybody wishes they had that. Just because I haven't found it yet doesn't mean it's not out there waiting to be found. It doesn't mean that other people haven't found it. Finding these treasures and imagining the love stories behind them is an escape. Objects can transport us from the everyday mundane reality of life and give us something to believe in. Whether they're true or not is less important than the hope they give.'

He's still looking at me like I'm an alien species he hasn't encountered until now, shaking his head in a despairing way. 'I don't know how you can go through everything you've been through and still come out with such hopefulness. I wish I was more like you. To quote a famous mermaid, I wish I could be "Part of Your World" and see things the way you do.'

'Why can't you?'

He makes a noncommittal noise and goes back to trying to reach behind a sideboard for something that's fallen down behind it.

'I told you about me the other day.' I prod because I can't help myself. 'What's *your* story, Ren? And if you don't want to tell me, rest assured, I will question you mercilessly about it on some other day.'

He looks up and meets my eyes across the shop and laughs – a laugh that was probably supposed to be sarcastic, but comes out sounding genuine when he recognises the repeat of what he said to me in the café.

'Don't have one. I'm the most boring, embarrassing person on the planet. Ava can attest to that, and frequently does.' He's trying to joke, but there's an underlying hurt in his voice, and like the other day when he stayed hunkered down in the café doorway to avoid embarrassing her, I have no doubt that he's struggling with Ava growing up and going through the perfectly normal phase where everything your parents do is the most embarrassing thing ever.

And I cannot stop myself pushing. 'You seem like a man who's been hurt...'

'Hurt?' He scoffs and stands upright to look at me. 'Oh, I haven't been *hurt*. I've had my heart shredded and fed back to me on a pair of sharpened chopsticks, along with any belief I ever had in love, magic, the goodness of humanity, and my ability to trust anyone or believe in *anything*. Does that answer your query?'

I didn't expect such honesty, and he probably expected his sharpness to deter me from questioning him, but such a jaded worldview has done nothing but make me want to go over and give him a hug. Now I'm even more determined to find out what he's hiding under his prickly shell. 'Seriously, Ren,' I say gently. He seems like someone who needs a bit of gentleness in his life. 'Messy divorce? Absent ex-wife?'

'Ah, yes, why *does* anyone have kids if not so they can tell people private things you didn't want them to know within moments of meeting them?' He rolls his eyes at the memory of Ava opening up too much when they first came in here last Tuesday, and then glances at me and seems to relent. 'And yes. Messy divorce. Absent ex-wife.'

'You could elaborate, you know.'

'I could.'

Despite that, he stays frustratingly silent. Just because he *could* doesn't mean he's going to.

'She's gone to Italy?'

'Mickey...' It's said warningly, but it doesn't sound like a warning – it sounds more like a plea. *Please don't make me talk.* And if there's one thing I know about men with a rod of tension *that* taut through their shoulders, it's that they need to talk.

He's gone back to trying to shift the upcycled wooden sideboard, and I decide to change tack. If he won't talk about his relationship, maybe he'll talk about his job instead. 'What's it like being a teacher?'

'Great, in July. Bloody awful once term starts again.' He's not concentrating on his answer, and I'm surprised by the inadvertent admission.

'Really? You don't like teaching?'

'I'm not sure I like anything lately,' he mutters, and then glances up at me as he seems to catch up with what he's said and backtracks. 'I mean, yeah, I love it. It's all I've ever wanted to do, since my first history lesson on my second day at secondary school. We had a teacher who brought history to life. I connected with his lessons like I was really there, seeing past events happen in real time, and from that moment, I wanted to do that. I wanted to be standing up there at the front of the class, bringing times gone by to life for other disengaged kids like me. But these days, it's a *lot* of pressure, and it's increasingly hard to get the ultra-modern smartphone generation interested in times long ago when most twenty-first century kids only care about social media stats and getting TikTok views. It's a lot of lesson planning, over-time, taking work home to mark on my own time, and the feeling of helping kids has been buried under pointless admin and endless paperwork. If behaviour is poor in class, it's framed as your lesson not being engaging enough. If pupils aren't getting good marks, it's because your lesson wasn't written well enough. There's so much stress and pressure, and I...' He runs out of air and trails off, but I can hear the unsaid ending of that sentence. He, once again, seems like someone who is barely holding it together, and if the rest of that sentence *wasn't* going to be '...can't take any more' then I'll eat my hair flower. The urge to go over and give him a hug tingles in my fingertips again.

I can see the way his chest is heaving as he struggles to keep his emotions under control. His eyes are wide, a deer-in-head-lights look like he doesn't know how I got him to say all of that, and I'm not sure if I should give in to the hug urge or push him further. I don't think Ren opens up easily, and this is a chance that can't be ignored. 'And you're dealing with a lot at home too...'

He sinks down and sits against the sideboard he was trying to move with the heaviest-sounding sigh I've ever heard. 'Ava hates me. She blames me. When we split up, her mother made no secret of the fact it was because she was bored of me. I wasn't exciting enough. I didn't make her feel alive. She wanted more. I was holding her back, clipping her wings, ruining her life, and she made sure Ava knew it was my fault for not being enough. Ava had a choice of whether she wanted to stay with me or go to live with her mum, and she chose her mum, and one of the worst things I've ever had to do is sit her down and explain that she *couldn't* go with her mum because her mum didn't want her, but not in those words because I didn't want her to think badly of her mother or feel unwanted. My ex wanted to travel, see the world, and she didn't want to be tied down by a daughter who needed her.

'At first there were visits. Her mum would take her to do something fun and exciting that dull old Dad would never do – ice skating or a shopping spree – but she started coming up with more and more excuses about why she couldn't be there, or if she did turn up, she'd be hours late. Then she started standing her up completely, arranging to meet and then just leaving her there, waiting. Gradually she faded out of our lives. Her parents told us she'd gone to Italy with a new boyfriend. She hasn't been in contact for over a year. I suspect her parents know where she is, they've mentioned that she's travelling and Ava says they have postcards from her, but nothing else. To my knowledge, she's never even *asked* how Ava's doing or made any effort to contact her, and I have no idea how to make that better for her.'

This explains so much. The prickliness and cynicism. Even the warnings about not wanting Ava to get her hopes up – I now understand how badly she's been disappointed before. And *he* is broken by this, I can see it in every inch of him. Torn between blaming himself and being rightfully angry at his ex. He's hurting, and trying desperately to keep all of that away from his daughter. No wonder he gives off a vibe of barely holding it together, and I feel such a swell of affection for him.

For a man who is juggling so many problems, he's gone out of his way to help me, and to get involved in the diary solely because it was what Ava wanted, and that says so much about what a *good* guy he is, deep down, even if it seems like it's been a long time since he felt that himself.

'Ava still thinks she's going to waltz back in and fill our lives with excitement again. She *still* thinks that I drove her away and then somehow prevented her from living with her mum, and it feels like she'll never forgive me.'

My teeth have cut through my bottom lip where I've been chewing on it as he talks, trying to stop myself interrupting – either with words or by throwing my arms around him. 'Can I say something?'

He looks up and blinks, and it's almost like he's forgotten I'm here and it takes a moment for him to nod.

I go over and sit beside him on the sideboard. 'You're the least dull person I've ever met. You're clever, and brilliant, and funny, and kind, and the fact you *still* try to hide the true extent of your ex's cruelness from Ava speaks volumes about you.'

'Oh, Mickey.' He laughs a thick laugh and bends forward like he's gone light-headed, scrubbing a hand over his face and taking long, deep breaths.

My thigh is pressing against his, and I force myself not to rub his back and try to comfort him in some way. 'You can't blame yourself for any of that.'

'It *is* my fault, though.' His voice is muffled through his hands.

'Your ex *told* you it was your fault. She strikes me as someone manipulative, narcissistic, and selfish. There is something fundamentally wrong with someone who'd leave a child and then blame someone else for their own failings. Do you honestly think anything you did would have changed that? You could have been an all-singing, all-dancing cowboy rockstar space-hopping billionaire, and she would still have wanted more.'

He sits upright and pulls back far enough to raise a sceptical eyebrow at me. 'A cowboy rockstar space-hopping billionaire?'

I grin and hold my hands up. 'I'm just saying, nothing would have been enough. It wasn't *you*.'

He shakes his head like he's unsure of what to do with that sentence, and I sit beside him for a while, because I get the feeling he's a bit shaken by sharing all of that.

'Ava still sees her grandparents though?' I ask when the silence grows heavy.

'Yeah. They still wanted a relationship, and they're the only family she's got. I would never discourage that. And honestly, I'm glad of the break sometimes, which is a terrible thing to say and probably disqualifies me from any Father of the Year awards.'

I laugh. 'Maybe it makes you Normal Person of the Year instead. Being a single parent is a *lot*, I know – I grew up with one too. Ava's lovely – you're doing a great job even if it doesn't feel like it.'

I know I've hit a nerve when his breathing hitches and he shakes his head in a disbelieving way. 'I don't know why I told you all that. I never share stuff like this with people I barely know. Actually, I never share stuff like this with people I know really well either. Are there mind-altering substances in this shop or what?'

He gets to his feet and looks around, like he's searching for any mind-altering substances that might be hidden somewhere. 'Suspicious incense! I bet you're burning suspicious incense, right?'

I laugh out loud. 'There's no incense in the shop, Ren, suspicious or otherwise. And even if there was, I don't think it's known for having an instantaneous psychedelic drug kind of effect.'

'I'll feel better if you let me believe it's suspicious incense.'

I laugh because I really didn't have him down for being *this* adorable.

He paces a couple of times, and then holds a hand out to pull me up too, and when my fingers slip over his, his hand tightens and we hold each other's gaze for a long few moments.

'C'mere.' It's barely a whisper and I'm not entirely sure whether it was me or him who said it, but before he has a chance to rethink it, I pull him closer and reach up to slide my arms around him again, and just like the other day, he instantly sinks into it. His chin settles over my shoulder and his arms slip around me, his hands spreading out and covering as much of my back as possible, and after a few moments of my hands rubbing up and down, his rod-straight spine curves towards me, and he stumbles and has to replant his feet on the floor as his body loses some of its tension. He makes a noise of contentment that I'm entirely sure he doesn't realise popped out, and it just makes me squeeze him tighter. This is a man utterly *desperate* for a hug, and time disappears as we stand there holding each other.

'Why do we keep doing that?' He sounds blissfully dazed as he pulls away.

'Hugging? No idea, maybe it's all the suspicious incense.'

He laughs out loud and his shoulders drop. 'Okay, okay, I'm

not very good at dealing with my feelings, but I *am* good at recycling and recognising rubbish. Now, about that dragon fruit table...'

I smack at his arm and defend my dragon fruit table again, and he laughs good-naturedly, and we go back to the easy companionship of him picking up things and commenting on them, me making the case for their right to stay, while also trying to tell myself I can't keep *everything* and the whole point of decluttering is to *throw things away*. He's somehow a little bit lighter, a bit warmer and more jokey, and now I have a better idea of what he's dealing with, it means even more that he's given up his free time to help me, and that's someone worth listening to.

7

'Serious question – *is* there likely to be anything else from the mermaid's property? Should we be looking?'

'I don't know.' I look over at him where he's found a box of old records and is rifling through them, but I've already decided they can go. They belong with someone who specialises in record collecting, and the chances of someone who's looking for that exact thing coming in here are slim to none. 'I gravitate towards ocean-themed things, so there's a lot, but I have no record of what things came from where, and yes, I *know* I need to start keeping one.'

'Don't feel bad,' Ren interrupts before my thoughts stray to my father's faultless record-keeping and how much I've let that slide. 'We've all been guilty of not keeping on top of paperwork.'

Instead of dwelling on it I think more about how keen he is. 'I didn't know you were so invested in this mermaid's diary... You *want* to believe in this, don't you?'

'I wish I could. I *wish* I could see that diary and not be as cynical as I am. I wish I could read it and simply believe in it rather than trying to pull the evidence to shreds, but that's not me. I believe in facts, and so far, there is *nothing* in that book that can be proved.'

'We could sneak another entry... You have *no* idea how hard it's been to stop myself reading the whole thing, but as it's both of us, and Ava would never have to know...'

'You mean, go behind my daughter's back and do something that would break her heart and crush her soul if she found out?'

Just as I'm feeling like the world's worst person for even suggesting it, his face breaks into a huge grin. 'Heck yeah, I'm in!'

He recovers his composure and turns serious again. 'What I mean is that I don't want Ava to be disappointed, and the sooner we prove this is fake, the better.'

I let him keep telling himself that rather than admitting he's actually quite interested and run upstairs to retrieve the book from my bag, and bring it back down again.

'If nothing else, this has been good for Ava,' he says as I find the page of the last entry we read. 'It's got her off social media. All she's been doing online lately is googling history of mermaids in Britain, rather than obsessively following her friends' feeds as they post photos from their sun-drenched foreign holidays that I can't afford to take her on.'

'Not everyone has that. My dad could never afford holidays – it didn't do me any harm. After a rainy weekend in a caravan my grandparents hired on a storm-ravaged clifftop, it was decided that holidays were better avoided anyway. Adrenaline-rush roller-coasters had nothing on the sway of that thing.'

He laughs, and comes to stand next to me at the counter, just a teeny bit closer than strictly necessary, and I get another hit of his aftershave, amber and dark orange, and so skin-close that you'd need your nose in his neck to smell it. I got a hint of it when we hugged, and now it seems like his skin has heated up enough to make it even more intoxicating.

11 February 1899

The sky is ablaze with forks of lightning and the thunder rolls angrily overhead, so close that it is shaking the entire island. The wind is so strong that it seems like it's trying to push him back into the ocean. This storm is brutal and unforgiving. He is drenched to the skin and his body is racked with shivers. He has got onto his hands and knees and attempted to brace himself against the gales, but it is of no use. I fear he will not survive until morning. I must get him inside.

'Inside?' Ren looks up in confusion. 'All this time, there's been an "inside" and she's only just mentioned it? There's a building or something on this abandoned island?'

It makes me feel like we're missing something. I was picturing them on a beach with nothing but waves and open sea, like Tom Hanks in *Cast Away*, but this new information throws me. What 'inside' is this? What kind of building would there be on an isolated island? I glance up at him and his blue eyes meet mine, and I know we're both thinking the same thing – if she really is a mermaid, how can she go *inside* any place?

I have never got this close to him while he was awake before. He says something to me, he has to shout, but I cannot hear him over the pounding rain and screaming wind. I have found a tree branch and I offer it to him to lean on in place of his broken leg. I help him get to his feet and try to support his weight. He puts an arm around my shoulders and leans heavily on me.

I have never been this close to a man before. My sister is courted by men, she giggles and fawns and acts silly around them, but men are terrified of me. This one knows what I am, but rather than being scared, he seems glad of the help.

His body is still battered from the shipwreck, and this is the first time he has tried to walk. He screams when agony over-takes him. It is excruciatingly slow to shuffle towards my shel-ter. So much of his weight is leaning on me that I am convinced I shall drop him. We are both gasping for air by the time we reach the inside, and he falls down, collapsing onto the floor in front of the fire.

Sweat is mixing with the rainwater that streams down his face and I feel guilty for leaving him outside as long as I have. He tries to thank me but he's shivering so much that the words don't make it out past his chattering teeth. He's panting painfully, like a fish that's been left out of the water, his body heaving, the pain making his face turn a concerning shade of grey. I can hear the wheezing noise his lungs are making from across the room. I have blankets that I take to him. I motion for him to take his clothes off – he will never warm up with wet clothes clinging to his body. Eventually he gets himself into a sitting position and peels his shirt off, and I find my eyes tracking the movement as raindrops run down his pale, bruised skin. I wrap a blanket around his shoulders and when I do, his hand slips over mine and squeezes it. I didn't expect the contact and it startles me. I pull my hand away quickly and take his shirt to hang it up to dry, but now it is hours later and I can still feel the imprint of his hand around mine, like he has branded me. I wish I had not pulled my hand away so quickly.

I make a motion of eating to ask him if he wants something to eat, but he shakes his head. He tells me how ill he feels. I boil some water over the fireplace for drinking, and he sips it gratefully, barely able to hold the cup because he's shivering so violently.

He falls into a fitful sleep by the fire, and I move closer. Once I am sure he is asleep, I take a cloth and use it to dry his hair, letting my fingers touch the damp strands. I am drying his hair, but really, I sit beside him and fantasise about a world where he is mine. A world where someone would love me enough to let me take care of them, where I could sit beside someone and show them affection and receive affection in return. Wouldn't that be a lovely world?

I put my hand on my chest and make a noise of longing. 'That's so sweet. She's really starting to care about him. A mermaid falling in love with a human.'

'You can't honestly believe...?' Ren mutters. It's another question that doesn't need finishing, and it's not the first time he's asked it as we've been reading this book. 'How is she helping him to walk when, if she had fins and a tail, she'd be unable to stand herself, never mind let him lean on her and move around a... presumably a house because we know they've got a fire, a way of boiling water... Unless, of course, this is a work of complete codswallop.'

'Codswallop!' I smack at his forearm in mock outrage. 'She doesn't say *what* they're inside of. Maybe she means a cave or something? A cave would have water for her and shelter for him. The fire could be a campfire. Maybe it's *us* who are interpreting this wrongly.'

'Seriously, Mick? You have an explanation for absolutely everything?'

It's the first time he's shortened my name, and it feels so friendly and easy-going, the opposite of how uptight he often seems, and it makes me feel all warm inside. Friends shorten my name and it feels like a significant step towards us being real *friends* rather than strangers. 'Anything is possible.'

He laughs, and his fingers slip over mine and he gives my hand a squeeze. He lets go all too quickly, but he shifts imperceptibly closer as we read the next entry, leaning over so his stubble is catching on my hair, and it sends a little tingle down my spine because I didn't think anything would ever make him retract his prickles at first, but now he *wants* to be this close to me.

12 February 1899

I watched over him all night. I tried to sleep, but all I could think about was him. It unsettled me and I found myself calmer when I sat on a chair in the same room. I tried to read a book, but my attention kept drifting to him, watching the way his hair fell from his forehead as it dried, the way his closed eyelids moved in his sleep, and I touched my fingers to the skin of his arm and felt it gradually growing warmer.

When the morning comes, the sun comes with it. I should help him back to the beach, but it is winter and the sky is both bright and filled with foreboding clouds that pass by. Another storm may arrive before nightfall. He must stay for now. I am unsure if he is strong enough to make it back to the sand.

He groans when he wakes. He makes noises of pain as he stretches his body and slowly sits up. The fire has died to embers, but the morning sunlight is streaming in the window and it makes me feel more hopeful than I did before. His stomach growls, and I laugh at the loud noise in the otherwise silent room.

We eat breakfast together without a word. It is the first time I have ever shared a meal with anyone, apart from my sister, who spends most of them berating me. He thanks me for my help last night. He tells me about a dream he had. He fills the silence that I am unable to fill with his lilting accent and deep, reassuring voice.

'Can you not speak or do you choose not to?'

I shake my head, unsure of how to answer him, and then I hold up a single finger – one, indicating the first answer – and he understands what I mean.

'You can't?' He waits for me to nod. 'That must be awful.'

I don't know how to answer so I nod again. It is awful. No one has ever acknowledged that before. I am not like others, and therefore, I am an outcast, a creature to be made fun of and teased or pitied. He is the first person who has ever tried to consider it from my perspective. He addresses me like I am normal. Like I am not a thing from another world. Most people act as though I can't hear them as well as being unable to speak, they treat me as if I am stupid and talk about me like I am not there. He talks to me as I have always wished someone would.

He looks much better this morning. His skin is a normal colour, his hair has dried, even his clothing has dried from the heat of the fire. He's holding the blanket around himself, trying to cling to the heat it provides.

His eyes flit around and eventually fall on the desk in the corner with my books and pen on it. 'Can you write?'

I nod and he motions for them, but when I pass them to him, he refuses and pushes them back to me. 'Write your answers. What is your name?'

I write it down and turn the book around to show him, and he tells me it's beautiful. My cheeks flush and I get a fluttering feeling inside my throat.

He asks me what I am doing out here, all alone, and I tell him by writing it in the notebook. He asks if it was me who saved his life on the night of the shipwreck. He has so many *questions, some I can't answer, but when we stop, the winter sun is much higher on the horizon, and pages upon pages of my notebook are covered in answers, and I feel like I've had a real conversation. No one has ever asked me if I can write before. No one has ever cared enough to try communicating with me.*

He drags himself to the window and sits beside it to look out. He tells me he is admiring the view from this vantage point, but I suspect that he is really trying to gauge the situation he is in, and he sees it is as hopeless as he fears. He asks me if I have signalled for help. I nod. Many times. No one can see a distress signal from so far out to sea. The very reason for being exiled to this island is so no one needs to think about me for six months, and my sister can pretend I don't exist.

Before I know what I'm doing, I've written that down and shown it to him, and he looks at me with eyes full of sympathy. He reaches his hand out, and I hold mine out too, unsure of what he's intending to do with it until he takes my fingers in his and holds them. 'Those people are fools.'

It makes me both laugh and cry, and my knees go so weak that it feels like I really am standing on my mermaid's fin. I look into his grey-green eyes and I feel my heart grow larger in capacity.

He is a good man, unlike so many of them, and we will survive this together.

'If I still believed in romance, I'd say that was one of the most romantic things I've ever read.' Ren clears his throat, sounding choked-up.

I glance up at him, feeling the same as the mystery mermaid – *he* is a good man, unlike so many of them, and from the soft look on his face, I'd say our unknown diarist isn't the only one with a heart growing bigger.

'I'm so glad Dad didn't throw out the dragon fruit table!' Ava hurls herself towards it and strokes the white-and-black pulp of the tabletop. 'I was sure he'd talk you into getting rid of it.'

'Your dad couldn't talk me into anything. And if you want to know a secret, I think he's a big softie at heart, and he loves that dragon fruit table really, but he's too embarrassed to admit it now after all the bad things he said about it.'

'Oh, you think so, do you?' Ren appears in the doorway, holding a cake box from The Wonderland Teapot and a tray of three takeaway cups, but he doesn't deny my observation.

I grin at him. It's been a few days since I last saw him and I've missed him enough to make it feel like much longer, and his matching smile makes my heart rate speed up.

Ava comes over and throws her arms around me. 'Thank you so much for the mugs, they're the best mugs ever.'

She's talking about the welly boot and cowboy boot mugs that Ren found the other day and how, when he went to pay for them as he was leaving, I refused and made him take them anyway. 'It's so unfair that he got to come and help you and I didn't.'

Ren steps inside and I move aside some of the stuff on the counter so he can put the drinks down, and he hands me a cup of tea, and Ava a chocolate milkshake, and takes a tea for himself.

'Well, today, you can stay and help Mickey while I take some of the stuff we threw out down the tip and to the drop-off point for charity collection.' He opens the cake box and we help ourselves to a red velvet cupcake each.

I wasn't going to accept his help with getting stuff to the tip, but he made a good point the other day that he's got a big family car, and I've got a tiny two-seater that my dad used to drive. 'I can help.'

'I have absolutely no confidence that you wouldn't rescue it all before it got thrown into the skips.'

I grumble but he has another good point. Agreeing to throw things away is one thing. Actually having to physically lob them over a railing and watch them smash to bits as they crash down into the skips below at the nearest tip is quite another.

'I could help,' Ava offers too. 'I want to see what you made Mickey throw out.'

'You'd be even worse! You'd rescue it all before I even got it out to the car!' he says with a laugh. 'Mick's said you can stay here, and I'll go and fold the seats down in the car to make more space and bring it to the door.'

I see Ava's ears prick up at the shortened name, and I take a sip of my too-hot tea to cover how red my cheeks have gone. Because Mickey is already a nickname, not many people call me Mick, and the ones who do are typically only people who know me *really* well, and I like the feeling that Ren is steamrolling towards that category.

'You can help me find ocean-themed stuff for the antiques fair at the end of the month, if you want,' I say to Ava. 'I don't know where to start. I was thinking of displaying the diary and telling people the story of the mermaid and the sailor, along with a selection of ocean-themed objects to tie in, so if I start putting stuff aside now, we just need to find out the truth behind the diary and it'll be a talking point to engage with customers...' I trail off because my heartbeat is speeding up again at the mention of the antiques fair, but not in the fluttery good way – in the sheer overwhelming fear and dread way. I'm an imposter in the world of antiques fairs. My dad *knew* his stock. He knew exactly the kind of customer who'd want to buy it and exactly the right words to use to talk them into it. I don't even know if I've got more than one item from the same house clearance. How can *I* ever do him proud at an antiques fair named in his honour?

I can sense Ren's blue eyes burning through me and it feels like he can see the thoughts inside of my head, and I turn away until he makes excuses about going to get the car.

'Dad says you went on a date,' Ava says as soon as we're alone.

I blink in surprise. 'Your dad said *that*?'

'Well, no, he said you had cake and tea in a café, and you're both single, so that's a date.'

'While we were waiting for you, you wally.' I laugh in relief that Ren *isn't* throwing around words like that. 'My friend Marnie owns the bookshop up the street and she sends people on platonic dates all the time because she thinks they'll get on as friends. It's only a date if there are romantic feelings involved.'

'He likes you. He blushes every time he talks about you, and Dad never blushes, not even when I talk to him about periods or this boy I like at school.'

And now *I'm* blushing at the thought of Ren blushing and she's absolutely going to notice if I don't redirect this conversation from the dangerous territory it's straying into. Yeah, Ren is beautiful, but he's very, very unavailable, and I don't want Ava getting any ideas about our friendship because that's all it is, and I'm not sure it's even that sometimes. 'You can always come to me if you want any advice about periods. Or boys, although I'm not so much of an expert with them, but I've got nearly three decades of period experience and I grew up with only a dad to talk to as well, so I know what you're dealing with there.'

'Did your dad put together a box for you? Every month, he finds, like, a shoebox, and fills it with different sizes of sanitary towels, and chocolate, and a book, and sometimes a new cover for my hot water bottle or a blanket or something, like a period care package.'

My heart melts. Now *that* is a guy who's stepped up when it comes to periods. 'My dad bought three books about periods and left them on the coffee table, right in the middle of the living room where anyone who came in would see them, because he wanted me to know it was nothing to be embarrassed about or shy away from. Every month, he filled the bathroom cabinet with supplies. I never had to ask for anything. It's not easy to grow up without a mum, but having a dad like yours is special. Not all dads are like that.'

The conversation is cut short by Ren's car pulling up to the door, carefully avoiding my mermaid's tail statue and the tables full of junk that are still outside. I used to think they'd entice customers to come in, but I'm starting to wonder if it makes the place look like a jumble sale, and the Dickensian feel my shop gives off is because only people from the mid-nineteenth century would deign to shop here.

Ren opens the boot, revealing an endless cavern inside his big estate car and comes back in, pulling on a pair of workman's gloves. Between the three of us, we carry everything from the area we'd cordoned off out to the car, while I try to make sure my second thoughts don't show on my face. Some of this stuff has been here since my dad was alive, it's *hard* to throw out things *he* chose, but I can also hear his voice in my head. *If it hasn't found a home by now, Mickey love, it isn't likely to here. Let it move on.*

When it's all in and the car doors are shut, Ren stands in the doorway. 'I won't be long. I'm not sure which one of you is more likely to lead the other one astray, but neither of you do anything I wouldn't do.'

'Daaad, that's *everything*,' Ava whines.

'Well, luckily the shop is open so we're a bit limited on things like going base jumping or wild-water kayaking in the hour it will take you to drop that off, but I'll tell you what, we won't do 99.5 per cent of the things you wouldn't do, and you'll forgive us for the rest, right?'

Ava laughs and so does Ren, his eyes twinkling as they meet mine across the shop.

'And thank you,' I add quickly. 'You don't have to do this but I really appreciate it.'

'My pleasure.' There's that twinkle in his eyes as his gaze holds mine again, and then he shakes himself and swings his car keys around on his finger. 'See you both later.'

'Do you like Dad?'

Ava's words catapult me out of the trance-like state I was in, standing at the window, watching his car pull away and then staring into space long after he's gone.

'It's okay if you do,' she continues. 'Everyone at school thinks he's hot. It's sooo embarrassing. Every girl in my year has got a crush on him, and so have some of the boys. Everyone calls him the hottie history teacher.'

'There are worse things they could say. It's better than everyone saying your dad is the teacher who looks like a walrus, isn't it?'

She giggles. 'I'm going to tell him you said that.'

'It's okay, I'm sure he'll take it in the spirit it was meant,' I say with a giggle too. 'And yeah, I like him, and I don't mind if you tell him that too. Why shouldn't I like him?'

'Because you're so alive and bright and young, and he's so boring and old!'

'He's actually only three years older than me. And I don't think he's boring. I think he's...' I hesitate before I say something I shouldn't and it takes me a moment to settle on a diplomatic answer. '...not having the easiest time since your mum left, but he's trying his best, and underneath his hard shell, he's actually very kind, thoughtful, and generous.'

'Because he's helping you with the decluttering?' She's going through trinkets on a dresser and comes across a ceramic seahorse and takes it over to the counter to put aside.

'Yeah, but also because he's... well, he always brings tea and cake even though he doesn't have to. He's brutally honest but that's not a bad thing. Like those mugs, he could have just let you think he paid for them but he openly told you they were a gift – there's something about someone who doesn't hide even little things like that. I spent a lot of years in a relationship with someone who was never straightforward – it makes me appreciate people who are. He's quick to apologise if he goes too far. And he makes me believe I can get a handle on the shop and face the antiques fair after all.'

'Why *are* you so nervous about the antiques fair?'

'Because it'll be the first one without my dad.' I was on my way out to tidy up the back room, and I stop to answer her question. 'He thrived on doing antiques fairs and talking one-on-one with potential buyers, and it was his suggestion to have it in the castle, but he died before everything could be put into place, so it's my turn to carry the baton and fulfil his idea. They've even named it the Philip Teasdale Antiques Fair in his honour, and that's a *lot* of pressure. Everyone on Ever After Street is going to expect me to have something spectacular. Witt – the castle owner and the guy who's set it all up – has got a news crew coming in and everything. There are going to be reports in newspapers and he's sent press releases out to antiques dealers and special interest websites because he knew that's what my dad would have wanted, but me... I'd rather stay in the background and hide in my shop.'

'That's sad.' She looks over at me. 'You're so lovely, you should be on the news.'

Tears spring to my eyes at how unfiltered she is, and I march over and give her a hug. 'So are you. Maybe your dad will let you come and help me out and we can *both* be on the news.'

'I'd like that.' She hugs me back. 'Dad will say no though. He never lets me do anything fun.'

'He's just trying to protect you. It's what dads do when you're thirteen. I was thirty-six when mine died and he was still trying to protect me, even then. One day you might appreciate it more than you do now.'

I let her go and go out to tidy up before I sob all over her. After I've crushed up a few cardboard boxes for recycling, and she's put a few more ocean-themed ornaments on the counter, she blurts out, 'What's it like not having a dad?'

'Horrible. Absolutely horrible. It's the worst feeling in the world. I would do anything to hug mine one more time. I hugged him every single day and it was never enough. If I could go back, I would hug him so many more times. Enough to make up for all the times I've wished I could hug him again since he died.' It's hard to think about my dad without getting emotional and I bite my lip to stop my eyes welling up again. Even two years later, the grief is still raw, lurking just under the surface, ready to be set off at any little moment.

She nods and thinks about it for a minute. 'I keep thinking he's going to leave too.'

It surprises me so much that the tears that were about to spill over stop in their tracks. 'Ava, that's something your dad is never going to do. You think he's dull and predictable, but that translates to being steadfast and reliable. I get the impression that your mum was fun and exciting, and while that might be exhilarating in the short-term, what you really need in a parent is exactly what your dad's built of. Strong and steady. There are worse things he could do than drink nothing but tea and go to bed early. I know he wasn't exciting enough for your mum, but you've got a good, *good* guy there and you're the most important thing in the world to him. Trust me, people like your dad don't walk out on people they love. Don't let your mum's actions cloud the reflection of your dad too.'

She gives it some serious thought, and then comes over and gives me another hug. 'Thanks, Mickey.'

We're interrupted by a customer coming in, and Ava immediately goes over and asks the woman if she's looking for anything in particular. I remember what Ren said about her lacking in confidence, and I get the sense that being here really has done her good. When she ends up buying a bell jar containing a model of a frog doing yoga, Ava brings it up to the counter and wraps it in tissue paper, and all I have to do is put the money into the till, wondering if I've accidentally fallen foul of child labour laws.

'You didn't tell her the story,' Ava says as the woman leaves.

'What story?'

'I don't know. Whatever story you've made up behind the frog in the jar.'

'Oh!' I laugh awkwardly. 'Your dad's made me wonder if I rely too much on stories and not enough on cold, hard facts. I don't think she minded too much.' I glance out the window and it brings my mind back to a thought that's been niggling lately. 'Speaking of cold, hard facts... Honest opinion – what do you think of the stuff outside?'

I ask her for a second opinion on the tables and crates beyond the window, with a few display pieces and boxes of stuff for people to rifle through. I *thought* it was a whimsical hotch-potch way of displaying things, but now I've started to wonder if it's looking like a junk overflow, the thought won't go away.

'Bad. It's sooo bad. It's ugly and cluttered and it looks like the shop has filled up with so much stuff that it's had to vomit the excess onto the street outside, and you don't tidy it often enough.'

I laugh because she's definitely inherited her dad's bluntness and then pull my sleeves up with a determined nod. 'Come on then, let's get rid of it.'

'Not the mermaid's tail though! You've got to keep the mermaid's tail, it's awesome!' she calls after me as I run upstairs to grab a couple of pairs of gloves and some binbags.

The mermaid's tail meets approval. At least I'm doing something right.

9

It feels good to be outside with Ava. We've both got on pink rubber gloves and we're throwing everything into binbags with reckless abandon, and it *is* freeing rather than daunting for once. The little bits and pieces I've thought people might look at and come to see if there were more inside have got muddled as they've been rifled through, but I can't remember the last time anyone picked something up and did anything more than put it down again hastily.

'At least you don't have to worry about anyone stealing it because no one would want it.' Ava empties a box of old marbles into the rubbish bag I'm holding open. There are also crates of other things people might collect, like tiny glass bottles, and vintage tins and cookware, a few ornaments, some pre-loved toys, and some artificial plants to pretty it up.

I can't help laughing even though she makes a good point, and it feels great to be making a noticeable difference in a short space of time. The decluttering inside is more of a long-term project, and even though Ren and I designated a lot of stuff for the tip or charity shops the other day, it hasn't made much of a dent yet, but out here, the street in front of my shop rapidly looks clear and inviting.

When we're done, I send Ava across to The Wonderland Teapot to get us another drink each, and while I fold up the tables, she goes back to looking for ocean-themed stuff for my stall at the antiques fair.

'We could photocopy pages from the diary and display them behind the stall,' she says as soon as I get back inside, hefting a table through the doorway. There are a few things that she's put ready for me on the counter, and I love how thoroughly she's checking everything for hidden nooks and crannies now. 'We could pin them all onto a big board side by side, so it looks like wallpaper, and then you could have the diary in a display case, and all this sea-themed stuff on the stall in front of you, and people could read the pages and ask about them without having to touch the real diary and risk damaging it.'

'You really do think of everything.' I chuck the folded tables out the back and when I get back to the main part of the shop, she's sucking her strawberry milkshake through the straw and looking at me expectantly, like she's waiting for some other penny to drop. 'What?'

'*Weee-eell*, you'll need to know how it ends, won't you? For the antiques fair, right? So we should read another entry. Only for the antiques fair.'

I can't help giggling. 'The antiques fair isn't until the very end of August. I've got over three weeks to find out how it ends.'

'Oh, come on! Before Dad gets back. He doesn't care, he thinks it's a load of nonsense, but you get it and I want to read it with you because you won't criticise every possibility.'

I admire her enthusiasm as I get the book out, because honestly, I've been itching to read more too, and restraining ourselves until Ren gets back suddenly seems too long to wait.

'Your dad cares more than you think he does though,' I add, because I think he does, just a little bit.

28 February 1899

Every time I look at him, I feel like I've spun in sixty circles and my stomach bounces around inside me. I am giddy with joy. I feel like there are little people tapdancing inside my body and my veins are thrumming with the thousands of taps of tiny little feet. He is the most wonderful person I've ever met.

I form his name in my mouth and act like I'm going to say it out loud. I keep trying, but my vocal cords don't work like a human's do, but his name is the first word I've ever felt like I could speak aloud, if I tried hard enough. Jeremiah. Jeremiah. Jeremiah.

It's written in three different styles of handwriting, and I glance at Ava in excitement. She's mouthing the word like it's written in the diary. This is *huge*! We have a name! We *have* to be able to do something with this. This is a gigantic step towards finding something, anything, that will prove this whole thing is real.

He has taken over my whole life, but it's more than that. He has taken over my entire soul. Every time I close my eyes, I think of him. When I am awake, I am talking to him via my notebooks. When I am asleep, I dream of him.

The other day, I sat beside the fire and he lay beside me. He rested his head on my lap and I stroked his hair until he fell asleep. It was the nicest thing I've ever felt. I continued stroking his hair until he woke and smiled at me, and I felt like I was dreaming too.

He does not seem to mind what I am. He treats me as he would treat any other human. He is kind and warm and he talks to me all the time. He asks me question after question about myself, even though he knows it will take me a long time to write the answers, and he waits so patiently while I do, like he has all the time in the world for me.

Like I am worth waiting for.

He's the person I wish had always been in my life. How much better would things have been if other people were more like him?

But something niggles at me too.

He grieves for his friend. He tells me about him. A brother, he calls him, a comrade. I have no words to say in response so he fills the silence, and I hope he hears what I say with my eyes. With my notebook, I can ask the question that has been playing on my mind since the moment of the shipwreck.

What were they doing that night? There were not supposed to be any vessels on the water in such a storm.

He reads my question and he nods, but he doesn't answer. It is the only question so far that he hasn't answered.

He is hiding something, and I am scared of what it might be.

'She's so in love!' Ava shouts as Ren comes back in the door just as we're about to turn the page and read the next entry.

'You read it without me? How could you!' He raises an eyebrow but there's teasing in his voice.

'Mickey told me you read one without me the other day.'

'Mickey is too honest for her own good,' he says with a grin in my direction.

'His name is Jeremiah,' I say, imparting the *important* information Ava and I have garnered. 'And she thinks he's hiding something.'

'She named him? At last!' Ren's face lights up and he gets his phone out of his pocket and comes over to the counter while his swift fingers type it in to Google.

'You think it's as simple as a first name and a shipwreck?'

'Well...' He's quiet as he scans through results, but the look on his face is one of disappointment, and he tries again with different wording. I get my phone out and try a few variations too, but nothing comes up in the results.

Mrs Moreno comes in at that moment, and Ava immediately goes to help her, unaware that she's about to get a full update on the gout-or-bunion saga and a seventeen-year-old cat's bladder issues.

Ren leans closer. 'Has she behaved?'

'More than. She's a godsend. An absolute credit to you.'

He meets my eyes with a soft smile, and I can *see* how proud he is, and we both go back to googling Jeremiah's name with various ways of putting what we know happened to him, but none of them bring anything up. 'Maybe it was too long ago to be on modern-day results,' I suggest when my fingers start cramping with how tightly I'm holding my phone, hoping against hope for a hit in the search results.

'Or maybe it's just—'

I cut him off by smacking at his hand where he's still holding his phone. 'Maybe it's just that we don't have enough info,' I finish the sentence for him pointedly.

He looks down at the place I touched him and then meets my eyes again, his dancing with mischief that makes *my* veins feel like they're full of tiny tap-dancers too, and I shake my head to clear it. 'Thanks for taking all that stuff. You didn't have to.'

'I brought some empty boxes back so we can start again some-time, maybe next week—'

He was probably about to suggest next weekend when Ava waves Mrs Moreno off and dances back over to the counter. 'She's so lovely. Look, she gave me a sweet!' She unwraps the humbug and pops it in her mouth and then speaks around it. 'Mickey let me serve a customer, it was awesome. I want to work here when I'm older! Actually I want to work here now but Dad would never let me.'

'You've got that right,' Ren mutters. 'This place is hazardous to health.'

'It's all that suspicious incense, right?' I give him a wink.

A loud and clearly unexpected laugh bursts out of him, and it takes him a few moments to compose himself afterwards. 'And I see you got to work out front. It's looking good.'

'Ava's been brilliant. Thanks for letting me have her.'

She throws me a wide grin and looks between us like she's plotting something. 'Mickey, how come you don't have a boyfriend?'

'Don't answer that.' Ren puts his phone down and shoots Ava a reproachful look. 'Please just ignore my overly inquisitive daughter who thinks it's okay to pry where she has no business prying.'

'Like you don't want to know too, Dad. You specifically said, "How can a girl like that be single?"'

'I don't! I did not!' Ren's cheeks are burning red and I can't help feeling a little thrill at the thought of them talking about me *and* of him wondering about my love life. 'Ava, if you're not grounded until Christmas, you will be a very lucky girl. You don't repeat something like that to the person it was said about!'

'Mickey doesn't mind. She likes you too. She said it was okay if I told you.'

Even though it *is* okay, my cheeks are also starting to burn with a hot tingling feeling as this conversation goes on. 'It's okay, I have nothing to hide. And I'm pretty sure your father has worked out that I like him by now. I would have thrown him out ages ago if I didn't.'

'How can you say that when he's standing right there and now he knows? Don't you want the ground to swallow you up and spit you back out as a different person? I like this boy at school and it would be the worst thing in the world if he knew I liked him. He'd laugh at me. All the other girls would laugh at me. I have to pretend I don't like him and laugh when the others make fun of him. It's so embarrassing.'

Ah, the minefield of teenage-girl-politics. I remember those days well. 'When you get to my age, you get past caring. If I like someone in a platonic *or* a romantic way, they should know. Life is too short to play silly games and keep people guessing.'

'Can't argue with that.' Ren meets my eyes again, his cheeks still tinged a sweet shade of pink. 'And for the record, I think you're...'

He's unable to finish the sentence, and the silence grows until it's an awkward cloud hanging over our heads with raindrops of awkwardness dripping from it.

'A hoarding madwoman with a dragon fruit problem?' I offer to ease the unbearable tension.

He laughs an awkward laugh. 'That's the one.'

I laugh too, but it's a fake titter and I undoubtedly fail at hiding the little sting I feel at his agreement. He's opened up to me a lot lately, I was thinking – *hoping* – that he understood me better by now too.

'Sooooo...?' Ava prompts me, going back to the earlier question that I wouldn't have minded her forgetting all about.

'I was with someone for a long time, nine years, we lived

together, he proposed eventually, but it was a "shut up ring"...' My cheeks are burning as I look between her and Ren, wishing she'd asked me while we were alone so I didn't have to go into my disaster of a love life in front of him.

'What's a shut up ring?' she asks before I can say anything more.

'It's when you've been with someone for a very long time, and you expect to get married, but it just... never happens. You get comfortable living together but never take that next step, but you want to, and you don't realise it, but you drop hints. Probably too many hints. You wonder *why* he's not getting down on one knee and why he keeps avoiding the topic whenever it comes up. And then there are outside pressures from family too. His parents already treated me like a daughter-in-law, they talked often about how badly they wanted to see us get married and give them grandchildren, and eventually the pressure gets too much and he proposes, and you're so happy, you think it's finally what you've always wanted, but then nothing else changes. He isn't interested in the wedding plans. He blanks you when you try to discuss potential dates, places, guests, or honeymoon destinations, and slowly, slowly you realise that he *still* doesn't want to get married, but he gave you a ring to shut you up so you and everyone else would get off his back for a while.'

Ren grimaces and sucks air in through his teeth. 'So we're kind of opposites then? You wanted to get married and never did, and I did but shouldn't have.' He glances at Ava and quickly adds, 'Apart from you, obviously. I will never regret marrying your mother because it gave us you.'

'Oh, I know that, Dad. Your life would be extra-dull without me,' she says with a cheeky grin and a self-assurance that only children can have and turns back to me. 'Did you break up with him?'

'I realised the relationship had stagnated. Realised we were more like flatmates than partners. I realised he'd made me feel insecure and needy and selfish for pushing for commitment when he wasn't ready, because he couldn't be honest about how he was feeling. Realised we'd fallen out of love, but believed that getting married would fix everything. Realised it was a conversation we should have had many years before, rather than *after* the most lacklustre proposal of all time and spending a week's wages on bridal magazines because he wanted to bury his head in the sand rather than being upfront.'

'That's a lot of realisations,' Ren murmurs.

'I also realised I felt defective and not relationship-worthy and made the decision to walk away, feeling like I'd wasted so many years and that things could have been so different if he'd had the courage to talk it through when he'd started having doubts.'

'You prioritised your own happiness and found the strength to start again – that's not a bad thing.' Ren's blue eyes find mine and he gives me a nod of solidarity.

'Except I didn't start again. I just sort of... stopped. I went back to live with my dad, and around the same time, he started experiencing symptoms that turned out to be cancer, and I... just haven't moved since. I still feel defective and not relationship-worthy, so now I hide out here, not looking for another relationship, ever. Instead, I invent stories to make up for the fact that my real-life relationship was the opposite of a fairytale, but I still want to believe that they do happen, just to other people, not to me.'

'Maybe that's why they say stories are made up – because they're making up for something in real life?' Ava says, showing a maturity surely far beyond her years.

'I'm sorry.' Ren looks serious and, actually, quite touched. 'It takes a *lot* to realise you deserve more than you have and to say, "I deserve to be happy" and to actually believe it, don't underesti-mate that. *I haven't got that far yet.'*

His hand slides over mine and he gives my fingers a squeeze, and then pulls his hand back quickly and leans on the counter to pinch the bridge of his nose with a groan. 'There is something seriously mind-altering in this shop. Are you sure you're not secretly running an illegal drugs farm from the back room?'

'Oi!' I smack at his forearm but when my hand connects with his skin, my fingers stay put just a little bit too long as I rub his arm to make sure I didn't hurt him.

Ava glances first at him, then at me, and then announces that we should read another entry and turns the page to the one we'd intended to read earlier.

21 March 1899

The best feeling in the world is to feel important to someone. At first, I think he is just being kind to me because we are isolated here, and he cannot manage alone with his broken leg, but as the weeks pass, I start to feel like he genuinely cares for me. I have always been good at knowing what people are thinking when they look at me, and I sense he likes me, genuinely.

He says I saved his life that night and that I have saved it again every day since. He calls me his guardian angel. I have never been called an angel before – a demon, a monster, a devil, but never anything good. People have always feared my kind, but when he looks at me, he has a look in his eyes that is the opposite of fear. It is warmth, and hope, and awe. He touches me sometimes, just a hand on my hand, or a leg against my scales. Sometimes, when I lean over him to dress his wounds, he winds his fingers in my long hair and caresses it, like it is the source of all life, and I am something to be admired, not feared.

When I brought his food the other night, he kissed my hand. His beard scratched against my skin and I nearly fell over. It was the single most delicious thing I have ever felt. It made me cry and he laughed and made me sit beside him so he could put his arms around me.

Senses are dulled underwater, but since I have been out here with him, inside our shelter, every colour, every touch, and every smell feels brighter and clearer than it has before. I feel like I could sing, if I wanted to. I feel like I could spin around in circles like the most elegant dancer. If he could stand, he would lift me up and twirl us around, and I'd feel like I could fly.

When we get back to the shore in Arfordir-Môr-Forwyn, he will be taken from me. I am sure of it.

I don't know what I shall do without him. What if I am wrong about the depth of his feelings? What if he only shows me kindness because we are in this situation? Alone, and he is injured and has only me to rely on. Back on land, there will be other women. Normal women. He will have his soft accent and his seafaring stories of dramatic mermaid rescues to tell, and he will be surrounded by beautiful women who look like I wish I could, with their pretty voices and enticing laughter, and I will be alone again.

Now I know what it is like to not be alone, I am terrified of ever facing my loneliness again.

We get to the end of the entry before I realise what we've just read and look excitedly at Ava and Ren. 'Arfordir-Môr-Forwyn! I've heard of this place! It's a little seaside village in west Wales. The name translates as "Mermaid Coast". It must be their nearest port! This is the most solid lead we've had so far – his name *and* a place.'

I pick my phone up again and google both things together, but nothing comes up, and I think about what we learnt about historical small boat sinkings – that our best hope would be newspaper articles from local authority archives. 'So if Arfordir-Môr-Forwyn is where they're going back to... it's also where the wreckage would have been reported, right? Where any reports of shipwrecked sailors would've made the local headlines...'

'That's odd wording though, isn't it?' Ren taps a finger on the writing in diary and I feel like he's deliberately ignoring my point. 'Taken from. Not "we will be parted", or anything along the lines of "he will leave, I will lose him, I will have to go". He will be *taken*. Is there something we're missing here?'

'Never mind that. This is it! Confirmation of *where* they are – somewhere we can go to check any official records and local newspaper stories from the time. This is what we've been waiting for! Let's go there!'

Ava gasps in delight. 'Oh my God! Can we?'

'We're not going there,' Ren snaps. 'Don't be so ridiculous.'

'I thought you wanted to prove this?' I say, confused by his reaction. From the moment we found out that local archives would be our best bet, I thought that if we found an exact locality, it was a given that we'd go on a road trip to see if we could find out something about our mysterious diary keeper and her sailor.

'Not by travelling 200 miles on a whim!'

I pick up my phone and google it. 'It's only about 120 miles actually, and it's not "on a whim", it's because we've already looked at official records and come up with nothing, so now our only chance is going to the local authority and seeing if they have any info about what happened...'

'Nothing *ever* happened, Mickey! This isn't real!'

'You don't know that. None of us know that. Which is exactly *why* we should go there.'

'This is nonsensical twaddle that could go on forever. First they're in Arfordir-Môr-Forwyn, but if we go there and it's a waste of time, what next? You reckon he's Irish, shall we go to Ireland too? If she's a mermaid, do we take a road trip in a submarine and try to find her? This is a series of endless wild goose chases and none of us are going anywhere.'

'Excuse me!' I scoff and fold my arms. 'I'm not one of your schoolkids. You can't tell me whether I can go or not. *I'm* going. I can take a weekend off and drive down there. It's not impossibly far.' I look between them and then sigh as the realisation sinks in that I'm going to be doing it alone. 'Don't make me do it without you two.'

'I didn't mean...' he sighs and shakes his head, but Ava interrupts before he can continue the sentence.

'I want to go! Mickey's right, we *need* to find out whether this is real or not, and we've already looked here and found nothing.'

He frowns at her. 'Absolutely not. My answer is final.'

'She could come with me...'

Ava nods excitedly and takes a step around the counter so she's standing next to me.

'Do you honestly think I'm going to let my thirteen-year-old daughter go alone on a weekend trip with a stranger?' He's got an eyebrow raised and his mouth is set in a hard and uncompromising line.

I wince at the sharp tone in his voice and try to ignore the jolt of disappointment that he still considers me a stranger. I thought we'd been getting closer. I felt like we'd opened up to each other and started to let each other in to our lives. Have I really got that so wrong? 'I'm not a *complete* str—'

'Nooooo!' Ava wails. 'Why do you have to ruin everything? This is so unfair. You're the worst dad in the world!'

Even I flinch at that. He's more sensitive than he lets on, and I know that would've stung. I risk a glance at his face and can see the hurt look he's unable to hide.

'Ava...' He tries to talk to her but she turns away, and then he fixes his frown on me instead. 'Well, thank you *so* much for making me feel completely inadequate. You might be able to pop off to Wales if you feel like it, drive over a hundred miles at the drop of a hat, but I can't. Some of us have adult responsibilities that aren't governed by fictional sea creatures.'

I can feel a surprising amount of anger building towards him at this unexpected reaction. '*I* have adult responsibilities. I'm the sole owner of my own business, Ren! I can't take time off without closing the shop, but things have to be balanced, and I think finding out something about this diary is worthwhile. In the long run, with the antiques fair, it's likely to bring in more customers over all than the few I'll lose by closing up for a couple of days.'

'Well, I can't be spontaneous and pop off here, there, or anywhere at a moment's notice. I need things carefully planned and—'

'—Executed with military precision,' Ava mutters. 'While having no *fun* whatsoever. *Whhhhy* can't you let us enjoy something for once?'

He glances at her without answering and then back at me with a withering look on his face. 'You don't need to find evidence of a fictional creature to make this shop work – you need to change it.'

'I *am* changing it.' I re-fold my arms, feeling knocked off-kilter by his sudden unexpected animosity.

'No, you're not. You've thrown out a few things, not even a car full, but this whole place needs an overhaul, and you're going to end up losing it if you don't get your head out of the sand and into the real world.'

I blink in surprise. 'Wow, that was harsh, Ren.'

'I *am* harsh. I'm not a big softie who secretly loves dragon fruit tables. I'm a responsible father with real-life responsibilities and a real world to live in. And you... you're focusing on the diary to avoid the reality of how alone you are. You've replaced truth with stories and people with things.'

'Because things don't hurt me!' I snap in retaliation. 'Objects don't die and leave me on my own. Objects don't promise a life together and then change their minds. So yeah, okay, recently it's been nicer to make up stories than to face reality, because guess what, reality is rubbish. As *you* know all too well. You're not exactly well-adjusted, are you? You've shut yourself down and pushed everyone away, and now you take your frustration out on people who have done nothing to deserve it. You pretend to be cold and unfeeling, but you're a ball of barbed wire twisted around a "please don't hurt me" sign, desperately wanting some love and excitement in your quiet life.'

His sharp blue eyes narrow as he looks at me. 'You don't know anything about me. About us. You don't know us. You're a stranger in a shop who we met two and a half weeks ago, and what *I* am is leaving. *Now.*' He turns around and stalks away. 'Ava, come on!'

'No, I—' She tries to protest but he's already stormed out the door.

'I'm so sorry about him,' she says to me with tears in her eyes. 'He's totally out of line. You're awesome. I'm going to yell at him on your behalf.'

'Thanks,' I murmur to the empty shop after she's left and I watch through the window as she rushes after him as he marches down the street. I feel like I've been verbally slapped round the face. That came out of *nowhere*, and it's made me feel uncomfortably bristly, because I don't think I did anything to deserve it, and yet, I understand Ren's got many layers of baggage, and something about my suggestion has rubbed him up the wrong way, even though it was unintentional.

I should probably be angry, but it makes me want to cry. I didn't expect that many home truths, or that his outburst would be so accurate. I *have* been hiding out in the shop since my dad died. I *have* spent too much time making up sentimental stories about objects because doing that has made the world a little bit nicer to live in since my dad died. I've felt less alone because I'm surrounded by things I've attached romantic stories too, and it's made me feel better about the fact that real life is the *opposite* of a romantic story. A coping mechanism, maybe, just like I think his blunt honesty and prickliness is a coping mechanism too, and mainly I'm sad and dejected because I really, *really* like that man, and I'd thought we understood each other better than that.

10

For someone I keep telling myself I'm angry with, Ren has moved into my head rent-free. It's been two days, and I'm in the shop but my attention is elsewhere, because I keep expecting him to come to apologise, but there's no sign of him. I refuse to text him after that argument, even though I should probably apologise for some of the things I said too, especially in front of Ava.

The empty recycling boxes he brought back are in the cornered-off area of the back room, so instead, I take his comments to heart and stalk around the shop, being brutal. He's right that I haven't fully accepted the idea of downsizing my stock, but I *have* been wholly committed to coming up with excuses about why I absolutely *must* keep something-or-other, rather than embracing the change and admitting that some of this stuff needs to go.

I pick up an ugly totem-like stack of tribal masks that, if I'm honest, probably *isn't* a good luck charm passed down through family generations as I've told myself, and in reality, is cheaply made by someone who, presumably, did it with a blindfold on, which is the only explanation for its quirky shape and question-able colour scheme.

I keep thinking about the diary too, and how much I want to spend a couple of days in Arfordir-Môr-Forwyn, but the thought of doing it alone, without Ren and Ava, has made the idea lose its shine.

The thing I'm loving most about this diary is the sense of the three of us being in it together. It's made me realise how lonely I've been, even though Lissa and the other Ever After Street shop-keepers make an effort to check in on me often, but it's only a quick hello at the start or end of each day. Ren and Ava are the first people I've shared any part of myself with in a very long time, and I miss them *both*, even though it hasn't been forty-eight hours since the argument yet.

I pick up a vase in the shape of a head with a crown of grapes, and immediately want to point out yet another fruit-based item, but there's no one to point it out *to*, and it makes the loneliness press down even harder, because I know Ren would laugh, and Ava would probably want to take it home.

I glance at it again and then add it to the charity shop box. Ava's taste isn't that bad, but maybe someone will love it one day, just not in this shop. It's one of the many things that have been gathering dust on my shelves for years. 'Stock turnaround, Mickey love,' my dad would have said. It makes me look around again with a more critical eye.

Some of this stuff really has been here for so long that it would take a miracle to shift it now, but instead of taking away things that haven't sold and keeping the stock fresh for my small group of regular customers, I just keep piling new stuff out and squeezing it into the very limited available spaces. No wonder this place is a disaster.

I lose track of time as I work. It's Sunday and the shop has been quiet, although yesterday was much busier than usual, maybe thanks to what Ava and I did to the pavement outside on Friday. The empty space out there seemed to encourage people to come in much more than the clutter ever had, so I decided to come back in today and apply the same theory to the inside of the shop. I've barely looked up since mid-afternoon, never mind noticed how dark it's getting outside, until there's a knock on the door, and I stop for the first time in hours and realise it's gone 8 p.m., my stomach is loudly announcing that I've skipped dinner, and my dry mouth is telling me how long it's been since my last cup of tea.

The knock comes again and I go through to the main part of the shop and unlatch the door, cautious of who would be knocking at this time of night when Ever After Street itself is long since closed to the public.

'Oh, thank God, I did *not* expect you to be here.' Ren is carrying a basket and pacing back and forth outside, and I breathe a sigh of relief because, firstly, it's not a robber, but mainly because it's *him*.

'I wouldn't have been, normally, but someone gave me a reality check the other day, so here I am, embracing the decluttering. Besides, you know where I live, you gave me a lift home after the library a couple of weeks ago.'

'That was my next plan, but it felt a bit stalkery and I wasn't sure you'd want to see me. And you probably have business insurance that would cover any grievous bodily harm on the shop premises, whereas if you disembowelled me on your own property, the home insurance premiums would be a nightmare.'

I didn't intend to laugh, but I can't stop myself. Typical Ren, always practical, even when it comes to his own potentially gruesome maiming.

'Before you slam the door in my face or dismember me in a

horrible and totally deserved fashion, I am a despicable human being who shouldn't be allowed to play with others, and I'm so sorry about the other day.'

It softens every inch of the annoyance that was still lingering towards him and I pull the door open fully and my breath catches in my throat at the sight of him. I've always thought he was gorgeous, but I didn't know there were *this* many other levels of gorgeous. 'Are you wearing pyjamas?'

'No. Um...' He stops pacing and looks down at himself. 'I suppose, theoretically, I could sleep in these, but I think they call it loungewear.'

'So you do wear sensible clothes sometimes then.'

'I wear sensible clothes all the time!'

'Sensible within context,' I clarify. 'There are times when you *don't* need to look like you're going for a board meeting with the headmaster.'

It's not just his clothes that are different tonight. He's wearing black jogging bottoms and a long-sleeve grey marl top, trainers on his feet, and there's no product in his hair, so instead of being held down, it's blowing around in the summer evening breeze, thick, straight, and choppy, and oh-so-touchable, and there's a smattering of black stubble darkening his jawline, which is also worryingly touchable because my fingers are twitching with the urge to reach out towards him.

'I don't always...'

'It's a shield, I get it,' I say – a throwback to what he said to me when we met at the library, and I suddenly understand how he knew that. He wears practical clothes and keeps his hair neatly battened down because it's something he can control when he feels like he's losing control of other aspects of his life. I under-stand that. I can dye my hair red and slip on Ursula's shell neck-lace and tuck a billowing fake flower behind my ear, and I feel like I *become* Ariel while I'm in the shop, and it's nice not to feel like me for a while. Ren clings onto being someone who *looks* like he's in control of his life, even when he *feels* like everything is spiralling out of his grasp.

He continues pacing. 'Sorry I'm so late. I wanted to come earlier, but it's *me* who owes you an apology and I didn't want to do it with Ava in tow. She's staying over at her grandparents' tonight and I was late dropping her off, then I was rushing to try to catch you before you left the shop to save turning up at your house uninvited, and between that and putting together the stuff for *this*, I forgot to change into anything else...' He stops pacing again and holds up the basket he's carrying, and I'm intrigued by how nervous he seems.

'What's that?'

'It's a "Sorry I was an arsehole" hamper.'

Despite my best efforts in trying not to, I burst out laughing again. He has no right to be this funny during what should be a serious apology. 'Is that the official name?'

'It should be.' He holds it out to me and my fingers brush against his as I take it, and then nearly drop it at the unexpected weight. 'Seriously, Mickey. I was cruel and *way* out of line. The feelings of inadequacy catapulted me back in time, but you didn't deserve my reaction, and I'm sorry.'

He's pacing again, and instead of pushing further, I lift one side of the basket lid and look through the contents. It's a little picnic hamper. There are shop-bought sandwiches, mini sausage rolls, savoury muffins, cocktail sausages, cheese bites, a box of fancy chocolates, and a bottle of wine. 'You didn't have to do anything like this, Ren.'

'I wanted to. I care about you, Mick, and I felt *so* guilty when I walked away on Friday. Ava will tell you it took me ages to drive off because I didn't want to leave it like that, but she convinced me it was better to give you some space because I'd probably have made everything worse by trying to patch things up there and then, so I left it, and time got away from me, and now it's late and... I don't know where I'm going with this sentence full of excuses.'

It makes me giggle again because I adore his honesty. He's *good* at apologising and he's endearingly nervous, and the hamper is so thoughtful that I can't help being touched.

'I think you're stunning.'

The words burst out of his mouth like an explosion and he stops pacing, flashes a look in my direction, and starts up pacing again. I concentrate on his feet traipsing across the pavement to avoid thinking about what that means as he hurries to clarify.

'I didn't finish that sentence the other day and I should have. I think you're *stunning*. Not in a beautiful way... Wait, I mean, *yes*, in a beautiful way, because you *are*. Your blue eyes, your smile that lights up this entire shop, your bright hair that I want to wind my fingers in...' He lets out a shuddery breath and shakes his head at himself.

He can talk with his thick, black *touchable* hair waving around like that. It may as well be screaming, 'Stroke me!'

'But also in the sense that I feel stunned when I'm in your presence. Every time I see you, I feel like I'm not myself, and when I said that sentence on Friday, I simultaneously realised all the most honest endings to it, so I picked a fight instead of confronting it like an adult, and I'm sorry.'

'I'm sorry too. I got too personal and said too much in front of Ava. Things I know you wouldn't want her to hear, and I shouldn't have presumed to know you better than I do.'

'You do. The stuff I've told you in the last couple of weeks, I've never admitted to anyone before, maybe not even myself. I...' He makes a noise of frustration and pushes a hand through his beautiful hair. 'My security is in planning and being prepared. My ex-wife was erratic and spontaneous and I can't deal with that sort of thing any more. I need to know what's going to happen – where, when, why, how – and Ava wants me *not* to be like that, and you suggesting we jump in the car and go to Arfordir-Môr-Forwyn is exactly what Ava wishes I was like and it made me feel inadequate and angry at myself that I can't be like that, and I took that out on you. It took me right back to the final days of my marriage, and Ava said exactly what my ex used to say – about being dull, no fun, and ruining everything, and I curled myself into a metaphorical ball and shot my angry spikes out as a defence mechanism.'

I hold my hand out and wait for him to stop pacing and reach out to take it, and when he does, I give his fingers a squeeze, because even though I'd gathered as much, it makes a difference to hear him say it so openly. Relationship breakdowns are a type of grief, and sometimes the most unexpected thing can dredge up unwanted flashbacks.

He makes an indefinable noise while staring at our joined hands, his fingers tightening slowly around mine. Eventually he shakes his head again without dropping my hand. 'I shouldn't have insulted your shop like that. Your shop is beautiful, it's very you and *you're* very unique and I *like* feeling like "part of your world" when I'm here, and you *shouldn't* change it because of my opinion.' He's short of breath because the words have spilled out so fast that it's like a form of physical exercise.

'Breathe, Ren.' I give his hand a tug, and he lets out a long breath and looks up at the sky for a moment, trying to centre himself.

'Do you want to go for a walk?' Watching him, my eyes fall on the Full Moon Forest beyond, the woodland area surrounding the castle and I blurt the question out before I've thought it through.

'A walk?' It sounds like he's never heard the word before.

'You put one foot in front of the other and aim for a destination? Often favoured by dogs and people trying to get fit? Also, this picnic won't eat itself, will it?' I reach down and pat the handle of the basket where I've put it on the floor.

He laughs a disjointed little laugh. 'I haven't heard of self-consuming picnics, no. But I wasn't trying to be presumptuous or imply you had to invite me or anything.'

'Well, any picnic will taste better shared, sitting by the river on a warm summer's night. Unless you need to get back for Ava?'

'No, she's at her grandparents' until tomorrow afternoon.'

'Good, because I'm starving. Come in while I get myself ready.' I give his hand another tug, hard enough to pull him towards the door this time, and then tell him to wait while I run upstairs to the bathroom. My hair is tied up in a messy knot to keep it out of the way, but I check it for dust bunnies anyway, and then grab two mugs from the kitchen because I'm not drinking that bottle of wine alone, and I'm pretty sure Ren is too refined to glug from the bottle neck itself.

When I get back down the stairs, he's in the other half of the shop, looking over the things I've put into the area for donating to charity. 'And still, the dragon fruit table survives...'

I poke my tongue out at him. 'Someone will love that damn thing one day and you'll be the first person I text when it sells.'

'It's not going to sell. Have you ever even *eaten* a dragon fruit? They're not easy to come by in the UK, I've never seen one down the local Tesco, have you?'

'You're hilarious.' I pick up the basket and manhandle him towards the door. As much as I appreciate him apologising, I've heard enough of his opinions on my stock for one forty-eight-hour period, even though I *haven't* ever eaten one. 'I have a candle that's dragon fruit scented and it's lovely, so it stands to reason that the dragon fruit table is rightly heralded by the person who made it for his dragon fruit-loving wife.'

He's laughing as he lets me shove him out the door, and as I stop to lock up behind us, he takes the basket from my hand to carry it, and when I turn back to him, he's got his arm hooked towards me, inviting me to slip my hand over it. The rational part of my brain tells me I shouldn't get any closer to him, but the other part of my brain is floored by how soft around the edges he seems tonight, and I can't stop myself slipping my fingers into the crook of his elbow and giving his forearm a squeeze through the thin material of his long-sleeve top.

He glances down at me and squeezes his arm closer to his side, so my fingers are held between his arm and his ribcage, and it doesn't feel like any words are needed.

* * *

Birds are singing their evening chorus, and the odd bat flits around the streetlamps as we meander around the edge of the forest behind the shop. The river runs fiercely below us, but as you get further out behind the castle in the hills at the end of Ever After Street, the land turns flatter and the river becomes a trickling stream with stony beaches perfect for picnicking on, even in the dark. It's not far from home, and when I was little, my dad and I used to walk our childhood dog down here all the time.

'This is so beautiful,' Ren murmurs as we wander along well-worn paths towards the lapping sound of the river.

I look up at him. *He* is so beautiful. After my last relationship and losing my dad, I felt like every part of me that looked at men in *that* way sputtered and went offline, but I can feel parts of myself tingling back to life because he's something incredibly special, and yet, also incredibly unavailable. He's still struggling with the hurt of the past, and he has Ava to worry about. She is rightfully his top priority, and after the strained relationship with his ex that still has a huge impact on both their lives, he's *never* going to entertain the idea of getting into another relationship. The thought is so bizarre that it's unfathomable.

'What?'

I realise I've been staring at him while lost in thought, about him, and about the shop and life in general. Sometimes someone comes along and gives you a new perspective on things when you didn't realise you needed it. 'You were right, you know. In what you said. I *have* been hiding in the shop, surrounding myself with *things* and convincing myself that they have magical stories behind them to avoid making connections in real life. I have my best friend, Lissa, but other than that, I keep people at arm's length. I don't want to open myself up again. You and Ava are the first people I've spent any significant time with or shared any *real* part of myself with, and it's made me realise how lonely I've been. I *have* replaced people with things and treated the things... almost like they were real?' I say it questioningly, hoping it makes sense to him. 'I invent the stories and then treat the objects like a physical incarnation of the imaginary people behind them, and I've put too much importance on that and treated them like stray animals looking for a forever home, rather than as things that someone needs to buy for my business to carry on, and stock that needs to be turned around semi-regularly, and I haven't wanted to admit that some of the things need to be thrown away.'

'Like the—'

'Not the dragon fruit table,' I interrupt before he can say it, and he dissolves into laughter that warms my heart. I squeeze his arm again. 'And you're the first person who's been honest enough to make me realise that, and I really appreciate it, even if it isn't easy to hear sometimes.'

'The way you treat things is endearing. You give objects a real importance and you care about them *and* the people who buy them. Don't change that because of what I've said. Your shop is full of *love* and that's what makes it special. Not *everything* has to be sensible and practical and dull and boring, like me.'

'I don't think you're like that at all.'

'What do you think I'm like then?' He glances down at me and slips into third person. 'He asks in trepidation, not sure if he really wants to know the answer.'

'Bloody beautiful.'

He lets out a half-snort half-laugh half-gurgle type of noise. 'Oh, Mickey...'

'No. Seriously. Ava is *so* lucky to have you.' I look up at him again. 'And your ex-wife is a twat. There are worse things someone can be than sensible and caring. And I think you've been hurt so badly that you struggle to see the good side now, and you've let other people's words influence the way you see yourself.'

He takes a deep breath and I can see his cheek dent inwards as he bites the inside of it.

Instead of saying anything, I give his forearm another squeeze and lean my head to the side until it rests against his upper arm briefly, just a touch that's not the hug I really want to give him, and he lets out another shivery breath and dips his chin until it brushes against the top of my head, and it feels nice, just the two of us on a dark summer evening, with no one expecting us to be anything other than exactly who we are.

11

By the time we reach the river, Ren's laughing at how loudly my stomach is growling, and he helps me down the shallow bank and we slip-slide over the water-smoothed stones of the riverbed towards the gentle trickling of the water. The moon has risen in the sky and is reflecting on the surface as we find a stone perfect for sitting on.

It's a big, curved boulder that you could recline on if you wanted a *very* uncomfortable recliner, and rather than squeezing onto it next to me, Ren untangles his arm from my hand and sits down on a smaller rock beside it, right at the edge of the water, close enough to dip our toes in.

The basket is between us, and while I go through it and pull out packets of picnic goodies, Ren gets out the two mugs I shoved in and opens the wine.

'Cheers.' He hands me a mug full of bubbling rosé, and then holds his own up to clink against it. 'To new friends.'

I tap my mug against his and take a sip. 'To *unexpected* friends.'

A wide grin lights up his face and he meets my eyes in the

dark evening light and his are positively shining, and his smile is a thing of beauty. He doesn't feel like a *new* friend. It feels like I've known him for years, not less than three weeks.

I rip into a packet of mini muffins and he opens the sausage rolls and we stuff our faces in comfortable silence, interspersed by throwing bits of pastry into the water and watching the ripples as tiny fish surface to gobble them up.

'I didn't do this with the intention of you inviting me to join you...' He looks up at me with eyes gleaming in the moonlight. 'But I'm really glad you did.'

I've kicked my shoes off and my feet are in the water, and I lift my foot until I can poke his knee with my toe. 'Me too. You *really* know how to apologise.'

'Maybe that should worry you about how often I have things to apologise for.'

Maybe it should, and it *does*. It niggles that this probably won't be the only time we'll ever clash, but I also appreciate that he's human and we all overreact sometimes and say things we don't intend to say, and when most of the food is gone and my stomach has well and truly stopped growling, I get out the box of posh chocolates and pick an almond praline crème, and then set the box on the rock where we can both reach it.

He shifts nearer, puts his arms up and folds them on my rock and lays his head on them, right beside me as he watches the water, and the temptation is just too much.

I let my fingers give his dark hair a quick ruffle. 'I like your hair like this. Usually it's so .. stiff.'

'Like me, you mean?'

'No, like it has too much product in it.' I probably shouldn't, but I stroke through it again, tugging gently on the longer part to the right of his parting that's usually stuck down, letting the dark strands slip between my fingers just one more time. 'You're perfect exactly as you are.'

I hear his breath catch and he lets out a shaky exhale of a sigh, and I *know* I should stop, I shouldn't be touching him like this, but he seems to be welcoming it. With every breath, his shoulders slump, shifting his head closer to my hand, so I carry on, gently brushing his hair to one side, trying not to watch the relaxation seeping through his usually taut body while trying not to overthink how good it feels to be this close to him.

'Sorry.' I go to yank my hand away when rational thinking returns with a vengeance. You don't stroke the hair of someone you barely know, especially when this, whatever *this* is, ends at the friendship we toasted to earlier. It *has* to.

'Please don't think you have to stop doing that.' He reaches up blindly until his hand wraps around my wrist and stops me from pulling away, and he swallows hard and lets out another breath. 'Please *don't* stop doing that, ever.'

His voice is a shaky whisper and the vehemence in it makes me smile. 'Well, you're going to have to give me a second because there's wine left and it would be a shame to waste it.'

I hold my hand out for his mug and he passes it up to me, and I empty the rest of the bottle equally between our mugs and pass his back, and then I shift nearer the edge of the rock and settle back, letting my fingers play with his hair again as he nestles his head against my thigh and his eyes drift closed.

It's the most gorgeous summer night. It must be about 10 p.m. by now, the air is warm but the breeze is keeping it pleasant, and there's no sound at all apart from the burbling of the river against the stones.

'I never used to be like I am now.' His voice is barely louder than a breath in the silence. 'Stiff. And uncompromising and dull, strict, a bore-fest as Ava would describe me. I used to be fun and spontaneous. I used to laugh.'

'You still laugh.'

'Not like I used to. I'm always holding back, never letting myself enjoy anything because I know it won't last.' He lifts his head to take another swallow of wine and then rests it against my leg again. 'I used to be like you. Easy-going, laidback, hopeful. I saw the best in people. I was the world's greatest believer in the power of love and the possibility of magic, and now... I'm sharp. Hard. Harsh. I lash out, I say things I don't mean to and see only the worst in people. I push everyone away, desperate to be left alone, and yet...'

'And yet you crave human connection?' I finish the sentence for him when he seems unable to find an ending for it.

At first I think he's going to deny it, but he sighs and moves his head against my leg, nodding gently. 'I didn't realise how much until I met you.'

I knock back the last of my wine and set the mug aside, and then let my free hand trail along his shoulder, until he reaches up to tangle his fingers with mine, and the fingers of my other hand continue carding through his hair.

'I know I shouldn't be sitting here, but that affection is like a drug. I haven't felt liked for so long. Ava holds so much against me. My relationship with her grandparents is strained – they blame me for their daughter leaving, even though we were already divorced by then. Friends pulled away – or I pushed them away,' he adds before I can interject. 'Every decision I make when it comes to Ava is the wrong one.'

'No teenager appreciates their dad. Don't take that personally.'

He sighs and untangles our fingers to take another glug of wine while being careful not to dislodge my other hand from his hair. 'I just wish there was somebody on my side. Somebody to tell me I'm doing it right, or at least, somebody to get it wrong with together. I've never felt so alone.'

I can *hear* the pain in his words. I want to say something to reassure him again he's doing a good job, but right now, it would seem like a pointless platitude. External validation makes very little difference when you're floundering this much on the inside.

He downs another glug of wine and then shifts, turning so he's leaning back against the rock, the back of his head resting on my leg as he turns his face to look up at the stars, and I go back to tucking his hair back and let the fingers of my other hand dance across his shoulder, because I don't know how long it's been since Ren opened up to anyone, but I have a feeling this is the very first time.

'I didn't ever expect to be divorced. I didn't think I'd ever be a single father. I was happy. I loved my wife, I thought she loved me. I thought we were in it together. I stupidly thought that marriage might make us a partnership for the rest of our lives, not only until she got bored of having a husband and daughter. All I wanted was love and a family and I had that. What I did wrong was being happy. Being settled. Not yearning for anything more. Apparently that's what you're supposed to do in a relationship, just want more all the time. Nothing should ever be enough.'

'Was there cheating involved?' I ask quietly, because it sounds like there must have been, but he's never said it outright.

'A lot. And I put up with it because I naively believed we could work things out and if I just let her do what she wanted, go looking for the "more" she believed was out there, maybe she'd eventually realise that what she had was enough all along...' He leans his head back and meets my eyes. 'See? I used to believe in fairy stories too.'

I give his shoulder a squeeze, awkward at this angle, because that tells me so much about him. He's been walked all over and then made to feel like he deserved it, and it gives me a real understanding of what I'd already worked out – that his straightforward manner stems from making sure no one else is going to get a chance to do that again. 'No wonder you don't now.'

'I come from a place of instability,' he says, like he's trying to explain why he'd put up with so much to try to save a relationship that clearly wasn't working for either of them. 'When I was a child, my parents split up, then got back together again, then split up, then got back together, then split up, then got other partners, then had an affair with each other again, got back together, split up... the cycle repeated endlessly. I never knew whether they were going to stay together from one day to the next, or whether they were going to have a screaming row in a public place at any given moment. I could go to school in the morning and they'd be all lovey-dovey and happy, and then I'd come home to find my mum in the upstairs window, hurling my dad's belongings onto the front lawn while he screamed up at her from the pavement outside. So I know what it's like to come from an unstable background. I know what it does to a kid to watch their parents have a blazing row in front of their friends. I know what it was like to go to friends' houses and see their normal, happy parents and want to stay forever. To wish I had a family like that. To never want to go home because I never knew what I'd be walking into. And I never wanted to be a parent like that. I wanted to find "the one" and be happy and settled and be *enough* for each other. I wanted her to *want* to come home and eat dinner together and go out for a family walk or cuddle up on the sofa and watch TV or read together. It's not much, but those small, simple things are the little stabilities that meant a lot to *me*. Knowing that someone *wants* to spend time together is special.'

He glances up at me, like he's aware that he's revealing too much, and I nod encouragingly because I've never been more desperate to hear something in my life.

'I wanted to be who someone else wanted. I wanted to be enough. And I wasn't. And now Ava has that instability and I'm trying, *so* hard, to be stable and steadfast, and maybe I've gone too far in the opposite direction, and now I'm too strict...' He trails off with a shake of his head where it's still leaning on my thigh.

'This isn't about Ava.' I card my fingers through his soft hair again. 'For right now, for *this* moment, we're talking about you. When you're a parent, especially a single one, you become nothing *but* a parent, but you're still you, Ren, you still have feelings and needs and wants.'

'Right now, I *need* to finish this wine and I *want* to hug you, and I'm pretty sure I know which one is the more sensible option.'

I grin as he sits forward to down the last of his drink and sets the mug down and then slumps back against the rock, and I lean over until I can slip my arms around his shoulders and give him a squeeze from behind.

It's the most awkward angle in the history of awkward angles but he laughs tipsily and snuggles back, as much as you *can* snuggle while sitting against a rock, and lets out a sigh that feels like a lead weight leaving his body. His hands come up and slip over mine where my arms are around his chest, and we stay like that until my back starts to protest the position just a bit too loudly and I have to pull away and straighten myself up.

He murmurs an apology and shifts again to look up at me without moving his head off my leg, and I look down and meet his glazed eyes and his answering smile is wide and definitely a little bit looser than usual.

Eventually, a fish jumps and reverts his attention towards the river, and I touch my reddening cheeks to see if they're as hot as they feel under his gaze.

'It's so beautiful here.'

'Ever After Street is a gorgeous place. My dad fell in love with it the moment he saw it. The area, the shopkeepers, the customers, even Mrs Moreno's cat.'

He laughs loudly. 'While I'm sure Mrs Moreno's cat is truly a delight, I didn't mean that, I meant *this*, in general. Being here, being here *with you*, being stuffed full of good food and even better wine, feeling this good. I know it won't last but it's been a long time since I felt this sense of contentment. Thank you for forcing me to open me up.' He holds two hands up and clumsily mimes opening a clamshell, and it makes me narrow my eyes at him.

There's a slight lisp to his words that makes me brush his hair back and look down into those glassy eyes again. 'Are you a little bit drunk, Mr Montague?'

'No! Nooo, of course not, don't be—' He lifts a hand and it flops back down onto his lap with a heavy thud, and he lifts his head and looks around in a way that suggests the world is spinning. 'Oh, bugger.'

I let out a peel of laughter. 'Never in the history of the world has anyone's reaction to getting drunk been, "Oh, bugger."'

'I've only had half the bottle! I can't be this much of a lightweight!' He sits forward and drops his head into his hands, scrubbing them over his face. 'I *never* drink these days. I always worry about Ava and what if there was an emergency and I had to drive somewhere, so it's been *years* since I drank anything at all. Oh, God! This is awful!' He flops back against the rock again, and I'm laughing so hard that I feel drunk myself, even though Lissa and I share enough bottles of wine that *my* liver is fully acclimatised to putting away half a bottle most weekends.

'You are *adorable*.' I lean over until I can hug him again, and he turns into me and hides his face in my shoulder and makes a noise of shame.

'I didn't even think...'

'You don't need to think. It's not a bad thing to relax and let yourself go. I'll take full responsibility for leading you astray.'

He groans and pulls his legs out from under himself and stretches out, half-reclining against my rock as he lies back, his head on my lap again, and looks up at the night sky. 'Is it hot in here or is it me?'

'It's you, my blootered friend, it's you.' I touch the backs of my fingers to his red cheeks, because *hot* doesn't come into it. He's by far the most gorgeous man I've ever met, with his ice-blue eyes and the dishevelled black hair, and that smattering of stubble shading his jawline, but it's not just how he looks. It's the beautiful, sensitive soul hiding underneath so many layers of pain and hostility and fear. Someone who wanted what we all want deep down in our souls – to be loved, to be wanted, exactly as we are – and there's something gorgeous about someone who can show enough vulnerability to admit that, even if he's got to be a little bit intoxicated to do so.

He scrubs a hand over his face. 'Oh, God, I drove here. My car's in the Ever After Street car park. I'm going to have to get a taxi home and come back to collect it tomorrow. I'm such an idiot.'

'Ren, stop. It's not the end of the world. People have done worse things than get a tad tipsy without meaning to. I'm within walking distance on the other side of the river, you can stay with me.'

He goes to protest but I interrupt him again. 'You've got nowhere to be, nothing to do, no one to be responsible for tonight, and I'm your designated adult. Let yourself go. Enjoy giving up a tiny shred of control.'

'Enjoy... I don't think I've enjoyed anything for years...'

'And *that's* a problem.'

'Yeah, I know.' It's a mumble as he reaches up and tangles his fingers with the hand on his shoulder, pulls it down, and brushes his lips across the back of my hand.

His stubble is soft rather than scratchy and it makes me feel even more overheated than I was feeling anyway, especially when he holds my hand against his lips for a long few minutes, and when he pulls away, he doesn't let go. Instead, he keeps hold of it, resting it against his chest, right over his heart, as he lets out another sigh and tries to relax, his thumb rubbing back and forth along the base of my thumb, and I get the feeling he needs something to hold on to. I fight the urge to lean down and hug him again, because he *is* adorable, and I feel ridiculously privileged that someone who tries so hard to be in control of *everything* has trusted me enough to let that control slip just for a little while.

We talk about anything and nothing, likes and dislikes, getting to know each other better while his walls aren't up, and time trickles past like the water, until it must be nearly midnight, but I'm trying to embrace this sense of peace too. Neither of us have anything else to do tonight, and there are worse ways to spend a warm summer's evening than on a riverbank with a man who, no matter how much time I spend with him, it's never enough, and this is the most serene and content I can remember feeling for a long time too, and I'd be happy if this night didn't end anytime soon.

Eventually, he starts to move. He shifts around to push himself into more of a sitting position with a few grunts and groans, and then leans back until he can catch my eyes again. 'You're not really going to Wales on your own, are you?'

'Yes. I'm not keen on driving, but the diary is important to me. I want to know the truth behind it, and if going there can help uncover something then it's worth it.'

'I'll drive.'

'What, right now?' I raise a teasing eyebrow, about to jokingly lecture him on the laws of drinking and driving.

'Hah hah,' he mutters and leans back to meet my eyes again. 'No. All three of us. Let's do it. Let's go to Wales. Not *right* now, obviously. Whenever suits you. Me and Ava are free until school starts again, but you've got the shop to work around. Figure out the best time for you and we'll go, get a hotel for a couple of days, see what we can find out.'

I squeal and he winces at the pitch too near his eardrum, suggesting he's sobering up *way* too quickly. 'You mean that?'

'Yes. It's not the sort of thing I'd ever do, but you make me want to be less... me, so yeah, why not?'

'For those of us who like you exactly as you are, I don't think that's a good thing. Being *you* is okay.'

He makes a disbelieving noise and looks like he wants to say something else, and I decide to lighten the mood. 'But so is not making me trek all the way to western Wales on my tod, so I'm going to hold you to that, even if you regret this conversation in the morning.'

He takes my hand again and lifts it to his mouth. 'Suspect I'm going to regret a *lot* of things in the morning.' His lips move against my skin, his soft stubble skimming across my hand, and then he lets go and sits forward. 'We should go, shouldn't we? This riverbank is having a detrimental effect on my ability to think straight.'

'I don't think it's the riverbank, do you?'

He laughs as he pulls his shoes over and puts them back on, which takes a few more attempts than it usually would, and then he groans as he pitches himself upright and I scramble up to wrap an arm around him in case he slips on the smooth stones.

I carry the basket in one hand and keep my other arm wrapped around his waist, while his arm stays around my shoulders, and as soon as the ground is solid again, he stops and pulls away far enough to hold both arms open, inviting a proper hug.

I step into his embrace instantly, because the half-squeezes and awkward angles have been nowhere near enough tonight. His arms slide around my waist and he pulls me tight against him, so every inch of our bodies are touching. One hand reaches up so his fingers can tangle in the falling-down knot of my hair, and I lose track of time as we stand there, just holding each other.

He starts humming 'Part of Your World' and moving us around in a blocky, unsteady dance that makes me giggle and hold on even tighter in an attempt to stop us both toppling over. One hand stays on his back, while the other creeps up to tangle in the thick hair at the nape of his neck, and he lets out a shuddery, guttural groan and curls even further around me. His feet stumble at the touch so I keep doing it, letting my fingers stroke through the hair at the back of his head and dance across the nape of his neck, until he buries his face in my shoulder and squeezes me tighter.

'That affection, I haven't had that for years. There's always an undercurrent of frustration running through me, and I don't feel that tonight. Thank you for making me feel so loved, even just for a little while.'

I can feel my heartbeat throbbing in my head and my throat is tightening as words fight to get out. He's *so* open that it's heart-rending and I have never wanted to wave a magic wand and erase someone's pain more than I do right at this moment. It would be so, so easy to lift his head and pull his mouth down to mine right now, and I *want* to. Oh, how I want to.

And I know he's feeling it too. 'It's been so long since I felt like this. I wish, just for a while, to feel wanted. Desirable. I wish you'd kiss me.'

He doesn't know what he's saying, I tell myself, as I let out a semi-hysterical laugh. 'I'm not kissing you when you're drunk. I'm not kissing you when you're sober either, for that matter.'

'Aww, why not?' He lifts his head from my shoulder and meets my eyes, sounding like even *he* isn't sure whether he's serious or not.

'Because you *are* wanted. You *are* desirable. And you *are* going to regret this in the morning. And so am I,' I mutter to myself as I reach up and let my thumb brush over the hair darkening his jaw as I cup his face. 'You have the softest stubble. Stubble by definition is prickly, but yours is like a layer of down covering your face.' I turn my hand around and let the backs of my fingers rub over his cheeks. 'And the most beautiful eyes. God, your eyes, Ren. They're so blue and so sharp. I've never seen eyes like yours before.'

Maybe it's me who should be more careful with what I'm saying. I don't know what's come over me tonight, but I suddenly want him to know *everything* I'm feeling about him.

His eyes are grey in the moonlight, and I know we're on more dangerous ground than the slippery river rocks just now, but it's physically impossible to look anywhere else. 'You have the most kissable cheeks.'

I know I should take my hands off him and step far, far away, but I cup his face again, my fingertips grazing along his jaw. His eyes close as I push myself up on tiptoes until I can touch my lips to his warm cheek. It's soft, lingering, and tender, and the tip of my nose rubs against his skin, and the noise he makes is full of longing. He slumps against me as his whole body goes boneless, making me wonder how long it's been since someone kissed this man.

'Didn't think I'd ever feel like this again.' After a while of holding him tight, he blinks wide eyes open and lifts his head so he can meet my eyes. 'Peaceful. Content. Happy.'

'Hammered?' I offer, making him giggle.

'I'm fine. Just a little bit… wonky.'

'Aren't we all?' I mutter.

'You're not.'

'Oh, I am. You know that. You've spent the past three weeks criticising my shop because of how wonky my approach to life has become. But the diary has inspired me. Whoever she was, she didn't have it easy, but she still…'

'…let herself believe in love?'

I pull back to look into his unfocused eyes again. 'I did not expect you to finish a sentence like that.'

'Seem to be doing a lot of things I never usually do tonight, and for the first time, I don't think it's a bad thing.'

'Neither do I.' Against my better judgement, I lean up and kiss his cheek again. 'Not at all.'

12

Ren is asleep on my sofa, and now the morning sun is streaming in the living room curtains, and I'm watching from the kitchen, hoping he stirs before I have to leave for work.

As the time gets later, my clattering around increases in volume until it has the desired effect, and he stretches with a groan and stays still for a few moments, a hand on his head like it's throbbing as he tries to get his bearings.

As he pushes himself into a sitting position, I go into the living room. I take his hand, open his fingers, and push two paracetamol out of the card and into his palm and put a glass down on the table in front of him. 'Paracetamol. Water. Kettle's boiling for a coffee. I think you're going to need all three of those things.'

'I wasn't that far go— Oh, God.' He drops his head into his hands and shakes it with a loud groan of shame. 'I asked you to kiss me, didn't I? I said we'd go to Arfordir-Môr-Forwyn, didn't I?'

'Yep, and you can't change your mind,' I say with a grin because I knew he'd regret those conversations this morning.

He swears and then groans again, and downs the tablets and half the glass of water in one. 'Can you just ignore everything I said last night? I don't think it was the wine, I think I got drunk on the affection.'

'Ah yes, affection. Well known for being 14.5 per cent proof and served in mismatched mugs.' I grin at him again, thoroughly enjoying every second of his discomfort. 'I can never mention it again, but I'm not going to ignore it. And if you think I'm ever going to forget the cute, snuggly, giggly version of you, you're sorely mistaken.'

'I feared you were going to say that.' His eyes meet mine and he smiles despite himself, and then looks away quickly and gets to his feet, and looks back at the fleece blanket that was covering him and murmurs a thank you.

He's given me a lift home before, but this is the first time he's ever been inside. He wanders around the room, taking in the mantelpiece with a couple of photos of Dad on it, and the one I still have of Mum, and goes over to the window to look out at the little patio area outside. 'Have you recently been burgled? Where is everything?'

He picks up a snow globe that's got Ariel inside it, sitting on a rock, and when you shake it, instead of snow, hundreds of tiny pink starfish swirl around her.

Instead of answering his question, I give him an explanation of the snow globe that he didn't ask for. 'Raff Dardenne made it for me. He runs the snow globe shop in the year-round festive part of the street, Christmas Ever After.'

I know what he's really asking. Why is my shop full of clutter when my home is only furnished by things that really matter to me?

'It's been comforting, I guess,' I say aloud, even though he never actually asked. 'To be surrounded by so many things that must have mattered to people once. It's made me feel less alone, like I'm not the only forgotten thing that's been left behind.'

'The shop would be vastly better if you applied *this* initiative to it. Things that have meaning and might mean something to someone else. Not just abandoned old things that you feel sorry for. This is beautiful.' He pokes at my little model of a carousel and winds the lever to make it turn so the old tinny music fills the living room. 'I know you can't know exactly what will mean something to your customers, but there has to be a better approach than just piling stuff up and hoping the right customer will come along and have enough stamina to see them through the hunt for it.'

I snort at his unfiltered way of putting things. 'Did you mean what you said the other day – you really think I'm going to lose the shop?'

'I shouldn't have said that. I'm s—'

'I know you're right.' I cut him off before he has a chance to apologise again, because he has nothing to apologise for. He *is* right. I've known it for a while and I've buried my head in the sand – he was right about that too. I can't carry on as I have been and expect things to magically improve, and Ren has a way of making me want to take action and *make* things different and rediscover the vision I once had and the shop I once loved so much.

'Your shop makes the world a better place.' He says it gently, like he can tell what I'm already thinking. 'There aren't many businesses like that in the money-grabbing retail industry. Ever After Street would be a much less magical place without you.'

I don't know if the implication on that last point is still about my shop or about me personally, but I appreciate him not being as pushy as he usually is. And he has a good point, as usual. Most of my stock these days is things that I think need rescuing, things that deserve a new home, rather than things I think will actually sell or that my customers might like. It's the opposite of how my dad ran things, and something's got to give.

'I feel weird this morning. Looser than I did before.' He rolls his shoulders around and shakes his arms out. 'It's the first time in ages that I haven't felt angry. Thank you for... I don't know. Listening, I guess. That kiss. I feel like you sucked out some of the poison in me.' He traces his fingertip along his left cheek like he can still feel it and then realises what he's said. 'I don't know why I'm saying this. Shut me up, Mick, please shut me up.'

His eyes drop down to my mouth and both of our minds go to the same place, the same *way* of shutting him up, because his cheeks flare red and I can feel mine start burning at the exact same moment.

'Not like that. Just stop me saying something I'll regret.'

'There's nothing to regret, I promise. I kissed your cheek, Ren. You make it sound like it was a lot more.'

'It was a lot more to *me*. You made me feel wanted. Cared for. No one's done that... For such a long time...' His voice breaks and he quickly turns away, probably praying I didn't hear it.

He swallows hard and squares his shoulders. 'I should go. Can you please not tell Ava about any of this? I should be setting a good example, not getting pissed and doing... whatever the hell this was.'

'Do you want to stay and have breakfast? Coffee?'

He thinks about it. 'Yes, I do, but I can't. I can't do it again, Mick.'

'Breakfast?' I ask, knowing he *doesn't* mean breakfast.

He shakes his head, taking a long while to come up with the real meaning behind those words. 'I can't not be enough for someone again.'

It's so exposed and vulnerable, and I can feel my heart splintering at the thought of him thinking it would be the same with us, with *me*, if this ever went further than a kiss on the cheek. No matter how much time has passed since the breakdown of his marriage, the scars of feeling responsible for it run *deep*. 'What if it was the someone who wasn't enough, and not you?'

'That's a... nice thought.'

He doesn't say he believes it but it's something.

After he leaves, I walk to work, filled with a new sense of purpose. I didn't get a lot of sleep last night, not just because of the beautiful man sleeping on my sofa, but because, in my mind, I couldn't stop turning over all the things we discussed last night, and that conversation this morning has reinforced my niggling thoughts. The shop has got to change, *now*, and the only person who can change it is me.

'We're going to *Way-els*, we're going to *Way-els!*' Ava sing-songs as she runs over and flings her arms around me for a hug. 'We're going to find out what really happened in 1899 and prove that mermaids are real! Best summer holiday ever!'

'We're really, really unlikely to prove that a fictional sea creature is real.' The voice of reason appears in the doorway behind her, looking suitably less excited about the prospect of a trip to the Welsh coast. 'Don't get your hopes up.'

Ava ignores Ren's grouching. 'It's no Disneyland, or Alton Towers, or Thorpe Park...' She continues reeling off a list of what are obviously her bucket-list summer holiday destinations, and while Arfordir-Môr-Forwyn is nowhere near the top, I guess anywhere that's *not* the Wye Valley is better than nothing.

'*How* did you persuade him? What spells did you cast?' She releases me and looks around like she's searching for the Fairy Godmother's magic wand. 'He never changes his mind about anything. And the most exciting place we usually go is to McDonald's.'

'Believe it or not, I didn't *have* to persuade him, it was his suggestion. I think your dad's much more of a great big softie than he'd have anyone believe.' I meet his eyes and grin at him across the shop.

'Oh, you do, do you?' Ren beams back at me and pushes himself off the doorframe he was leaning against without dropping eye contact.

My grin gets implausibly wider. 'Good morning, Mr Montague.'

His cheeks redden at the throwback to the riverbank last week, and even though it's impossible to tear my eyes away from Ren, I can sense Ava's head whipping back and forth between us before she eventually declares, 'Oh my God, get a room!'

'We've got a room,' Ren mutters. 'Unfortunately it's only *one* room.'

It's Friday and once we'd decided on this weekend for our road trip – leaving this morning, staying three nights, and then coming back on Monday afternoon – he tried to book a place to stay. Unfortunately, it's a small coastal village with only one hotel and it's smack-bang in the middle of the summer holidays, so every room was booked, although they'd just had a cancellation for *one* room, which he sensibly snapped up, but still.

'It's giving "classic rom com"!' Ava squeals.

'It's giving "Ren sleeps on the floor and ends up with a bad back because Ren is too old to sleep on the floor."'

'Ren is too young to complain this much,' I counter. 'Ren is like a forty-one-year-old with a ninety-one-year-old living inside him.'

'Touché.' He grins, but it's with a teasing, jokey wink and he can't stop smiling. 'The receptionist said they could provide a folding camp bed, so I'll have that while you girls share the nice, comfortable *real* bed.'

'Thanks, Dad,' Ava calls from where she's looking around the shop, before she reappears with a concerned look on her face. 'What happened in here?' She turns to her dad. 'What did you make Mickey do to her shop?'

'Actually nothing,' I answer for him. 'That was all me.'

'I thought it was odd that I didn't get concussed by a Victorian birdcage on the way in.' Ren looks around with an approving nod.

'You've made me realise where things have gone wrong lately. Everything has got so cluttered and I've lost sight of what I always wanted this place to be. It's supposed to be an undersea treasure trove with an ocean theme, and that's got lost along the way. I *love* mermaids and all things oceanic, *that's* the direction I was intending to go in when I took over while my dad was still alive, but when he died, the waters got muddied, and *you've* made it seem clear again.' I nod to Ren, loving the way his cheeks redden.

'I know that feeling,' he mumbles, out of Ava's hearing.

'I want my stock to be more curated. More selective. Lissa's the curator of the Colours of the Wind museum, and she's going to help me decide on what to keep and what to sell off. I've talked to Witt – the guy who owns the castle and has organised the antiques fair – and he's agreed that we can have a big sale in the castle grounds on that weekend. I'll display the diary as we've planned to give people something to talk about, and Lissa and some of the other shopkeepers are going to run separate stalls full of the other bits and pieces and sell them at a reduced price in an attempt to get rid of them, so loads of stuff is boxed up ready to be taken up to the castle, and—'

'You haven't chucked the dragon fruit table, have you?'

Ava's anxious interruption makes me giggle. 'No. That's staying put until it finds a buyer who *loves* it, just so I can rub it in your dad's face when it does.'

They both laugh, and if I'm not mistaken, they *both* breathe a little sigh of relief.

Ren dips his head towards me. 'It sounds like a good idea. About the shop, I mean, *not* about the dragon fruit table, no one in their right mind would buy that thing, but you seem... happier? Lighter?'

'It's the right decision. I can't throw all of this stuff away, or give it all to charity shops because I've spent the business money on it and I need to get *something* back, and Witt's convinced the extra stalls won't give the antiques fair too many "car boot sale" vibes, and with the extra space in here, I can choose more important things to showcase – things like the diary – with real stories behind them that deserve to be known, and it really does feel like a weight has been lifted. So thank you. For all your help and your input. You might be harsh and blunt but you make the occasional good point.'

He blushes hard, and it gives me a little tingle to remember what Ava said about Ren blushing. For someone who never blushes, he's been getting red-faced a lot in my company lately.

'I've always said we never really own objects, we're just looking after them until their real owner arrives, and I've lost sight of that and stopped considering whether their potential owners are likely to be part of my customer base or not, and as you can see, they're not. This has become a home for unwanted things rather than a halfway house for things waiting for their new owners. I need to start matching my stock to my customers rather than rescuing every object I see.'

Ava picks up a blue and gold balloon dog ornament. 'Can I own this one?'

'No,' Ren says at exactly the same moment as I say yes, and we meet each other's eyes and break out into laughter.

'Go on then,' Ren acquiesces, but I stop him when he goes to get his wallet out to pay for it, and Ava comes over and gives me another hug.

'I think you should own this one too.' The diary is in my bag on the counter, and Ava is fiddling fondly with the strap, so I slip the bag off and hang it over her shoulder. 'Whatever happens in Arfordir-Môr-Forwyn and after the antiques fair, you should keep this. No one loves it more than you, no one's been more invested in it than you, and you *did* find it fair and square. It's yours now. May it always remind you that, truly, anything is possible.'

She gasps and looks in the bag that's banging against her side and then squeals. 'Seriously? *Eeeeeek*! Thank you, Mickey! It's my most favourite thing ever. I'll treasure it for the rest of my life. One day I'll have children and they'll treasure it too!'

'Mick, don't. It could be valu—'

'So are you. Both of you.' I cut off Ren's protest. 'It's too special to sell, no matter what it's worth. Better it stays with someone who loves it and realises that value doesn't just come from monetary price.'

Ava's jumping up and down on the spot. 'Can I read it in the car? We need to know if there are any more clues before we get there!'

I give the shop a final glance, surprisingly glad to be getting away from it for the weekend. I can't remember the last time I went away anywhere, and the possibility of solving the mystery of the diary thrums through my veins. Getting close to the place where it actually happened will give us the answers we need. It has to.

Ava has taken my suitcase and headed for the car park, and Ren is rushing to catch up with her. When we reach the car, he unlocks the boot and Ava hefts my wheeled case up into it, and organises their bags around it, and I look up at him as we stand aside and let her get on with it.

It's the third time I've seen him since the other night, and the third time there hasn't been any product in his hair since then either, which I like to think I had a little something to do with. 'I like your hair like this. The softer look suits you.'

'I'm not so sure. Bad things happen when there's no product in my hair.'

'I'm not convinced it was entirely the fault of your hair gel.' I can't help laughing even though he's clearly still embarrassed, and I nudge my elbow into his arm. 'And I don't think they were bad things.'

'Good or bad, they were things that can't happen again.'

The sharpness of his words makes me flinch, but I can't deny he's got a point. It would have been *far* too easy to kiss him the other night. It was hard enough to *only* let myself kiss his cheek when what I really wanted was to go much, much further. He might be embarrassed, but I told him he had beautiful eyes, the most kissable cheeks and the softest stubble, and *I* can't blame the wine. Of all people, I'm the one who should be in absolute agreement that nothing that happened the other night can be repeated, ever.

'How did you ever get me to agree to this?' he says as Ava slams the boot closed.

'You wanted to!'

'I was... d-r-u-n-k!' He glances towards Ava before spelling the word out under his breath.

'Shouldn't need to be drunk to throw caution to the wind once in a while, Ren.'

'Can't argue with that,' he says with a huff, looking very much like he wishes he *could* argue with it.

Ava dives into the backseat, and I slip into the front next to

Ren, he sets the Sat Nav and makes sure everyone's strapped in, and Ava cheers as we pull out and start leaving Herefordshire behind. She puts her headphones in and pulls the diary out of the bag, and I glance at Ren.

'Thanks for coming. I really didn't want to do this on my own.'

'You're welcome,' he says in response, because so far he's even refused to accept any money towards the cost of petrol for this trip. 'This has been good for her.'

His voice drops and his eyes flick up to the rearview mirror and focus on Ava behind us. 'She's not on her phone as much. She seems less worried about what people think of her, and more open about her feelings, and I think that's your influence. Your confidence, your upfrontness, your courage in telling people how you feel, your... *youness*.'

A few weeks ago, I'm pretty certain this would've been an insult, but right now, he can't stop his lips twitching into a smile, and it fills my heart with joy because I *know* he means it in a good way.

'I even got a hug this morning,' he continues. 'And maybe that's something to do with you too.'

'Hugs engender hugs?'

'I guess we need to put that theory to the test?' he says with a grin, and I reach over and rub his thigh, and he smiles to himself in a way that suggests it's a good thing he's not going to take his hands off the steering wheel any time soon.

'Oh, noooo, he's really ill. What if he dies?' It isn't long later that Ava rips her headphones out, and when I turn in my seat to look over at her, she looks distraught.

'He's not going to die,' I reassure her.

'You don't know that. Not every story has a happy ending,' Ren says. 'What does it say?'

Ava paraphrases the entry, and Ren huffs. 'It sounds like he has an infection and they have no medical intervention. He might die, Ave. You need to prepare yourself.'

On the one hand, I *understand* why he's saying it, why he doesn't want Ava to be upset if the mystery sailor *does* die, but on the other hand, a bit of hope wouldn't go amiss, would it? 'Can I read it?'

Ava passes the book over and I spread it open on my lap, trying to ignore Ren's eyes flicking sideways as I read.

3 April 1899

His leg is causing him pain. I fear the broken bone will not heal, but I don't know what to do about it. It has been many weeks. If he was under a doctor's care, it would be mended by now.

His skin is too warm and his teeth chatter even though he is burning hot to the touch. I do not know if I should try to cool him down or keep him warm. My hands shake as I try to tend him, and my mind is flooded with all the worst possibilities. What if he is unable to recover? What if he is to die right here in front of me? What if I am not good enough to save him?

What if I could have got him help, but I have not, simply because I like him being here, and I had not realised how lonely I was until he came?

He does not want food. He cannot keep water down. I go out to the shore and ask my friends for help. If there is any magic in this boorish world, please let me find it tonight. I must save him.

I have done so many things wrong in my life, and tonight, I regret all of them. If I had not been so heartless, as selfish as my sister calls me, maybe the gods of the sea would see fit to save him. I will do anything. If I could give my life for his, I would.

My heart is in my throat as I turn the page to the next entry, wondering how the hell *I'm* going to cope if the next entry reveals the worst possible scenario.

6 April 1899

In my fear last night, I confessed my part in his shipwreck. I wrote the words that I had been hoping never to write – it is my fault you are here. I was supposed to prevent this from happening, but my mind wasn't focused, and I caused this. Like all mermaids, my song ensnared you into the arms of danger.

He has accused me of luring their ship to its doom, and of murdering his best friend.

He is less warm today, but he pushes my hand away when I try to lay my fingers against his forehead. His leg is red and blotched. The bone is not healing properly, and the rope I have used to tie on the wooden boards is cutting into his skin, but I do not know how else to hold his leg straight while it heals.

He blames me for his predicament. It is my fault, after all, but I am glad that he does not look as unwell as he did yester-day. There is colour in his cheeks again, even though it is the putrid colour of anger, and it is directed at me.

He calls me a monster, and it makes me angry. I thought he was different to the others who label me with that name. I am not a monster, am I? I am different. It is he who has made me feel unlike a monster, and it hurts so very deep inside that in one angry exchange, he can undo all the good he has done.

I do not speak to him for the rest of the night. I am crying too hard. I didn't want to cry in front of him, so I go out to the water where I have always been safe. I am weak and afraid. I

will never be anything but a monster, and now, if he is to die,
will I become a murderer too?

I suck air in through my teeth because it's painful reading.
You can *feel* her hurt in every word. You can sense the emptiness
inside her now he's called her the one thing she thought he didn't
see her as. Even her writing has changed, like he's broken something inside her soul.

'If someone doesn't tell me what's going on, I'm going to pull
over so I can read this thing too,' Ren snaps.

'I thought you didn't care, Dad.'

He glances at me and then meets her eyes in the rearview
mirror. 'Turns out your old dad's a bit of a softie after all.'

10 April 1899

He says he is sorry. He was angry, in pain, and scared, and
sometimes words come out when he doesn't intend them to. I
don't understand this, but maybe I would understand it if I had
a voice of my own. Maybe it is like when I go to speak and
forget that I cannot. If the words were able to, might they come
out, even if I didn't wish them to?

I am both sad and frightened. I am frightened of how
deeply I feel for him, and even more frightened of losing him.
He is everything I have ever wanted, and yet, he is not mine to
keep. Is love only ever supposed to be temporary?

I cannot get all my thoughts written down. They are too
complicated to show to him. He will think me mad.

He is sitting on the floor in front of the fire and I sit down
beside him. Sometimes, when words fail, I put my head on his
shoulder and he puts his arms around me and that is all that
needs to be said.

Tonight, we kiss. We go further than kissing. I have never gone that far before. I always believed such an act would be painful and immoral. My sister would surely die on the spot should she ever find out.

He says that if he is to die, he will be able to die a happy man.

And I might die a happy woman. I feel like I am soaring. I didn't know it was possible to feel this good.

I will do anything for this man. I will do whatever it takes to save him – to keep him.

'What the...?' Ren's knuckles turn white as his grip on the steering wheel tightens and he shoots me a frown. 'Has this just turned into mermaid porn? Ava, don't you dare read that!'

'I'm thirteen, Dad. I know what happens when two people love each other.'

'*I'm* scarred for life!'

'I thought you didn't believe in mermaids...' I say, because he seems increasingly invested in this book, and increasingly willing to believe there's something real behind it.

'I don't, but I don't want to think about the logistics of... *that*! That's just disturbing!'

'Oh, stop it. She's a young merwoman in love. There's nothing wrong with that. Who knew that even mermaids have fights and make-up sex? These are her innermost thoughts, her most uncompromised feelings, and we have the privilege of reading them, even so many years later. This is something so special.'

Ren looks over at me. 'You really are part of another world. How can anyone see so much good in something? Is there *anything* you don't like?'

I give it some thought before answering. 'Slogan bathmats.

You know those ones that have words like "nice bum" or "get naked" on them? I *hate* them.'

He laughs so hard that the car is in serious danger of crossing into the wrong lane. 'You are something else, Mickey Teasdale. Something else.'

'Maybe she's part mermaid?'

'It's beginning to seem like a distinct possibility.' He glances over at me. 'She's definitely something otherworldly.'

'Unlike you, Dad, you're just a dinosaur.'

We laugh all the way to Wales. I've closed the diary because I'm laughing so much – and just in case things do get any more risqué between the mermaid and her mystery sailor – but mainly because these two make me want to be present in the moment and not lost in words from 1899, and it's been a while since I felt like that.

For the first time in ages, real life is better than fiction.

* * *

'Oh my God, there's a mermaid!' Within moments of pulling into the car park at the harbour in Arfordir-Môr-Forwyn, Ava has dived out of the car and run to the edge of the promenade.

'Well, that was quick,' Ren mutters sarcastically as he folds himself out of the car and stretches. 'If we've found her already, shall we turn back and be home by nightfall?'

'That's The Little Mermaid.' I stand on tiptoes and strain my neck to see the statue on the waterfront that Ava has gone over to. 'It looks like a replica of the one in Copenhagen to honour Hans Christian Andersen.'

'So we're in the right place then?' Ren looks around as I shut the car door and follow Ava across the tarmac to the statue.

'Do you think that's her?' she asks me.

'I don't know, but maybe it means the people around here know something we don't.' I lean on the railings and look out at the ocean. There are the silhouettes of small islands in the distance, far out to sea, and when I look down at the water below, I half-expect to see the iridescent scales of a mermaid's tail disappearing into the depths. Rer's face shimmers into the reflection as he comes to stand beside me and looks over too.

'Can we go out to those islands?' Ava looks around. 'Do you think one might be *the* island?'

From here, the islands off the coast look like craggy, rocky outcrops, but considering how many are on the horizon, surely there's a distinct possibility that one of them could indeed be *our* Little Mermaid's island?

'Are you interested in the Arfordir-Môr-Forwyn mermaid, dearie?'

There's an elderly man sitting on a bench nearby, looking out to sea, obviously near enough to overhear our conversation.

'Yes!' Ava goes over to talk to him. 'Was she real? Do you know anything about her?'

'It's been said that these waters were full of mermaids, once upon a time. They say that if you walked on the beach on a quiet night, when the wind was dancing across the sea from Ireland, you'd be able to hear them singing. Mermaids sing songs to find love, you know.'

'Can you still hear them now?'

'My wife used to say that all the ships and marine traffic these days has scared them away, but maybe if we're really quiet, they'll come back one day.'

Ava is watching him like he's an oracle on all things mermaid.

'They used to rescue sailors who got into difficulties. The sea out there is treacherous. Where the Irish Sea meets the Atlantic, there's a maelstrom of tidal currents, and there are rocks and sandbanks lurking not far beneath the surface. Many a ship met its maker in those waters, but the mermaids would drag the drowning sailors to the safety of the beaches. They saved count-less lives. That's why we chose that statue – a tribute to not just one mermaid, but *all* mermaids and want-to-be mermaids.' He looks at her. 'My wife wanted to be a mermaid. She was just like you when she was a youngster. Every night, we used to walk along the sand, listening for the sounds of a mermaid singing in the distance.'

'Did you ever hear one?'

'I didn't need to. My wife sang the only songs I ever needed to hear.'

I feel my heart jolt in my chest, because he's obviously talking in the past tense and his eyes have taken on a watery look, and it makes my heart thump harder as I think of my own mum, who spent many a night on the sands of darkened beaches, wishing to see something magical. When I glance at Ren, he's looking more touched than I expected him to.

'That's why I sit here now. My wife always said that when she passed, she'd come back as a mermaid, so I come here every day and watch the waves, hoping I might see her, and I feel like she's still here with me, in these sands, in every shell that washes ashore, every breeze that whispers off the sea. The statue is a tribute to everyone who's ever stood on the shore and wondered if they belong out there rather than on land.'

Ren goes to speak but his voice doesn't work and he has to clear his throat to hide the emotion in it. 'Any of those islands occupied?'

'Aye, some of them, others are rare seabird colonies that are off-limits to the public, but there are regular boat trips around them, weather permitting.'

'Anywhere a mermaid might have lived?' Ava asks him.

'Well, mermaids live in the ocean, young lass. I don't think they have much use for islands.'

Ava looks disappointed, but it's a good point. Our mermaid is seemingly living on an island. I glance out at the rocky silhouettes again. They all look like the kind of places you'd need a good pair of sea legs to climb on to. How would it ever have been physically possible if she really did have a tail?

'Do you know anything about a shipwreck around these parts?' I ask the man.

'There have been many ships run into trouble around here, dearie. Narrow it down?'

'End of the nineteenth century. Two men on board. We don't know any more than that. We're trying to find out.'

He thinks about it for a while before shaking his head. 'As I said, these waters are perilous, even more so in the days before modern technology. The local council office will have records, just along there, up on the hill.' He gives us directions to a building that Ren has already marked on his map.

Ava looks like she wants to question him further, but Ren cuts her off. 'Thanks for your help, enjoy the rest of your afternoon.'

'What a lovely young family. Enjoy your stay!'

'Oh, we're not—'

Ren cuts me off by dropping an arm around my shoulders and leaning his head against mine. 'Thanks, we will.'

It's a deliberate non-correction of the man's assumption, and at first I think Ren is just trying to hurry away, but when his arm stays around my shoulders, I wonder if there's a deeper meaning, and get a little flitter-flutter inside that there might be.

The hotel is a short walk along the promenade, right on the harbour front, and a cuddly looking middle-aged lady greets us with an enthusiastic welcome when we walk into the reception area.

'What brings you to Arfordir-Môr-Forwyn?' After introducing herself as Caryl, she gets us checked in on the computer.

'We're looking for a mermaid,' Ava tells her.

'Well, you've come to the right place. We have a lot of mermaids around here. Look.' She points out the canvases of mermaids hanging around the walls, and Ava goes over for a closer look at the paintings by local artists.

'What about real ones?'

'Hmm, more like stories. It's always been said that mermaids swam in the waters around our coast. They used to use their voices to tempt sailors towards the shore so their boats would run aground on the shallow rocks, and the seafolk below would steal their bounty.'

Ava gasps in horror. 'But the old man on the bench said...'

'Ah, yes.' Caryl clearly knows who we've been talking to. 'Some people have overly romanticised views of them, but I think they were just creatures, like any other animal that has to survive in a challenging environment. I don't think they had palaces on the ocean floor and crabs putting on concerts for them. I think they had to fight for survival, and they ended up going extinct because things were so tough for them.'

'But they were real?'

'I like to think so. You'll find a lot of people round here who believe so. Maybe one day we'll find some proof, eh?'

Ava makes a high-pitched noise that suggests she's moments away from exploding with delight.

By the time we've checked in, taken our bags up to the room, and got Ren's fold-out bed set up, it's too late in the afternoon to head to the council offices, so we go for a wander around the village instead. There are local people everywhere who are all too happy to tell us their opinions on the mermaid stories, from those who think Hans Christian Andersen got his inspiration from this very place, even though to everyone's knowledge, he never actually visited, to those who believe mermaids were real but were driven deeper and deeper into the ocean by human curiosity, and eventually became extinct when they couldn't survive in such depths. One thing made louder by its absence is the total lack of anyone who seems to think mermaids *aren't* real, which buoys mine and Ava's confidence and makes Ren roll his eyes.

By the evening, we've walked around the village, met locals, eaten ice cream and handmade fudge and sticks of rock, had dinner in a pub called The Mermaid's Tail, and to be honest, I've almost forgotten that we came here for any purpose other than to enjoy ourselves.

As it gets dark, we stand at the harbour's edge and watch the lights of the boats coming back and the ones leaving on night-fishing expeditions, and when it gets later, Ava and I sit up in the double bed we're sharing and read another diary entry. There aren't many pages left to read now. The unread portion of the book is getting thinner by the day, and I can feel my hope waning with it. There is still no resolution, and the more time that passes, the more unlikely it seems that the mermaid and her sailor are going to have a happy ending.

20 May 1899

As the promise of help comes nearer, I hold onto him a little tighter. The months are getting warmer. Soon it will be time for me to return to my old life under the water, and he will no longer be with me. I'm unable to bear the thought of such a thing. I don't want to be alone again, but it's more than that. I don't want to be without him. Life was different before he came, and I cannot imagine anything more heartbreaking than it going back to the way it was before.

He is spending more and more time outside. He uses a stick to aid his walking, but it is more of a limp now. He says he will never be able to walk normally again, and my guilt grows larger. When I write these thoughts down, he assures me that had I not tried to immobilise his leg, he would never have walked again at all.

Mention of that night brings me back to a topic of conversation we have so far avoided. The night of the shipwreck. He doesn't tell me much, but I know his intentions were not honourable on that night.

He has begun to tell me that I must send him away, for if I am caught harbouring him, I will be accused of being a party to his misdeeds.

I cannot do so. He will die if I send him away. There is no way off this island. There is nowhere to send him but back to sea, and there is no boat. He will drown, from the swell of the waves or the temperature of the water, or the pain of his broken leg, which will prevent him from swimming strongly.

I tell him that help will not come for six more weeks. He will have time to recover. We will think of a story that we will tell to save him.

He shakes his head as I write suggestions down. No one will believe us. They will know of the dishonour he will bring to his family. He says he will not bring dishonour to my name as well. He has begun gathering driftwood and tying it together with rope. He is intending to form a raft and sail away for good, and I cannot let him.

It is both his and my fault that we are in this situation. If there are consequences, we shall face them together. He has promised me that we will spend the rest of our lives together, somehow, and I will not give that up. That is what people do when they love someone. They stand by them.

No matter what.

'That's sooo romantic,' Ava gasps. 'He's willing to sacrifice himself to keep her safe. She has to stop him. She will stop him, won't she? They're going to be okay, right, Mickey?'

Ren gives me a warning frown, and I think about my answer before giving her false hope. 'All we can do is hope they are. They found each other in this completely random, fateful situation. We have to believe that they were meant to be, and somehow, they overcame all the odds so they could be together in the end.'

'I hope so.' She leans over to give me a hug and then snuggles down on her side of the bed, and Ren turns the light off and the fold-out bed creaks under him.

'Night, girlies,' he says, and it makes my stomach do a little flip-flop. Or so many flip-flops that I'm not sure how I'll ever get any sleep.

14

After such a long day, I must've been worrying about sleep for nothing because it's a couple of hours later when I wake up again, lost for a moment in the unfamiliar surroundings. I lift my head and check on Ava, who's sleeping soundly on the other side of the bed, and then check on Ren, who's *not* lying on the fold-out bed where he was when I last looked.

I push myself up onto my elbows to look around, and he lifts a hand in silent greeting from where he's sitting on the window seat. I could lie down again and try to get back to sleep, but a far more attractive prospect is the gorgeous silhouette outlined by the moonlight shining in the window behind him, and I slip out of the bed, being careful not to jostle it and wake Ava, and pad across the room.

He holds up his mug and gestures to ask if I want a cup of tea. I glance towards the kitchenette, and at this time of night when I was asleep two minutes ago, it seems very far away, and like he can tell what I'm thinking, he puts his own mug down and clambers off the window seat, and I listen to the click of the kettle boiling, and within minutes, he's back, holding a steaming hot mug for me too.

My fingers brush his as I take it, trying to remember the last time anyone did anything so thoughtful without so much as a second thought, and I take a sip to try and get my brain functioning properly and murmur my thanks as he sits back on the window seat, pulls his legs up, and pats the space on the opposite side.

I have never known a man who can look so ridiculously sexy in a pair of baggy blue check pyjama trousers and a plain blue T-shirt, and I can't resist sitting on the other side of the window seat, facing him.

He smiles at me as I pull my legs up too, bent at the knees, so I fit alongside him and our arched legs rest against each other's.

He takes a sip of his tea and lets out a sigh, letting his head drop back against the wall. His dark hair is mussed up and sticking out in a few directions, there's a few days' worth of stubble peppering his jaw, and he looks half-asleep and soft around the edges.

'Can't sleep?'

'Only the recently deceased could sleep on that thing. If one of my ribs starts poking out of my neck tomorrow, you'll know why.'

I hide my giggle behind my cup of tea to make sure I don't wake Ava up, and he turns his head to look out of the window again, a distant look in his eyes.

'Watching for mermaids?' I ask quietly.

He makes an affirmative noise in response, and then blinks a few times. 'Er, no, I meant... just sitting, watching the water. It's perfect here, like a fairytale town. I could get used to a view like this.'

He rolls his head against the wall until he's looking directly at me again. 'I haven't enjoyed life for a long while, but I've had such a good time this summer – because of you. Thanks for making me come here, no matter what questionable persuasion tactics you had to use.'

I go to protest and jokingly smack at his leg, but he catches my hand and squeezes it, and his cheeky grin lets me know he's teasing.

He jiggles my hand gently to make sure my attention is on him. 'You make me feel hopeful again. I'd given up on the idea that life could ever be good again, but since I met you, it... just *is*.'

I nod in recognition. I hadn't realised how muddy my waters had got until he cleared them, but this has been the most enjoyable summer I can remember, and for the first time since losing Dad, I've started to feel normal again. Hopeful, like there really is something to look forward to.

He lets go of my hand, but before I can be too disappointed, his hand lands between our knees where they're resting together, and his fingers start marking out mindless patterns on my knee, trailing warmth through the thin material of my pyjama trousers as he goes back to watching the glittering lights of the boats moored in the harbour, and the more distant lights of houses on the occupied islands on the horizon, and the silence is comfortable and so peaceful that I could fall asleep right here.

I wrap both my hands around my mug like I'm trying to warm up, not because it's cold tonight, but because it would be too easy to take his hand and draw those patterns on his skin too and the constant movement is making me want to shift nearer to him.

'Thank you.' It's nothing more than a murmur and he says it to the view outside the window before turning to look at me.

'What for?'

He shakes his head like it's a question he doesn't have an answer for, and then turns towards where Ava's asleep in bed.

'How you are with her. You've been good for her.' He pauses for a minute and turns back to me. 'In a weird way, I think you've made *me* better for her.'

'The highest form of praise,' I say with a smile.

'You're confident in what you like, and you aren't afraid to like things other people would laugh at, and *that's* been good for her. You're unequivocally you, unapologetically you, she doesn't have many adults like that in her life, and it's been good for her to realise you can be who you are and people will like you for that, and anyone who doesn't like you isn't worth your time anyway. All I've ever shown her is that if someone doesn't like you, you should change yourself to please them, and *I* hadn't realised how harmful that is until I met you either.'

He's obviously talking about his ex, and I reach over and let my fingers brush over his hand where it's stilled on my knee.

'Even having the courage to talk so freely to the old man on the bench today, and to Caryl on reception, and to see her helping customers in your shop has been fantastic. I hadn't realised how much confidence she'd lost until I've started to see her regaining it. And that's *you*. Making her believe in herself and trust her feelings and just... *know* that you like her. That you *want* to spend time with her. After her mother...'

He doesn't finish the sentence, but I know what he's getting at. Her mum not showing up for arranged visits, and then leaving without the slightest bit of contact. 'I honestly can't imagine what it's like to face that kind of rejection at her age, and I can only imagine how much it must destroy someone's self-worth. One of the most powerful things in the world is being wanted, *as* you are, for *who* you are, and one of the worst feelings is being unwanted, and being made to feel like you're not good enough, when *you* are.' I add a pointed tone to the last two words so he knows we're not just talking about Ava.

He holds my gaze as a tired smile creeps across his face, growing wider with every second that passes, and his fingers twitch towards mine, barely grazing them, like he's trying to stop himself holding my hand.

My hair is loose, long waves that cascade down to my lower back, a bit haywire where I didn't bother to smooth it down when I got out of bed, and rather than taking my hand, he reaches over and lifts a section of my hair and then sits back with it still in his hand, his thumb rubbing back and forth over the red strands.

'Maybe I've gone too far,' he murmurs. 'Tried to be too cautious. There are worse things in the world than having coloured hair. Yours is... beautiful.'

He meets my eyes again as he says it and the word sounds so heartfelt that it makes my breath stutter. 'Why are you so against it?'

'Because her mother would've let her get her hair dyed, and I don't want to be *anything* like that woman.' He answers without thinking about it, and then looks surprised, like he didn't intend to answer so openly.

'There's such a thing as compromise,' I say. 'You can let her express herself without giving the impression that you're about to swan off into the sunset too.'

'All right, you know a lot about hair colour – what if it goes wrong?'

'What if it does? Every woman has many hair disasters in her life, we've all got to start somewhere. Besides, why should it go wrong? Her hair is brown and she wants it purple. There's no bleach or other harsh chemicals involved. They'll use a vegetable dye and it'll probably wash out within three weeks. You're over-thinking it.'

'Yeah, I do that.'

'Oh, really? I hadn't noticed.'

A laugh bursts out of him and he clamps a hand over his mouth to keep quiet, and then chuckles to himself, and it makes a huge difference to see him not taking himself too seriously for once. I can't help giggling too, consistently surprised by how easy it is to enjoy simply spending time with him.

He picks up my hair and starts playing with it again, and I squish my legs tighter against his because the position is impossible for a proper hug, and his hand slips over my knee again and he gives it a tight squeeze, and we smile at each other in the darkness, and it doesn't feel like anything else needs to be said.

I lose track of time passing as we sit there. His hands are resting on my knees and his fingers are twiddling in my hair, plaiting and un-plaiting the section he's holding, and it feels like such a gentle and intimate thing, and it's only a movement down in the harbour below that makes me sit up so fast that my hair falls out of his grasp. 'Did you see that? It looked like a tail diving into the water!'

'Dolphin.' He rolls his head along the wall and looks down again, but I scramble up onto my knees and cup my hands around my eyes to block reflections and look out onto the water.

'Okay, firstly, dolphins are something to get excited about too, and secondly, it could have been something else.'

'A harbour porpoise or a large fish, maybe even a nocturnal seabird catching a late-night feast,' he suggests, making it obvious that he's deliberately trying to avoid what I'm suggesting.

'It *could* have been a mermaid.'

'It *could*...' He smiles an indulgent smile, and then yelps under his breath when I accidentally kneel on his foot as I try to press my face closer to the window. There's a gentle lapping of waves against the hulls of moored boats, but no other movement now. 'What do you want me to say, Mick? *Oh yeah, that was definitely a mermaid's tail disappearing under the water*? It wasn't. We *both* know it wasn't.'

I sigh and sit back on my knees, and he pokes my thigh with his toe until I look at him.

'I want you to believe it could have been,' I whisper eventually. 'I *know*, okay? I know they aren't real, but there's no harm in believing in magic, even for a moment. Everyone's life is better if they're open to possibilities. And there's something about the diary that feels real.'

'It does feel real.' He holds eye contact so intensely that I feel like there's a hidden meaning. 'A lot of things have been feeling real lately...'

Eventually, he looks away and back out to the distant sea. 'Historical reports of mermaid sightings have been proven to be manatees. I believe there might be some truth in the diary – the boat sinking, the island perhaps – but I cannot, not even for a moment, believe that she's really a mermaid. I agree with your assertion that the ocean depths are vast and there are undoubtedly things out there that we don't know about, but I don't believe they're half-human, half-fish affairs who sing songs of love and rescue princes from drowning.'

'Okay, what is she then?' My attention is half on him and half still looking out the window, hoping for another glimpse of whatever we just saw in the water. 'Based solely on the diary, if she's *not* a mermaid, what do you think she is?'

'My honest, sceptical opinion that you've heard before and won't like?' His teeth pull his lower lip into his mouth as he waits for me to nod. 'I think she's a novelist. A good novelist writing a first-person point-of-view story. Within thirty seconds of arriving, we were told a fairy story about a mermaid. This isn't the origin of that story – this is someone who's been here and heard that same fairy story and written a tale about it. They probably employ that bloke on the bench to sit there and spoon feed that junk to tourists.'

'Oh, don't be so cynical.' I smack at his knee and he catches my hand again and holds it between both of his, his fingers playing with mine, pressing, squeezing, stroking, and I sit back down again and scooch nearer to him, because no matter how cynical he is, he *isn't* anywhere near as contemptuous as he was a month ago, and tonight, he's touchy-feely and soft, letting me see a tired, vulnerable side, and I get the feeling that he *wishes* he could believe in mermaids in a metaphorical sense.

He's still holding my hand but he leans his head back against the wall and his eyes drift shut. I watch the water for a while longer, but whatever it was that splashed down there, it's long gone, and the hands of the clock on the wall have moved past 2 a.m. now.

I give his hand a gentle shake. 'You want to go back to bed?'

'Nah.' He blinks hazy blue eyes open and focuses on me. 'I'm going to stay here. The window seat is more comfortable than that folding contraption.'

The look he gives the offending fold-out bed makes me chuckle to myself, and I reach over to squeeze his knee. 'I'm going back to bed. Give us a shout if you see any mermaids out there.'

Even half-asleep, he manages to raise the most disbelieving eyebrow and I have to bite back laughter again.

I slip off the window seat and he reaches out, silently asking if he can pull me in for a hug, and I step into his arms and lean down to give him a squeeze. His arms slide around me and his hands splay on my back, his fingers warm through my pyjama top making me shiver in a definitely-*not*-cold way.

'You know what's powerful?' His voice is muffled against my shoulder and his lips graze my neck with every word. 'You got out of bed to spend time with me.'

I'd think he was teasing if I didn't know how much little things mean to him. 'I can sleep anytime. How often do you think I'll get to drink tea and watch for mermaids in the middle of the night with you? That's a better option than any dream.'

He makes a noise that sounds like someone's just punched him really hard in the solar plexus. His face is still buried in my neck, and his arms squeeze me impossibly tighter.

'Night, Ren.' I let my fingers slide through his hair and tuck it back once, and then press my lips to his forehead, right on his hairline, and I hear his breathing stutter, and his hands tighten in my pyjama top, holding on so tightly that there's the sound of fabric stretching, and he keeps his arms around me for an abnormally long time, so long that I half-wonder if he's gone to sleep in my arms, and honestly, although going back to bed is the *only* option, I could quite happily stand here and hug him until morning.

15

'Dad, the archives are that way.' Ava points up the road towards the council building because we've come out of the hotel and Ren is taking us in the opposite direction.

'Ah, but *one* of us has got an appointment elsewhere first.' Ren steeples his fingers in an evil overlord sort of way, complete with matching 'mwhahaha' laugh.

Ava looks to me, silently asking if I know why he's lost the plot, but I'm as in the dark as she is.

He's following a map on his phone, and we cut through a couple of small streets full of touristy souvenir shops, cafés with gorgeous smells wafting out, and galleries displaying the paintings of local artists, until we come to a quaint shop with a pink and white striped awning and images of models with fancy hairdos on the windows.

'A hairdresser?' Ava looks between the two of us and then gasps as understanding dawns on her. 'A hairdresser! Oh my God! Are you letting me dye my hair like Mickey's?'

'If you want to. You've got an appointment at 10 a.m.'

'Daaaaaad! You're the best!' She throws her arms around him

so hard that she nearly knocks them both into the road. 'Thank you, thank you, thank you!'

When she releases him, she jumps on me for a hug too. 'Thank yoooou, Mickey! I don't know what you did to persuade him, but you're also the *best*!' The last word is squealed at a pitch that, somewhere out in the Irish Sea, has got several dolphins turned around and wondering if their sonar is on the blink.

She rushes inside and drags us both in with her, and Ren goes to talk to the receptionist. Ava is going through their dye selection when he comes back.

'Do you want to go up to the council place and start looking?' he says to me. 'There's no point in us both wasting a couple of hours here when we've only got until Monday.'

'I want Mickey to stay!' Ava speaks before I've had a chance to answer. 'Can *you* go to look through the archives and we'll stay here? You'll only sit there and moan constantly and tell them not to do it too bright!'

Ren laughs. 'All right, fair point. If that's what you want...' He double-checks it's okay with me, and then goes to pay upfront, with instructions to call him if we need anything, and waves as he leaves.

We're the only customers and a hairdresser comes to take Ava to a chair, shows her colour charts of the shade each dye is likely to go on her brown hair, and she chooses one, has a trim, and then we have to wait for an hour for the dye to take effect with her hair wrapped in a plastic cap.

'Best day ever!' Ava declares as we sit in the waiting area, leafing through the selection of glossy magazines. 'Thank you so much for whatever you did. I'm going to have purple hair because of you. You definitely have Fairy Godmother magic powers!'

I giggle at her childlike innocence. 'Believe it or not, it was nothing to do with me. He must've booked that appointment before we even woke up this morning.'

'Yeah, but you loosen him up. You make him see another point of view. That, and he thinks about you so much that he forgets to think about the evils of dyed hair.'

It's a sweet, over-simplified point, but I get a little thrill at where she's coming from – the idea that *I* am somehow responsible for loosening Ren up and that he spends so much time thinking about me.

After the hairdresser has washed the dye out, straightened and blow-dried Ava's new Cadbury-purple hair, she's over the moon and keeps stroking it and twirling it round her fingers. It's nearly lunchtime when we step outside and the August sun is high in the Welsh blue sky.

'Hear me out,' I suggest. 'We could go straight up to the archives and see how your dad's getting on, or we *could* get ice cream and go for a walk on the beach and—'

'You had me at ice cream! He won't even miss us! We can just tell him the dye takes hours to work and he'll never know!'

There's an ice cream van on the seafront, selling the most obscenely gigantic 99s with two flakes, drizzled with strawberry *and* chocolate sauce, and I get us one each, and we kick our shoes off and skip down onto the sand. The tide is coming in and families under umbrellas and behind windbreakers are gradually moving their way up the beach, but Ava and I head down to the water's edge and paddle along the shallow lapping waves.

'Thanks for this, Mickey.' She holds up the ice cream, and then waves her shoes towards the general area. 'Dad would never have done anything like this without you, and he'd *never* let me eat an ice cream this size before lunch!'

I laugh. 'Maybe we should downplay quite how huge it is when we see him...'

'He won't mind, really. You're the best thing to ever happen to him!'

'Oh, I wouldn't say that. He's... um... well, he's been pretty good for me too. You can't deny my shop looks a lot better because of his input.'

'Yeah, but our *life* looks a lot better because of your input.'

My heart is melting faster than my ice cream in the summer sun, and I nudge my arm against hers gently, because we've both got ice creams in one hand and shoes in the other so a proper hug is unfeasible.

'He likes you. So much,' Ava continues, licking dripping ice cream off her cornet. 'He's so different with you. More like the old dad he used to be. I hadn't realised how much Mum had broken him. She criticised him all the time, and he changed because of it, and she still complained about him, but then he wasn't himself any more. And you've mended him. You like him just as he is, and you told him that, and it changed something inside him for the better.'

Who knew it was possible to tear up while eating the world's biggest ice cream? I sniffle and turn away, pretending to be fascinated by the coiled castings of a sandworm while I get my emotions under control.

'It's really easy to feel unloved sometimes, and to take it personally if someone doesn't stay,' I say carefully, aware that they're both struggling with the way Ava's mother abandoned them. 'It can make you feel like you're not good enough or like you did something wrong, when really it's the other person who was wrong to do what they did, and it can be really hard to reframe it as being a problem with that person and not with you... you understand that, right?'

Ava nods, the cornet forgotten in her hand.

'And the greatest thing in the world is to be loved for exactly who you are. To know someone wouldn't change any aspect of you. And in a strange way maybe that's part of why your dad wouldn't let you get your hair dyed and doesn't always want you to do grown-up things – because he loves you exactly as you are, and he's worried that you're going to change and grow up and stop loving him too.'

'Everyone has to grow up, except Peter Pan.'

I can't help giggling at the analogy. 'It can take dads a while to get used to the idea of their little girls growing up, and for what it's worth, he's trying. It's not easy to be a single parent, I know his job is stressful – for you both,' I add before she can say it's stressful to have a parent working at your school too. 'Maybe he doesn't always get things right, but he is trying his best.'

'Did your dad get things wrong?'

'All the time. But we only had each other so we got through it together. He apologised when he was wrong, and I apologised when I shouted at him and slammed doors, and things did get easier. Even when it doesn't seem like they will, things will always get easier.'

Ava nods and we finish our ice creams in comfortable silence, and then she hands me her shoes to carry and starts collecting shells to take home.

'I wish he'd stop treating me like a child and be honest with me about Mum,' she blurts out. 'He says he drove her away, but I know it was her. I know she never wanted to spend time with us. He'd make special dinners and she wouldn't come home in time, and sometimes we planned special outings for the three of us and she never bothered to come. And then after the divorce, when I was supposed to see her, she never wanted to see me. I knew she wanted to be somewhere else when we were together, doing something else, with someone else, and I just want him to admit she was a selfish cow and we're better off without her.'

I probably shouldn't laugh, but I can't hide the half-snort at her straight-talking wisdom.

'He's always trying not to take sides and he doesn't want me to think badly of her, but *she* made me think badly of her, and it should be okay for both of us to be angry and hurt and upset.'

'I... cannot argue with that, and I actually think your dad could learn a lot from you. Maybe you could say all that to him sometime? Because from what I've gathered, he takes responsibility because he thinks everyone blames him, so maybe it would be good for him to know that *you* know it was a problem with your mum and nothing that either of you did.'

'Oh, I know that. Look at this.' She shoves the handful of shells she's collected into her pocket, and when they won't all fit, hands them to me to juggle with the two pairs of shoes, and gets her phone out.

I bend down so I can see the screen she's showing me as she cups her hand around it to block out sunlight. She's opened her text messages and is showing me the conversation thread with 'Mum' at the top, except... every single message is from Ava.

She's been texting her mother often. I catch a glimpse of a few dates as she scrolls up the endless message thread, one message a week, sometimes two or three, going back months. Some are chatty, telling her mum what she's been doing at school, complaining about her maths homework, and some are raw and painful, begging her to come back, telling her she misses her, and not one of them has had a reply.

My heart feels like it's being torn apart in my chest. This is the most heart-wrenching thing I've ever seen, and it does make you wonder about the heartlessness of a woman who could get so many texts from her young daughter, who clearly desperately needed her at the time some of these messages were written, and never once bothered checking up on her in any way.

She sighs and scrolls back to the bottom and my eyes focus on the most recent one that's telling her mum they're going to Wales with Dad's new girlfriend.

'Ava, me and your dad aren't...'

'Well, you should be. See?' She changes message threads to the one with 'Dad' written at the top and shows me one of the most recent ones from Ren, telling her what a good time he'd had with me while she was at her grandparents'.

'Scroll up a bit,' I ask, and she does, and although I don't want to read her private text messages, I want to prove a point. Even though they live together and probably don't have much reason to text each other, *every* single message has a reply from Ren, because that's what good parents do.

'Do you want my advice?' I ask as she puts her phone away and nods enthusiastically. 'If it were me, I'd text your mum less often and text your dad more often. After all, the best people in your phone are the ones who always want to text you back. If someone doesn't make room for you in their lives, sometimes it's worth backing off and letting them see what they're missing.'

'Like you, you always text me back.'

'Why wouldn't I text you back? You're a little ray of sunshine in my lonely life.'

'Thanks, Mickey.' She throws her arms around me with such force that we both overbalance and end up on our bums in the wet sand, both pairs of shoes splash into the sea, and her shell collection scatters everywhere.

We're both giggling as I quickly rescue the shoes and Ava gathers up her shells.

'And maybe give your dad a few extra hugs too? I think he needs that.'

'Maybe *you* should hug him more often too.' She stops shell collecting long enough to look up at me with waggling eyebrows.

'Hah hah,' I say out loud to cover the fact I'm blushing *bright* red. 'I think I've probably given him enough hugs lately. He's bound to start complaining sooner or later.'

We're still laughing about it when my phone rings and Ren's name flashes on the screen. 'See? He's starting already.' I hold it up to show her before answering.

'You two need to come up to the archives,' Ren says down the line. 'I've found something.'

16

I'm still brushing sand off my trousers and my shoes are squelching when we go through the revolving door of the Arfordir-Môr-Forwyn council building and the receptionist directs us to the archive room, where Ren is sitting at a computer, waiting.

Ava goes straight over to give him a hug, and he pulls back to admire her new hair colour. 'Very nice. Very *bright*.' He glances at me, and when I frown at him, he backpedals. 'Which is good, obviously. It looks like there should be a bar of chocolate inside.'

'What have you found?' I ask before he says anything worse.

'The boat was stolen. Look.' He pulls an article up on the screen and Ava and I lean over to read it.

It's dated March 1900, and in the days before photographs were commonplace, it's accompanied by an artist's impression sketch of a boat, called the *Síolta*.

Wreckage of a boat, stolen from Wexford, Ireland, has been recovered off the coast of Wales, more than a year after it went missing. Suspected to have been taken by two smugglers to facilitate the illegal trade of contraband goods between Ireland and the United Kingdom. Two men who were seen acting suspiciously were later identified as Jeremiah O'Maher and John Murphy. Neither man has been seen or heard from since, and there has been no trace of the Síolta since the night of the theft – the same night a vast storm rolled in unexpectedly.

At first it was believed the Síolta had sunk in dock, but a timeline placing the two men nearby was later put together. The owners had given up hope of ever discovering the vessel's fate, until now.

Shadows spotted and later raised from the seabed revealed the wreckage of a boat run aground in bad weather, and the remains of an illicit alcohol cargo destined for illegal trade. It is now believed that the boat never made it to shore and both thieves are expected to have lost their lives in the incident.

'Well, I guess his intentions that night really *were* dishonourable. He wasn't kidding when he told her that.' I stand back upright from where I was leaning over to read the screen and take my hand off Ren's shoulder.

'You don't think he drowned, do you, Mickey?'

'No, of course not. We *know* his friend didn't survive, but he did. Our mermaid saved him.'

'He doesn't seem like a thief,' Ava says. 'He seems so nice. He's so kind to our mermaid. He treats her better than anyone else in her life treats her, she says so.'

'A person can be both. Just because he does one bad thing, it doesn't mean he was an awful person. We have no idea what his motivation behind it was – he could have been desperately trying to provide for his family or something. Or maybe he *was* a bad guy but he changed because of love. Maybe she made him reconsider his life choices and he made amends for it afterwards. He could've been a bad boy turned good, like Flynn Rider in *Tangled*,' I insist, despite the fact we still don't know how their story ends, and I've got a niggling feeling that we never will.

'Is there anything else?' I ask Ren.

'Not that I've found. I've searched his name too, but there's nothing. The archives have got a birth certificate, but nothing more. No marriage or death records, and no census information including that name. It's another dead end.'

'It's not a dead end. We've proved that the boat was real. The diary is *real*. It's an account of what really happened that night. It isn't fictional – this is genuinely the boat that sunk. The mermaid was *there* that night – she's writing the truth, so we have to believe that *every* part of her story is true.'

'Again, she could have just heard the story. If she was here at the time, there was probably a lot of talk about this boat – gone missing in a storm, suspected to have been stolen by smugglers – it would've been quite the scandal. She could have made up something about what she was hearing.' Ren looks up at me hopefully and then purses his lips into a pout when neither me nor Ava share his cynicism. 'And I hate to break it to you, but we have his full name now, and there is *no* record of him being alive after that night. It's reasonable to assume that both sailors – thieves – drowned in January 1899, and what we're reading in the diary is a fantasy about what *could* have happened.'

'No, no, no.' Ava folds her arms. 'What about the rumours of mermaids around these shores?'

'Where she got the story idea from.'

'Nope. Mickey and me are going to prove it, together.'

I sit down at the next computer and Ren shows me how to load up the newspaper articles from the turn of the century, and both of us scan through more. He goes forwards looking for mentions of the boat or any other info about the sailors on it, and I move backwards, looking for reports on earlier sightings of mermaids or anything to suggest our diary keeper was really what she says she is. Ava stands between us to see if she can spot anything, but it's as fruitless as I suspected it would be. Ren has already found the only article that exists about the boat, and despite all the stories we've been told about mermaids, there doesn't seem to be any written evidence of anyone ever encountering one, and surely something like that would have been reported to local newspapers. So what are we missing here? Has Ren got a point – that if she was ever real, someone somewhere would have seen her and it would've been headline news?

After an hour, the receptionist comes to tell us they close mid-afternoon, and it doesn't seem like we're going to find anything more. At least we have the mystery sailor's full name and proof the boat was real and really did sink that night. We can continue googling when we get back to Herefordshire.

'We have to read the last entry,' Ava says as we leave the building and step back out into the late-afternoon sun.

'We left the diary in the hotel room.'

'No, not now. Before we go. Just in case there's anything else that needs to be investigated and we can stay a bit longer. Caryl said the boat trip around the islands doesn't leave 'til Monday. We should go on that, just in case.'

'In case of what? A mermaid pops out of the water and introduces herself?' Ren snorts.

'It *might* happen.'

'Well, keep your phone at the ready because *that* clip will make us a fortune. Now, is there anything else you want to talk about, for instance, what colour that hair dye is going to stain the bathtub?'

'*Yeh-ess*,' Ava says in a wheedling sort of way. 'When are you going to let me get my ears pierced?'

'You see?' Ren holds his hands up in defeat. 'You give them an inch... I know exactly how King Triton felt!'

17

When we get back to the hotel, Caryl accosts us and hands Ava a flyer. 'Ah, there you are! Did you know it's teen night tomorrow?'

'What's teen night?' Ren reads the flyer over Ava's shoulder.

'Once a week during the summer holidays, we run an evening for our young guests to meet and socialise. This week, we've got a film screening of *Splash* in one of the function rooms, and there will be snacks and games and prizes. It's only five pounds, and it'll give Mum and Dad a chance for some *peace and quiet* on their holidays too. Dinner out, a romantic walk on the beach...'

She puts an intonation on the words that suggests 'peace and quiet' is very much a euphemism and I quickly say, 'Oh, we're not—'

'We've got a few teens staying at the moment.' She ignores my correction. 'And eighties movies are retro-cool, so I'm told. There's a candyfloss machine and you can pop your own popcorn!'

'That sounds ah-maze-zing! Can I go, Dad?'

He shrugs, looking like he's not really sure what's happening. 'Sure, if you want to. Mickey and I will...'

'...go mermaid hunting?' I suggest, which is definitely *not* a euphemism. 'I want to know what I saw splashing in the harbour last night. Even if it was a dolphin, I've never seen a dolphin in real life before.'

Ava looks torn for a split second, but at that moment, a teenage boy walks past with his parents and from the look on her face, he's the hottest teenage boy she's ever seen, and as Caryl waves them over and accosts them with a flyer too, she yanks Ren's arm enthusiastically, obviously hoping the boy will be roped into teen night too.

'Fine, fine.' He gets the money out of his wallet and hands it to Caryl. 'But if that candyfloss gives you a sugar rush that keeps you awake all night, you can sleep in the hallway and I'll have your *comfortable* side of the bed.'

'Nothing could be better than the ice cream Mickey bought me! It was *mountainous!*'

'Was it indeed?' Ren ruffles her hair and she tells him off for messing it up after the hairdresser has straightened it, and then he grins at me. 'See? You can always rely on this one to drop you right in it. There are no secrets with a thirteen-year-old about.'

* * *

'We're not really hunting for mermaids, are we?'

Far from the romantic meal for two that Caryl implied, Ren and I have had fish and chips on the seafront while Ava is at her teen night, and after sitting and watching the lights of the boats in the harbour for a while, now I've dragged him down onto the sand for a walk further around the coast, leaving the harbour and the hotel behind us as our toes squidge into wet sand and the edge of the waves lap at our feet.

'There's no harm in seeing what we can see. You saw something from the window last night too.'

'*I* saw a dolphin playing. The issue is that not everyone agrees.' He glances over at me. 'However, there's no harm in walking on the beach with you. It's actually quite a pleasant way to spend an evening.'

I can't help giggling at how formal he sounds, and it seems like a good time to bring up something I keep thinking about. 'Speaking of doing things with me, this is the first chance I've had to ask you – the old man on the bench – why didn't you correct him when he assumed we were a family? Or, more specifically, why did you go out of your way to *not* correct him?'

'And there was me hoping you hadn't noticed that.' He looks at me with a raised eyebrow, and then shakes his head and looks back out to sea. 'I don't know. I liked it. I liked the thought of someone believing that a livewire like you would look twice at an old curmudgeon like me. *I* wanted to believe it too, just for a moment.'

'Curmudgeon, really?' I look at him curiously. 'I didn't realise people still used words like that in this land of the twenty-first century.'

He laughs, but I can tell he's trying to put a jokey spin on something that there's a hint of truth behind. His ex made him feel inadequate for enjoying a quiet life, and when he says things like that, it emphasises how deeply those scars run.

'Firstly, you're only forty-one, you haven't reached curmudgeon status yet, and secondly, look *twice* at you? I can barely *stop* looking at you. You must have noticed that...'

His eyes are twinkling with mischief as they flick up to look at me again, but he doesn't give me a proper response. Instead, he says, 'I also wanted an excuse to put my arm around you.'

'You don't need an excuse for that.' I hold out the hand that's not carrying my shoes and he tangles our fingers together, and then I lift our joined hands so his arm loops over my head and settles around my shoulders, and he squeezes me closer to him, and then leans over to rest his head against mine for a moment. He rubs his chin against the top of my head so his stubble catches on the dark roots of my hair, and I breathe in his subtle orangey aftershave with every step, but he doesn't try to put any space between us, and every so often, his fingers give mine a little squeeze, and I can't remember the last time anything felt as nice as this feels.

We've walked far enough away from the town that it's absolutely silent this far down the beach, and it feels like we could be the only two people on the planet, and I'm enjoying every moment of simply *being* with him.

'Look at that.' His voice is rough when he goes to speak after being quiet for so long. He disentangles our fingers and bends down to collect something from amongst the seaweed gathered at the tideline, and when he stands back up, he's holding a beautiful pearly white conch shell. He holds it out to me, clearly remembering what I said so many weeks ago about how my dad and I used to speak into them, like Mum really was a mermaid and could hear us somehow.

He nods encouragingly when I don't take it from him. My eyes have filled up at his thoughtfulness and if I release my lip from where it's held between my teeth, it's likely to unleash a swell of tears, and I see the moment he realises, closes his hand into a fist and hides the shell inside, and then holds his arms open, silently asking if he can hug me. When I nod, his arms encircle me from behind and tug me back against his chest without a word, and it feels like he's giving me a moment and protecting me from the rest of the world while I take deep breaths and force myself not to cry again, although I'm not sure if it's the memories of my mum, or if it's the sheer gentle kindness of this gorgeous man.

Eventually I cover his hand with mine and open his fingers

and he lets the conch shell drop into my palm. I brush my fingers over it and then hold it up to my mouth and whisper 'I miss you' into the opening, and then I step out of his arms so I can throw it as hard as I can and watch it plop back into the ocean, far out in the waves. 'I like to think she's still out there somewhere. I feel like she is sometimes.'

I stand with the waves lapping over my toes and he comes to stand beside me. He doesn't say anything, but I appreciate the calm, reassuring presence of his height next to me, and without a word, his fingers tangle with mine and he squeezes my hand, and then holds it, his thumb brushing my skin, and we stand there, right at the edge of the waves, looking out at the ocean, for an endless time, and he makes me feel like nothing is more important than just appreciating nature and the magnificence of the ocean. 'It feels like we're listening for the sound of mermaids singing.'

'Maybe we are.'

I glance up at him, but he keeps looking forwards and his face doesn't give away whether he's joking or not, but it doesn't feel like he is.

It's darker when we walk off again, and more glittering lights have come on in the houses on the shore. Boats are heading into the harbour behind us, making it look like the ocean itself is sparkling with moving fireflies, and the summer breeze rustles through the grasses on the dunes.

'I feel like there should be a crab singing "Kiss the Girl" and fish spurting water all around us,' Ren murmurs.

It makes me giggle, although unlike Ariel and Eric, I don't think a gang of musically inclined sea creatures are going to be encouraging *us* to kiss each other.

'I feel like we're walking in a blue lagoon. This is so beautiful.'

'You always say that.'

He squeezes my hand again. 'Maybe it's the person rather than the place.'

I make retching noises to cover how unbalanced those words make me feel, and he laughs, but quickly turns serious again. 'Maybe it's the feeling rather than the surroundings. We could be at the bottom of a stagnant well and it would still be a great night out with you.'

Butterflies fill every inch of my body in an instant, and my heart starts pitter-pattering, despite the fact that the bottom of a stagnant well would *really* not be a great night out.

'What are you getting at, Ren?' My voice is shaky because I *want* him to mean what I think he means, but at the same time, I'm sure he *can't*.

'I don't know. You've always said I'm too blunt, and there it is, bluntly. I don't know, but I *do* know this is something special and I'm *terrified* of it ending.'

'Why should it end?' I swing our joined hands between us, trying to shake loose the words he doesn't seem able to say.

'Because I don't know how I'm going to keep getting my Mickey fix every day when school starts again. Summers are great. Summers are easy. I don't have to go to work every day. I don't have to spend half the evening marking and lesson planning and the other half trying to corral Ava into doing her maths homework, but the rest of the time, I start school at eight o'clock, if not earlier. I have to drag Ava in with me and she *loathes* hanging around until her friends get in. Some nights, I have to work overtime and she has to wait for me, which she also *loathes*. It doesn't leave us much time for coming to Ever After Street, and I don't know how only seeing you at weekends is going to be enough for either of us.'

'Ava could always come to me after school. Hang out in the shop for a while rather than waiting for you. I've got an excuse to see you when you pick her up then. I'm a bit rusty at maths homework, but I could give it a go. And we could have dinner together then or something. I don't want to let this go either. You've lit up my life in a way that's made me realise what was missing, and how much I've shut people out and replaced them with made-up stories behind unwanted objects. Just seeing you at weekends isn't enough for me either.'

He uses his grip on my hand to tug me to a halt, and pushes his other hand through his hair, looking out to the ocean like he's searching for the right words. 'All right, I said that wrong just now. It's not that I'm scared of it ending – what I'm really terrified of is it *not* becoming more.'

I let out a breath and I can feel my face break into the biggest grin as he continues.

'I'm not listening for the sound of mermaids singing now – I've been hearing mermaids sing since the moment I walked into your shop.'

I reach up and tuck his hair back and brush my fingers across his forehead. 'The bang to the head from the Victorian birdcage wasn't that hard.'

His laugh is a slightly unhinged cackle that *really* shows me how nervous he is. 'Do you have any idea how much I've laughed this summer? I can't remember the last time I laughed like I do with you, but you make everything feel easier and more fun. You make me feel different, and at the same time, you make me feel like I don't need to *be* different, and—'

'You *don't* need to be different. You were never the problem. We all understand that relationships end, but parenthood never does. Anyone who can walk out on a child *is* the problem. But in a way, she did the best thing she could possibly have done – because she freed you. She gave you the freedom to find someone who's a better fit, someone who loves you exactly as you are and doesn't *want* you to be any different. And Ava too.'

'Ava won't find another mother.'

'I'd venture that no mother at all is better than one who strings her along, plays with her emotions, and never puts her first. Having a mother who makes you feel so unimportant is arguably more harmful. Feeling like an inconvenience is worse than being alone. And now Ava gets to have a relationship with you that she otherwise wouldn't have had, and she gets to feel *real* love from a parent rather than tiptoeing around one who doesn't want to be there.'

He doesn't hide the emotions that cross his face. His eyes close and he shakes his head and then blinks them open again, and reaches up to stroke his fingers through my hair. 'And *that* attitude is why I've fallen for you so hard. From day one, you've taken me out of my own head and given me a different perspective, and I never want to *not* have that perspective in my life again, and the biggest disservice I could do to you, Ava, *and* myself, is to not open my heart and beg you to come in, with your fairytales and your belief in magic and your bright hair that lights up every room, and—'

I push myself up onto tiptoes and cut him off by pressing my lips against his, and he stumbles backwards and makes a noise of surprise, and then returns the kiss. It's just a peck, but one of his hands is still holding mine and his fingers tighten so much that broken bones might be on the cards, and I pull him closer, stroke through his hair, and *love* the little shiver that runs through him, and the one he sends up my spine when his other hand settles on my back and his fingertips press into my skin.

Even though it's just a peck, we're both breathing hard when we pull back, and his forehead drops to rest against mine. He lets out a *huge* sigh of relief. 'You feel it too.'

'Of course I do.' My fingers curl into his shoulder where my arm is still around him, trying to make sure that he *feels* how much he's reminded me of all the good things in the world.

'For the record, next time you can tell I'm overthinking something, feel free to stop me in exactly the same way.'

I laugh and lean up to press my lips to his cheek, exactly like I did that night on the riverbank, and his hands settle on my hips to hold me close, and his forehead rests against mine as another shuddery breath leaves him.

'Ariel rescued Eric from drowning, and so did you. I've been trying to hold it together on my own for so many years, and that first hug in the café started unravelling something inside of me, and I feel like you're the only person who's ever seen past my walls and realised that I wasn't holding it together at all.'

I think of that guy who came into my shop the first time. It didn't seem like he *could* hide it. The only thing that would have made it more obvious is if he'd had a Post-it note stuck to his forehead saying 'I'm barely holding it together', but somehow, somewhere, he *let* me see that and unintentionally letting someone in when he was so closed off has chased away some old ghosts.

'Maybe you are some kind of ethereal sea creature because you've bewitched me. From the moment I met you, all I wanted to do was see you again. Every day we spent time together, all I wanted was to spend *more* time together. I get excited at the thought of seeing you. That night on the riverbank aside, I've been feeling the same way around you every time we're together – completely and utterly intoxicated. You soothe something inside me, the part of my soul that's so broken. You cover all the sharp edges with warm and soft glue and stick them back together again.'

I pull back until I can look up into his eyes and cup his face, letting my thumb brush against his cheek. 'All right, how much have you had to drink?'

'Nothing, as you know,' he says with a laugh, turning his face into my hand. 'I'm not drunk, I'm *desperate* to kiss you. I can't think about anything else.'

'Well, I can. Where is this going, Ren? I'm not kissing you if this is a one-time thing. If you're going to wake up in the morning and realise you need to dedicate your time to Ava and you haven't got the room – headspace or *heart*space – for a relationship, then no. I'm not doing this. I *can't* do this. I like you, you know that. *Really* like you, probably more than *like* you, and Ava too, but... she's your priority, as she should be. She and I get on great, but she might not be open to you getting into a relationship again – it could change things.'

'It won't change anything. She's been on at me to ask you out since the first day. She loves you to bits and fully supports anything happening between us. She's told me 11,762 times and been disappointed when I've told her to forget it.'

I laugh, but the last bit of that sentence gives me pause. 'And what about you? I know how much you've been hurt. I know it isn't easy to open up again. Are *you* ready for something more? *Really* ready?'

'Honestly? I never thought I would be. Five weeks ago, I *knew* that I'd never get into another relationship ever again. And then I met you. I've fallen *so* hard for you, I feel like I'm in freefall and you're the only thing stopping me from hitting the ground. I regret so much about my marriage, but I already know that the greatest regret of my life would be not seeing where this goes. I *need* you to be part of our lives, and if we carry on as we are, I'm going to end up kissing you and ruining everything, so please give me permission to kiss you and *not* ruin everything...'

'It wouldn't ruin anyth—'

He cuts me off with a kiss, and this time, it's the furthest thing from a peck. His mouth touches mine, gentle at first, but quickly becoming more forceful when my arms slide around his shoulders and drag him closer until my fingers tangle in the hair at the nape of his neck, and the noise he makes is probably the hottest noise I've ever heard in my life. If I was to lose my hearing tomorrow, I would still die happy that I ever got to hear that noise. It's like the loosening of a thousand tightly wound screws that burst open all at once, and the kiss is like a mutual sigh of relief.

I can't imagine what it takes for someone who has been so badly hurt by love to ever open himself up again, and I never thought I would either, but Ren has inadvertently got under my skin from the first moment I saw him.

One leg hooks around his to pull him impossibly closer, and his thigh presses in places that make my hands grasp his hair harder, and my teeth nip his lower lip. His legs stumble for purchase in the wet sand as the waves wash over our feet, and he ends up holding me under the thighs as he fails at keeping us upright and sinks down onto his knees without breaking the kiss, groaning in both pain and pleasure as my legs wrap around him. It feels like the whole ocean breathes a sigh of relief as we land in it, and we just keep kissing.

I'm unable to tear my mouth away from his, even though I can feel seawater seeping through my jeans. His hands are rubbing up and down my back, one is gripping my hip to hold me in place when we finally pull back, gasping for breath, our chests heaving like we may *never* get our breath back again.

'Wow,' he breathes the word, and a tingle goes through me because the feeling is absolutely mutual, and I've never kissed someone who simply says that afterwards and doesn't try to hide how deeply affected he is, and I can't remember the last time I felt so much emotion just from a kiss.

We sit there on the wet sand, breathing hard, my knees on either side of his legs, occasionally he leans forward to brush his lips across mine, and he takes my shaking hand and tangles our fingers together, holding our joined hands down in the lapping water, making me giggle at the tickling sensation, as I rest my forehead against his and tuck his hair back, and just breathe in sync with each other.

It's a bit like when Ariel saved Eric from drowning, and watched over him on the beach, except Eric didn't suddenly swear and say, 'Oh, bugger, my phone!'

Ren scrambles to his feet and manages to pull me up in the same swift movement as he yanks his phone from his back pocket and tries to dry it off with his T-shirt.

He's breathing hard and I'm breathless, and after that kiss, the water lapping over my feet is not the only thing that makes it feel like the ground is shifting underneath me. 'One thing Disney mermaid movies didn't make allowances for was modern technology.'

He laughs, even though the phone he's holding is dripping with sandy seawater.

I nod to it. 'We should head back, try to dry that out.'

'You think my legs are steady enough to *walk* after that? Also, time to ourselves is going to be rarer than you think. This is just a short interlude to resuscitate my phone, but I'm not done kissing you yet while I've got the chance *without* a thirteen-year-old watching on.'

We share a few more kisses on the darkened beach before I realise that it *really* is getting late, and we need to head back before someone sends out a search party.

'Can I say something?' he says as we start walking back the way we came. 'If I have to pay a few hundred quid to replace my phone, it was worth every penny for a kiss like that.'

'That might just be the most romantic thing anyone's ever said to me. You can have as many kisses like that as you want, just make sure they're on dry land next time.'

'Ah, where would be the fun in that? And you make life a lot more fun than it was before.' He glances down at himself, taking in his wet trousers and sandy T-shirt. 'And much, much wetter.'

'I'll take that as a compliment.'

He takes my hands and twirls us around, and we run, dance, and skip back along the beach, and I feel like the luckiest Ariel who's just found the real-life Prince Eric who filled my young romantic dreams, and that's better than finding all the dinglehoppers and snarfblatts in the world.

18

The following morning, we go on the boat trip around the coastal islands, but the journey reveals nothing but squawking seabirds, the sea-battered remains of a defunct lighthouse in the distance, and rocky islands that no one with a mermaid's tail *or* a sailor with a broken leg could ever plausibly reach, and by the time we get back to the shore, I've got to admit that even *I* have started to wonder if Ren's right – if our mystery diarist is someone who has heard a rumour and made up a story behind it. A basis in reality, but mostly, complete fiction. If anyone has an understanding of making up stories in place of reality, it's me.

We have one last holiday ice cream each, and Ava makes us sit on the seafront in the midday sun and read the final diary entry.

10 July 1899

He is gone.
When I awoke, the island was empty, and he was gone. Only the words 'I will leave my heart with you until I find you

again' remain, scrawled in my notebook in writing that is not my own.

I do not know if he is alive or dead. I do not know if he will make it to safety, or what will await him if he does.

He is gone, like water that I try to hold in my hands. It slips away as if it was never there.

As I stare out at the open ocean, watching the slow approach of the boat that is coming to take me back to the mainland, I wonder if I imagined the past six months. Was he ever really here at all?

The Welsh men shout at me. I linger too long for their liking, but I cannot leave our island without saying goodbye to the place that has been my home for so long, and has made me realise what a home truly feels like.

Eventually, I step into the boat and I feel like I disperse, like seafoam across the waves.

'Oh, come on! That's literally the ending of the original Little Mermaid story. She lets the prince live and turns to seafoam. This is nothing but a storybook, as I've said all along! And step! Step, Mickey!' Ren taps his finger on the page. 'On legs! Not on bloody flippers!'

Everything I was before is different now.

I leave part of me behind on this island. I am unlikely to ever see this place again. When they discover the vessel I am responsible for destroying, I will not be permitted to return. I do not know if I would want to. Now I have seen what life is like when I am not alone, I do not want to be discarded for such a long time again.

My heart aches for him. Maybe it would have been better if

*I had never met him at all, for now I know what I am missing,
and I don't know how to return to life as it was before.*

*I don't know if I will ever discover his fate, but he has
changed my life forever, and both of our hearts will always be
on this little island, for good.*

'That's it?' Ren says. 'We did all of this and we don't even get to
discover the outcome? He's just gone?'

'That *can't* be it.' Ava desperately flips through the rest of the
pages, but each one is frustratingly blank. 'Maybe she kept her
notebooks! Maybe you have them in your shop too! I know we've
been through everything, but they might be *reeeeally* well
hidden!'

I tell her she's welcome to have another look, but a lot of my
stock has already been taken up to the castle ready for the
antiques fair next weekend, and we *all* triple-checked for
anywhere that other diaries or notebooks could possibly be
hidden.

'Maybe that really was *it* for her too,' I say carefully. 'Maybe
we're never going to know because *she* never knew. Maybe he
never did come back. That's the problem with real life – sometimes you don't get a neatly wrapped-up movie-ending. Sometimes things happen and you never truly understand why. That's
why I've always made up stories about the things in my shop –
because I have to accept that I'm never going to know the real
truth behind them, and stories are nicer. In stories, people who
deserve happy endings always get them. In real life, sometimes
they don't, and feelings are ugly, messy, and complicated, so it's
nicer to believe in a ribbon-wrapped neatly tied up happy
ending.'

'So we just have to believe that he got back to her? When he left, maybe he headed to the mainland, and was waiting for her on this very beach when she got back?'

'Well, it's certainly a possibility.' My eyes flick up and catch Ren's, and I'm torn between buoyant enthusiasm and false hope. It might've been summer by then, but the mystery sailor was still injured, and whatever raft he'd managed to cobble together, it probably wasn't the greatest feat of engineering. Ren and I share a look that suggests we also share an idea of the sailor meeting a watery grave that night, but I can't rain on Ava's parade like that. 'Maybe she was so deliriously happy that she didn't have time to write any more in her diary because they were so busy planning their future and living happily ever after.'

'That's a much better ending, Mickey. Let's keep that one.' She closes the diary and hugs it close to her chest. 'Thanks for only reading an entry or two at a time. If we'd read the whole thing on the first day, Dad would never have let us come back to your shop. I purposefully dragged it out so we could spend more time together, but it doesn't matter now he's in love with you.'

It takes a few seconds for my brain to catch up with what she's said.

Ren, who was leaning over the bench from behind to read the diary over our shoulders, pushes himself upright, his face blazing red enough to rival the centre of the sun. 'Ava!'

'But you are. Have you seen the way you look at her? And did you see the sand on your clothes last night? And your phone's sitting in a bowl of rice! It doesn't take a genius to work out how that happened! Honestly, I can't leave you alone for five minutes...' She clicks her tongue and sounds like such a scolding parent that it makes me giggle, and what she's implying has made me feel fluttery and tingly anyway. 'Besides, you're always telling me to be honest, so you've only got yourself to blame.'

She knows exactly what she's doing and is loving every second of winding him up.

'Ava, there is a difference between being honest and saying things in front of people when *they* weren't the intended listener.' He's come round to this side of the bench and is pacing in front of us. He glances at me and then back to her. 'Would you mind? Hypothetically? If I was?'

'I'd be so happy! Mickey's the best thing to happen to us in foreeeeeever!' She throws her arms around me from the side.

I squeeze her close and tug gently on her purple plaited hair. 'You'll always be his number one priority, and this doesn—'

I was trying to reassure her that this doesn't change anything, but she interrupts me. 'Are you kidding? I don't want to be his priority! If he's distracted by you, maybe he'll let me do something fun for a change!'

'Oi! I'm not that bad!' Ren protests, and we're all giggling as we walk back to the car with Ren in the middle, an arm around each of us, with Ava carrying the giant teddy bear she won from Caryl last night.

'Does this mean we get to spend more time in your shop, Mickey?'

I grin over at her. 'Yes. And hopefully a few customers will spend more time in my shop now too, after your dad's input and advice.'

'And as a bonus, all three of us will actually *fit* in there after some of that stuff has sold next weekend,' Ren quips.

'I'd really dislike you if I didn't like you so much.' I give him a jokingly scathing look, and he responds by leaning over to drop a kiss on my cheek.

'Oh my God, get a room!' Ava repeats for not the first time this weekend.

As we head homewards, it feels like even though we didn't find out the *real* outcome of the diary, maybe, just maybe, we found something even better.

19

'These are the coolest mugs I've ever seen!' Franca, who runs The Nutcracker Shop on the year-round festive end of Ever After Street, loves mugs as much as I do, and she's volunteered to look after a stall at the antiques fair selling off some of the mugs I've gathered over the years. 'Never mind selling these, I think I'll end up buying the lot! I've been in your shop hundreds of times and I never knew you had mugs in there!'

It's another thing that rams home how much of a mess I'd let the shop get in to, and how right Ren was in everything he said.

It's the opening day of the Philip Teasdale Antiques Fair, and all my fellow Ever After Street shopkeepers are covering stalls selling off some of the shop's treasures. I've kept the most valuable things, and the most sentimental things, and the things I like the most, like the dragon fruit table, but I've been utterly brutal with everything else. If it doesn't add actual, real-life value to my stock, then it goes. If it hasn't sold in over two years, then it goes. This fair will be a great way to reach new clientele, customers who enjoy shopping for antiques and vintage treasures, and who wouldn't dream of coming to Ever After Street usually. I want them to *know* The Mermaid's Treasure Trove is here, and for it to give them a reason to come back after the antiques fair is over.

Marnie, who runs the Tale As Old As Time bookshop, is manning a stall filled with random ornaments and knick-knacks, and Imogen who runs Sleeping Beauty's Once Upon A Dream bed and bath shop is in charge of a stall of tableware. Cleo and Bram have got a Wonderland Teapot stand with cakes and baked treats, and Ali, the chef at the 1001 Nights restaurant, is providing refreshments. Even Mrs Moreno has volunteered to keep an eye on the larger furniture items as long as she's got a seat and no one minds her knitting a jumper for her cat while she's on duty. Apart from the cat, presumably.

And then there are the other antiques sellers with shops and businesses far and wide, who travel around and sell at various antiques fairs throughout the country. Most of them knew my dad and have set up booths to support the idea of a local antiques fair being held here on a yearly basis. Witt and Sadie have gone to great lengths to advertise this, and I'm certain the castle grounds will soon be filled with antiques buyers ready to find some bargains.

The stalls are dotted throughout the castle grounds, which are beautifully maintained by Marnie's other half, Darcy, at this time of year, and the perfume of roses is heavy in the air. The grass is so neat that it looks like it's been cut with a beard trimmer, the topiary hedge shapes have been maintained so perfectly that there isn't a single leaf out of place, and I'm honoured by how much work everyone has put in just to make this fair held in my father's honour as perfect as it can be.

Our stall is up a couple of steps, on a sand-coloured gravel ridge of the gardens, surrounded by neat hedging and stone planters full of tall, purple flowering verbena plants. We've got a small marquee set up to protect the ageing pages of the diary from strong sun, and behind us, we've put together a wall of foam boards and photocopied the pages and pinned them up, so the whole story is repeated in A4-sized enlarged prints, that people can read without the risk of damaging the ancient diary. Most if it is Ava's doing. She painted the shells we collected on Arfordir-Môr-Forwyn beach last week and has scattered them around, and decorated our printed pages with shell-shaped ink stamps, stickers, and decorative stems of blue leaves she found in my shop, and I've been happy to give her free rein. Having the help and not being alone has given me more confidence in my ability to handle the antiques fair, and no one is more invested in the story of this diary than she is.

'I can't believe he sacrificed himself to protect her.' Lissa is poring over the diary before it gets put back in its locked plastic box to display it to the public but protect it from curious fingers.

She's stroking its aged pages with the pads of her cotton-gloved fingers. 'I want to display this in the museum when the antiques fair is over. It's the most romantic thing ever. It could be Ariel herself writing this.'

'I don't think Ava will let it out of our sight. She loves it so much, she keeps reading it over and over again, trying to spot hidden meanings or clues we might've missed. And we don't know that the mystery sailor sacrificed himself. He *could* have survived.'

'A barely healed broken leg, and even in summer, that Irish Sea is vicious and *cold*. If he did make it to shore, he was a wanted man. Theft, destruction of property, smuggling... His Victorian rap sheet was never-ending. There's no way this ended happily. If he survived, he was probably thrown in prison for years, and if he didn't, then...' She trails off, leaving the prospect of the most likely outcome wide open.

Lissa sighs and puts the book into its box, open on the entry of the shipwreck, and slips the key into the pocket of her shirt. She's staying here to cover this stall today, so I'm free to go anywhere I might be needed, and talk to the journalists Witt and Sadie have got coming.

The more coverage, the better, I keep telling myself. My dad would have been *delighted* to think of his idea coming to fruition, and even more so to have it named after him – I owe it to him to talk it up as much as possible, no matter how far outside of my comfort zone it is.

Our elevated platform in the castle garden gives us a top-down view of the rest of the area, and I spot Ren and Ava heading up the stone walkway towards the castle gates, Ava waving madly when she spots us.

'How's that going?' Without me noticing, Lissa has moved until she's standing beside me to see who I'm waving at, although she answers her own question when I don't respond quickly enough. 'Good, judging by the grin on your face.'

'Yeah, really great. He's *perfect* even though he's the furthest thing from perfect, and Ava is the sweetest little muffin. She's like me when I was thirteen. I can't pretend I'm not worried about how things will be when school goes back, but we can all cross that bridge when we come to it.'

'A real-life Prince Eric.' Her eyes follow them as they disappear into the winding paths through the castle grounds, before reappearing at the bottom of the steps up to our flat ridge.

Ava bounces up them faster than a lemur on a pogo stick. 'Hiiiiiiiii! It's antiques fair day! Maybe someone will know something about the diary! Maybe one of those antiques dealers will collect mermaid stuff and have her other notebooks!'

'Don't get your hopes up, Ave.' Ren huffs up the two steps behind her, looking positively worn out from all the bouncing he's had to put up with so far today, and all week since we got back from our holiday. Ava has been *really* excited about this weekend, and her enthusiasm has rubbed off on me, whereas school starts again on Tuesday and Ren has been more concerned with the practicalities like uniform shopping and lesson planning and preparing for the new term.

She throws her arms around me, and then Lissa, before going to inspect the diary pages on our wall, and double-checking the diary box is locked and that Liss and I haven't done anything to wreck her decorating handiwork in the hours since she left yesterday.

Lissa offers to take her for a private tour of the Colours of the Wind before customers start arriving, and they skip off together, with Lissa promising she has an exact replica of the statue of Prince Eric that Ariel tries to save in her fairytale museum, and Ren sinks down on one of the stone benches between two planters with a groan that sounds like it's been a *long* morning considering it's barely 9 a.m.

'Look on the bright side, maybe all this historical stuff will inspire her to give history lessons her full attention from now on,' I offer.

'Maybe. And she hasn't even complained about being out with me lately. You've single-handedly turned me into a cool dad.' He raises an eyebrow and pats the empty space beside him. 'Good morning.'

I go over and sit next to him, and we share a gentle kiss that's nowhere near long enough *or* steamy enough, but I'm hyperaware of being above the rest of the sprawling gardens and visible to *everyone.*

'Did you know there's a guy down there selling genuine Victorian outfits? And someone selling vintage musical instruments, and artwork from years gone by? This place is a historian's dream. A millionaire historian, but still. I've never seen so many pieces of history in one place before. I got quite excited walking through just then. And quite worried about what Ava's going to make me buy when all those dealers open their shops.'

'This is what my dad loved. He used to drag me round to antiques fairs at weekends. I hated it at the time, I thought it was all so old and boring!'

'He'd be so proud of you. Look at this place. Everyone's gone so far out of their way to make these next two days a success – in his honour. That's special, Mick. The things you loved have got a much better chance at finding their new owners now, and the shop is like walking into a different space. It's already attracting more customers, I can tell from how little alone time we've had this week.'

He's not wrong there. Every moment I've had with Ren this week, it seems like a customer has come in, and judging by the takings in the till when I cashed up last night, most of them are buying things too.

'What can we do to help?'

'Nothing. You've both done more than enough already. Witt and Sadie are handling the event itself. Lissa's going to stay here with the diary, and I'm going to flit around where anyone needs me. All of the other shopkeepers are doing this for nothing in return – the least I can do is keep them well supplied in tea and cakes.'

'I can help with that.'

'Aww, I've always said you'd be the best boyfriend ever.'

'Am I your boyfriend?' His face breaks into a huge grin. 'That makes me feel like I'm about twenty again. At what age does the term *boy*-friend become an unfeasible description?'

I can't help giggling at the giddy look on his face and the twinkle in his blue eyes. 'Curmudgeon-friend then.'

He laughs so hard he nearly falls off the bench. 'You make me feel like I should be back in school, and *not* in a teaching position. I feel like a hormone-fuelled teenager whenever I'm with you. In a good way.'

We laugh and enjoy the sunshine together, and I tell myself to stop worrying about what might happen. *This* is worth fighting for, even if life is easier in the summer holidays, it's not like I'm never going to see him again. This is the most *right* thing I've ever felt, and Ren *and* Ava are worth fighting for because spending time with them is the only thing that's improved my life in recent years.

When Lissa and Ava come back, Ava has already taken on the job of assistant manager of the stall today. She sticks with Lissa, and when customers start trickling in, she excitedly tells them the story of the diary, how we found it, and points out key entries on the wall of photocopies behind us, and politely declines any offers we get from collectors who want to buy it, telling them firmly that it's our most prized possession, and swiftly turning it into a shop plug. 'It's not for sale, but you never know, you might find even better treasures in The Mermaid's Treasure Trove!' she trills at one man who's just offered to buy the diary. 'Be sure to come back soon!'

It's a shame she's got to go back to school because I'd happily take her on as a shop assistant.

Quite a few journalists come over, taking notes about the diary, taking photos of it, and Ava handles them like a pro, chatting away like her life depends on it. I see Ren hovering in the background, looking proud of how much confidence she's gained. Each one leaves with assurances that the Philip Teasdale Antiques Fair will be getting rave reviews from their publications.

'This is the best fun ever,' Ava says as she comes with me when I walk round the castle gardens to check on everyone running stalls on my behalf.

'Not Alton Towers?'

'Way better!'

It makes me laugh. There can't be many teenagers who'd rather go to an antiques fair than a theme park.

When Witt comes over just before lunchtime to check on us, and I introduce Ren and Ava, he offers to show them around the castle, and when they come back from their private tour, Ava is buzzing because a local news crew have just arrived, and I stand on tiptoes from our raised spot to peer over the hedge and watch as they get out of their van with cameras and filming equipment.

A reporter and film crew gradually make their way through the grounds, filming every stall as they go, and while my palms are sweaty and I think I might throw up before they make their way to us, Ava's practically vibrating with excitement, and she chats away to the reporter, seemingly oblivious to the guy holding the camera right behind him. I almost don't have to say anything as she waxes lyrical about our find, and the possibility that mermaids once existed in UK waters.

I get the diary out and flip through it on camera, and give a little background story about my dad and how the Philip Teasdale Antiques Fair came to be this year.

When evening comes, Witt and Sadie have dragged a TV into the main hallway of the castle and ordered a takeaway for everyone, and we all gather to watch ourselves on the local news, and we go home happy, and exhausted, and looking forward to doing it all again tomorrow after a truly successful first day.

* * *

Sunday dawns dry and warm, and after the news broadcast went out last night, it's *much* busier than yesterday, and the antiques themselves are dwindling fast. Ren, Ava, and I have brought some more stuff up from the shop, and all my fellow shopkeepers have volunteered to come back for the second day of the antiques fair too.

It's mid-afternoon and Lissa's gone for a tea break, and Ava is in her element with me at the diary stall, while Ren has gone off with fellow history geek Witt to talk about, I don't know, historical points of architectural interest in the castle or something like that, when a woman approaches, clutching a wooden chest that's decorated with seashells and has an anchor-shaped padlock on the front. It gives me an immediate flashback to the one we found the diary in, and the hairs on the back of my neck stand on end.

'I think you have something that belongs to my family.' She puts the chest down on an empty spot on our table and points to the diary in the locked display box.

Ava's attention was on a goth-type teenage boy trailing behind a parent down in the courtyard, but her head suddenly whips around and I see her clock the similar chest and the woman's finger, pointing towards *our* diary.

'We've spent months searching for it. Imagine my surprise when I saw you on the news last night and there it was!'

I place my palm on the box. 'You're saying this is yours?'

'It was sold off in the house clearance by mistake, wasn't it? That's how you came by it?'

I nod, trying to ignore the sinking feeling coming over me. Did we say that to the news reporter last night? I don't think we did. I don't think she'd know that if she didn't have a legitimate claim to the book.

'It's a family heirloom,' she continues. 'My mum had possession of it, and when she passed away last year, although we looked for it in her house, we couldn't find it anywhere. In the haze of grief, my sister and I assumed our aunt must've had it, and our aunt assumed one of us had it, and it was only weeks after the house clearance sale when we all got together that we realised none of us had it, and it must've been in Mum's belongings all along. We've been desperately trying to trace the buyers who purchased bundles from the house, but the auction company have been most unforthcoming in sharing details. My sister and I have been trawling antiques shops in the area, my aunt has been mounting an online search, and there you were on the local news, waiting for us to find you.'

'We don't know if that's true!' Ava snaps. 'We talked to a ton of journalists yesterday, we definitely told some of them that it came from a house clearance, you could've just seen their articles and now you're trying to claim it because you know it's valuable.'

I wince at the panicked-angry tone in her voice. She *loves* this diary, and like I am, she's realising that it isn't ours, and this woman is most probably the rightful owner.

'What's your name?' I ask, trying to defuse the situation and find out more, because Ava's got a point, she could just be a chancer, trying to get her hands on something of value, but the chest she's carrying is almost identical to the one we found the diary in, and there's no way someone trying to pull a fast one would know about that.

'I'm Pamela. Mayme was my great-great-great-great-aunt.'

'Mayme? That was her name?' Ava steps closer, her interest obviously piqued.

It adds a whole new layer to this. We've never known her name. How often do you write your own name in a diary? You write about the people around you, the things that happen to you, but never include your own name.

Mayme. I'm almost afraid to ask my next question. 'Was she really a...?'

'Mermaid?' Pamela laughs. 'Oh, heavens no, of course not. She was born with deformed vocal cords so she was never able to talk. Mayme means "drop of the sea" and family legend goes that she always loved the ocean and when she read the Hans Christian Andersen story, she felt it was meant for her. She connected with the mermaid who couldn't make herself heard. We think it gave her comfort to believe she was really a misplaced creature from another world rather than a human so different from all others, and so incapable of this most basic thing that *everyone* else can do without a second thought. Everyone around her, seemingly everyone in the world can speak, but she couldn't, and in those days, doctors were at a loss. Apparently no one knew what to make of her – her parents babied her, looked after her, protected her from the world, and when they passed, she was left in the care of her sister, who had no time for her. Her sister had always thought she was playing up for attention, and she trotted her around to various witchdoctors for potions and herbal remedies and eventually a real doctor realised there was something physically wrong, but medical operations in those days didn't have the advantages of modern technology and there was no treatment.'

'That's what she meant about doctors poking and prodding her and humans coming to look at her.' Ava is listening intently; the prospect of finding out the truth has overtaken all her other doubts.

This suddenly makes so much sense. Of *course* she wasn't a mermaid. Of course she was just a normal person who must have felt anything but normal. She found sanctuary in this ocean-themed idea that she was somehow different from everyone else. The idea that there was something – by choice – that set her apart. It must have made the rejection and the feeling that no one understood her easier to cope with.

'And the island? The boat sinking? The sailor? We've been to Arfordir-Môr-Forwyn so we know that actually happened...'

'She was a lighthouse keeper.'

I gasp and grab Ava's hand. 'We saw it! On the boat trip, we saw the ruins of a lighthouse in the distance, didn't we?'

Ava nods excitedly, and I carry on, because now we know, it all seems so obvious. 'Of course she was a lighthouse keeper. *That's* why she felt responsible for his boat running aground – not because she was a mermaid luring him to a watery doom, but because she'd...?'

'Got caught up in the book she was reading and forgotten to light the oil lamps until it was too late.'

'I always knew she was my kind of person,' Ava says. 'How could we ever have *really* thought she was a mermaid?'

'It's an easy mistake to make,' Pamela says kindly, and I can't help thinking about how strange this must be for her – to see her family heirloom displayed for all to see, photocopied pages from it enlarged and flapping around in the summer breeze. It's quite possible that no one outside of their family has ever read it before, and here we are, broadcasting it on the local news and talking to every reporter under the sun, about the possibility of it really being written by a mermaid.

Lissa returns from her break at that moment and comes over curiously, and I explain what's going on.

'What about Jeremiah?' Ava's hand squeezes mine, sounding like she's not sure if she wants to know the answer or not. 'Please tell us he survived!'

'He survived.' Pamela looks bemused by how invested we are in this. 'Months later, he came to find her in England, they were married and had four children.'

'Oh my God, I can't wait to tell Dad!' Ava throws her arms around me. 'I *knew* it couldn't end like that! So did you! It's proof that love can overcome everything! Did they stay together forever?'

'They were happy together until she died in the 1940s, and him not much longer after. It was said that he died of a broken heart.'

Ava pulls away and puts a hand on her chest and lets out a wistful sigh. 'That's the most romantic thing ever!'

Pamela is watching like she can't quite believe she's having this conversation about something so personal with a couple of strangers. 'I love how much this mattered to you. We often thought about sharing the story outside of the family, but we didn't know how to or if our relatives from times gone by would want us to. Can you imagine what a Victorian lady would make of things like the internet and the idea of so many people from all around the world reading her intimate thoughts?'

'We did think of that.' Ava sounds immediately defensive again. 'But we thought she was an actual mermaid and it was important to share that.

'Oh, I know. I didn't mean you'd done anything wrong. I think what you've done is lovely. All of this information you've found out. You even went all the way to Arfordir-Môr-Forwyn? You saw her lighthouse? Even *we* have never done that.'

'I wish we'd known about the lighthouse. We'd have found someone with a boat to take us closer to it. It was miles offshore, past the other islands around the coast. I can't believe none of us put two and two together and realised what she was doing out there. Even when we *saw* the lighthouse remains, it didn't occur to me...'

'It's nice that people still believe in magic in this day and age,' Pamela says. 'I never knew her obviously, but I think Mayme would like knowing that her musings could have such an impact, even so many years later.'

It makes me look around for Ren. He should be here too,

hearing this, counting out the ways he can say 'I told you so' because he was annoyingly right on the mermaid front.

'Our mum used to read me and my sister those diary excerpts as bedtime stories. She had grown up with *her* mum doing the same, and her grandmother telling her tall tales of the mum before her, passing the story down for generations. My sister and I used to talk about it all the time. It bonded us as children. Everyone who overheard thought it was something we'd made up. I'm honoured that you've all fallen in love with it like we did...' Her kindly smile turns awkward as she looks between me, Lissa, Ava, and the diary. 'And I'd really like it back...'

Ava recoils instantly. 'You can't have it back! It's not yours! You gave it away!'

'Not intentionally, pet. We were all struggling after our mum died. Sorting her house out was one of the hardest things we'd ever had to face. We knew the book would be somewhere safe, but it had been passed between her and our aunt over the years, depending on the ages of the children they had to read bedtime stories to, so we just thought...' Her fingers rub over the wooden crate she brought with her. 'We assumed it was in this box with everything else, and we didn't find out that it wasn't until it was too late.'

'Oh, Dad! Thank God you're here!' Ava spots Ren coming back up the steps before I do and races over to grab his arm and drag him over. 'This lady is trying to take the diary! Tell her she can't have it! It's ours, right? You paid for it!'

'I didn't...' Ren looks as surprised as he might if he'd meandered back over and been walloped round the face with a wet mackerel. His eyes flit between us all with a bewildered look. 'Can someone explain what's going on?'

Ava rushes through a garbled explanation, and I try to fill in the gaps in her haste.

Ren turns to Pamela. 'Well, she does have a point. Anyone could come here and make up a story from what they've seen on the news last night, although...' He glances at the wooden crate and then at me, and he can clearly tell from my face that I'm pretty certain she's for real. 'We can't even ask you to tell us what's in the diary because it's printed behind us in enlarged font. Is there any way you *can* prove it?'

'Well, I do have some of her other diaries.' She opens the wooden box and we all step closer to peer in, and sure enough, there are other books in there, notebooks that are clearly old and look very similar to this one.

It's a real *Cinderella* moment, like at the end of the animated film when the glass slipper smashes and Cinderella tells the duke not to worry because she has the other one. With everything she's said, I had very little doubt about her claim anyway, but no one can argue with proof like that.

'Can I have a look?' Ren asks politely.

Pamela takes out a thicker book and hands it to him. 'This is her diary from 1900. The first entry in particular might interest you.'

Ren brushes his hands on his trousers before he takes it from her and opens it carefully, laying it on the plastic display box so all three of us can see it with Lissa peering over my shoulder.

27 June 1900

I never thought I'd see him again. I have spent so many nights crying over what was lost. I have been certain that he died on the night he left the island.

It is Wednesday, another dreary day so like each one before it, and I am asleep when my sister shouts from the stairway. I am always asleep these days – what reason could there be to get up and face life? I know they have found his ship. I know they believe him to have perished – as do I.

My sister tells me that I have a visitor and I must get up to greet him immediately. I do not know why anyone would want to visit me, but I pull a robe around myself and descend the stairs.

It is him.

He is standing in the doorway. He was wearing a cap but has taken it off to come in, although my sister has not permitted him entry further than the front hallway. He looks up as I come down, and the smile that blazes across his face could illuminate the lamps of a thousand lighthouses, and suddenly, the whole world feels brighter.

He is alive. He is here.

Enough tears to refill the ocean are pouring down my face and I momentarily forget that no noise will be heard and let out a scream as I run the rest of the way.

He catches me at the bottom and lifts me from the last stair. He picks me up and spins me around and I feel so happy that I could explode all over my sister's front hallway, although I must not, because she would consider me even more of an inconvenience than she does currently.

He waits outside while I get dressed and we walk in the local park. He remembered enough information from our time together to come to my village and make enquiries until he came upon my sister's home. His leg is better – he still limps, but not as badly as almost a year ago. He has had to falsify his last name so as not to serve a prison sentence. He has what he calls 'friends in the wrong places' and they have provided him with false paperwork for his journey by ferry across the sea. He must never return to Ireland, but it does not matter. He says he doesn't want to return there because I am not there. I feel like I do explode right there in the park and a million butterflies come bursting out of me.

At nightfall, as the streetlamps are lit and the stars glitter above us, he sinks to one knee and asks me to be his wife.

I say yes. No sound comes out, but it is the most important word I've ever spoken in my life.

We flick through further entries. Mayme and her sister are fighting about the wedding. Her sister wants a big society wedding. Mayme wants a small private one. She writes about how Jeremiah stands up for her where she is used to being overruled by her sister. How he becomes the voice she never had, and she and Jeremiah end up eloping. He is able to get a job, and so is she – as a typist who types an author's dictated words. They move in together. The stains of happy tears have splashed the page on the day she writes she has fallen pregnant.

It is documenting the happy life she dreamed of, and this time, there is no question that any of it is a fairy story. It's all as real as she deserved it to be.

It's amazing to read the further entries and find out the ending that we never thought we'd know, but there's an undercurrent of tension around the table. Ava *loves* this diary. I knew that even Lissa would have trouble persuading her to let it be on display in the museum, but it's rightfully Pamela's, and Ava is going to struggle to let it go.

The crate is filled with photographs and letters. Endless notebooks where Mayme wrote down the words she couldn't voice. As cameras became more accessible, there are photographs of the two of them together. Photos of the children they had.

I've got tears in my eyes as we leaf through them. I feel like we've got to know this woman over the summer, this stranger from so many years ago, and her life *matters* to me. To *us*. I glance over at Ava, who's given up trying to hide the tears streaming down her face, and Ren's eyes are watery and he's got his lower lip clamped between his teeth.

'Thank you for sharing this with us.' I carefully place the last of the notebooks back into Pamela's wooden crate and go to unlock the case displaying the diary, but Ava stops me.

'No!' She turns to Pamela. 'You can't just waltz in and say, "Oh, that's mine, that is!" and take it!'

'Ava...' I start.

'No! It's not fair! This diary is the best thing that's ever happened to us, and it's not for sale! Go away!'

'I'm happy to buy it back if need be.' Pamela goes to get out a purse, but I hold up a hand to stop her as Ren puts a hand on Ava's shoulder and turns her away. 'We don't want anything else back from the house clearance. Everything else was supposed to go, except the diary.'

'*I* found it! Finders keepers!' she sobs. 'Mickey gave it to me!'

'It wasn't mine to give.' I realise now that this was a monumental mistake on my part. The very essence of my dad's business was to reunite owners with things they'd lost. I should have been more aware of the fact that this book was sentimental to someone and, sooner or later, they'd come looking for it. 'I'm so sorry, Ave. I should have made it clear from the start that it wasn't the sort of thing someone would have thrown out. I thought someone would be looking for it one day, I just didn't know it would be so soon or that it would become so important to us.'

Ava's crying so hard that she can barely catch her breath, and Ren has taken her to the side, crouched in front of her with both hands on her upper arms, and is trying to persuade her to take deep, calming breaths.

He looks over his shoulder and catches my eyes, his flicking between the diary and Pamela.

He's telling me to give it to her *now*, while Ava's not watching. Maybe he thinks it will be easier that way?

Lissa's looking like she desperately wants to do something to help, and when I risk a glance down at the shoppers in the grounds, Ava's howling sobs have attracted far too much attention.

'Is there anything I can do?' Pamela asks awkwardly.

I shake my head as I turn the key and extract it from the display box. 'She's had a tough time lately and finding this diary helped a lot. I'm sorry. It wasn't meant to end like this.'

I cling onto it for a moment too long as I hand it over. It feels like the end of *Gremlins* when Billy has to give Gizmo back to the old Chinese man. He doesn't want to, even though he knows it's the right thing to do.

Pamela clearly wasn't expecting the scene this has caused as she takes it from me and settles it into her wooden crate with the other things and murmurs a quiet thank you, but she hesitates, looking like she's having second thoughts about taking it. 'Maybe I should come back another day instead?'

I look over my shoulder to where Ren has still got Ava turned around so her back is to us. On the one hand, leaving the diary here now would make things better today, but then what? Get Pamela to return when Ava's in school and take it then instead? That would feel even more underhanded and like I was stabbing her in the back. She'd still be just as upset when she found out. Surely it's better to rip the plaster off in one go than keep picking at it all week?

'Thank you for looking after it so well.' She reaches out to shake my hand when I tell her to take it now, and I shake hers too.

'Thank *you* for inadvertently sharing a piece of your family history with us. It really has made it a very special summer.' I glance at Ava and Ren as I say it, filled with a sense of trepidation that our special summer is well and truly *over*.

Pamela lifts her wooden crate and hurries away, and as she disappears into the crowd, Ava finally escapes the hug Ren has been trying to give her, and realises the diary and Pamela are nowhere to be found.

She lets out an eardrum-piercing scream. 'It's *gone*? It's *gone*? You distracted me so *she* could take it?' She slaps Ren's hand away when he tries to comfort her and then turns on me. 'You haven't got Fairy Godmother magic powers, you've got Wicked Step-mother evil powers!'

'Ava!' Ren has got that helpless look on his face again, the one I haven't seen for a few weeks now. 'Don't talk to Mickey like that. Apologise now, please.'

'She should apologise to me! She's ruined everything!'

'I'm so sorry, Ava,' I say again. 'It wasn't ours. It was never ours.'

'Yes, it was! All you had to do was tell that stupid cow to do one!'

'Ava!' Ren admonishes again, but she's so upset that it doesn't make any difference.

'It wasn't ours to keep. No object is ever ours. Old things came into the world before we did, they're ours for a while, but ultimately, they live on after we're gone, and someone else will take care of them for a while too. That's what my entire shop is about – taking things that were once loved and looking after them until they can be loved again. The diary stayed with us this summer, it brought us into each other's lives, and now it has to go back, like a really good library book that you wish you could keep, but you know you can't, because other people deserve the joy of reading it too.'

'You can buy a really good library book on Amazon!' she mutters, swiping tears away.

'I know it's not the same, but just because we no longer have the book, it doesn't mean we don't still love it and have it in here...' I put my hand on my heart because I know where she's coming from. I feel the gut-wrenching pang of not being able to keep it too, but it's warring with happiness at being able to reunite someone with something they must have been devastated to lose. 'We still get to keep the experiences it gave us, but it has sentimental value to someone else and her family deserve that back. Sometimes we have to let things go for the sake of someone else, right?'

The more I talk, the more she cries, and her howling sobs are attracting even more attention. All I want to do is pull her into my arms and hug her until she feels better, but I'm definitely the last person she wants a hug from right now.

'I thought we were in this together, Mickey, but you let me down. Everyone always lets me down and what I want is never important. I thought you were different, but you're just like everyone else. You don't fight for the things that matter. You don't care about the things that are important to me. You give up when things get tough. Just like *everyone* else.'

She means her mum, obviously, and the comparison makes me wince, but I have no idea what to say in response. Everything I say is only serving to make Ava more turbulent.

I can *see* how she feels, like she desperately wanted me to stand up for what she wanted, to be on her side for once, because I don't think she feels like many people are. I didn't when I was thirteen either. But this was a situation with only one possible conclusion, and when Ava calms down and thinks it through, she'll see that. I'm sure she will. She *has* to.

My stomach is churning and my hands are shaking because I feel so bad about this. 'I'm sorry, Ava. I'm so sorry.'

'I hate you! You're the worst!' It stings even harder than usual because of the number of times she's told me I'm the best, and the distance between us feels like it's several miles wide and expanding by the second. I don't know how she's ever going to get over this, and there's nothing I can do to make it better.

Ava's breath is gasping, rasping, and hitching every time she inhales and her pink T-shirt is soaked with the tears dripping down onto it, and I see the moment she looks around and realises people are staring at us, and again, I desperately want to hug her.

'Why don't we go and get a chocolate milkshake and take a breather from all of this?' Ren sounds like he's balancing on a knife edge and has no idea what to do either.

'No! I hate you! I hate both of you!'

'Ava!' Ren bellows, but she's already turned around and stormed off down the steps. He goes to run after her, but he turns back to me, looking torn, and throws his hands up and makes a noise of frustration. 'I'm so sorry, I've got to...'

He points in the direction that Ava went, but Lissa stops him.

'Let me go. I'm more neutral, and you two need a minute.' She grabs a photocopied page and rips it off the foam boards behind us and dashes after Ava. 'And look, we still have some parts of the diary. All is not lost.'

Ren swears and kicks at the gravel under our feet. 'Sorry about that, she was out of line to say all that and to cause such a scene.'

'No harm done. She's upset and hurting. Lissa's amazing with kids, and she's not involved in this like we are. It'll be okay.' I don't believe my own words – a feeling that's further intensified when I reach out to take his hand and he yanks it back and stomps away, gravel crunching under his boots.

'No harm done?' He repeats my words in a nauseating tone. 'Do you honestly think that any of us have come out of this summer unscathed?'

'The diary was never ours to keep...' I start, feeling knocked off balance by both his tone and the pinched look on his face. He seems to be getting at something much deeper than the diary, and he looks like he's aged ten years in the last five minutes. 'You agreed. You knew she should have had it back too.'

'Yes, but it's not about that. It's about Ava needing to feel like she comes first – like she matters.'

'Of course she matters. I tried my best to defuse that situation, but what was I supposed to do – tell Pamela she couldn't have her family heirloom back because Ava wanted it more?'

'I don't know.' He pushes a hand through his hair, sounding more desperate than frustrated now. 'It's not just about that, Mickey. It's about everything. Everything that's happened these past six weeks. Everything that shouldn't have happened.'

He paces for a minute and I can see his anger building, and I'm filled with an overwhelming sense of dread that this is all about to come crashing down. 'You *should* have made it clear from the outset that someone might come back to claim it one day, not "given" it to her and let her think it was hers forever.'

'You could have made it clear too! It wasn't all my doing.'

'I'm not the expert on curiosities and reuniting owners with their lost treasure.'

'No, but you *are* the father obsessed with micro-managing your daughter's expectations. You were *glad* to see her enjoying something – neither of us thought through the possible outcomes. No one ever *really* thinks that someone's going to turn up and claim something back. My dad reunited, like, three objects in thirty years. It's not a regular occurrence.'

'Yeah, well, you had no right to let *either* of us believe in bloody fairy stories and magical nonsense.'

'What?' I raise both eyebrows because he's not just talking about the diary. He's loosened up so much this summer – I never expected to hear him say something so cutting when I *know* he's enjoyed every moment too.

The gravel crunches under his feet as he continues pacing. 'There's a reason I don't get involved with anyone, and this is it. People are reckless, spontaneous, and never think through the consequences of their actions – everything that I am not. Because, guess what, you *can't* be like that when you're responsible for a child. When you've got someone who looks up to you, you have to be a role model, not a bloody mermaid!'

'Or you can show her that it's possible to be both. Everyone can still be a well-rounded adult while saving space for a touch of whimsy in their lives. The last thing anyone should be showing *any* child is that there is such a thing as too old to believe in magic, or that there is something wrong with being *both* sensible and level-headed and fun and whimsical!'

His hands swing out as he turns around and paces in the other direction. 'Ava didn't need any more trauma in her life, and now this thing that's brought her so much joy has ripped her heart out – exactly what I was trying to prevent happening, I just thought it was going to be when we found out the writer wasn't really a mermaid or the sailor had died, I didn't foresee it being like *this*.'

'What was I supposed to do, Ren?' I ask again, defiantly, because that was a no-win situation and I have no idea how I could have handled it differently.

'I don't know. But I do know this was a mistake. I got so tangled up with you that I let myself make it anyway, even though I knew it would end in tears. Or a bloody great hormonal meltdown, in this case. What we need to do is forget *all* of this and go back to how things were before we met you.'

'You don't mean that.' Tears I was fighting to hold back spill out of my eyes, and he hesitates, and for half a second I think he's going to throw his arms around me and tell me that he doesn't, of course he doesn't.

He shakes his head, but it's a gesture of resignation, not a rebuttal of those words. 'Yes, Mick, I do. I *have* to. Because I have a daughter who needs me to put her first, and I should never have forgotten that. Now, if you'll excuse me, I've got to go and undo some of the damage this summer has caused!'

As he marches down the steps and back into the castle grounds, Cleo races up them and pulls me into a hug. 'Oh, that was *painful*. I'm so sorry, I thought he was "the one".'

'So did I,' I mumble, trying and failing to fight the tears that are running down my face.

'Anyone who buys that amount of tea and cake is a good 'un at heart. Emotions are high at the moment. Don't take it personally.'

How many times have I said the same to Ren this summer? I never expected to have someone saying that to me when it all went wrong. Because it *has* all gone wrong, hasn't it?

Ava will never forgive me, and Ren... never wanted to get involved in the first place, and this is his perfect excuse to shut himself off again.

Cleo rubs my back and lets me cry into her shoulder while I try to come to terms with how quickly this all went south. With the way I've been feeling about Ren, I expected them both to be in my life forevermore, but somehow, we didn't even make it to the end of the summer holidays, and I suddenly wish we'd thrown that diary into the fathoms below as soon as we found it, and stayed well and truly *not* a part of each other's worlds.

20

'That was totally unfair and out of line, you know that, right?' It's a couple of mornings later, and Lissa has come to check on me for what is probably the seventieth time this week. 'If he hadn't been dealing with a messy teenager, I'd have thumped him for talking about my best friend like that.'

She punches a fist into the open palm of her opposite hand, making me laugh despite myself, as only a best friend can. 'He was angry. He's a protective father and his daughter was upset. Emotions were magnified and I *did* tell her she could keep that diary when I had no way of knowing that.'

'*You* didn't upset Ava – the situation did. Kids of that age aren't always mature enough to separate the two. She'd attached an importance to the diary that was unrealistic and it shocked her when she realised it belonged to someone. Children have no idea how to regulate their emotions and meltdowns like that are common. We're not *that* old – you must remember being that age. Everything feels bigger than it is and every situation makes you feel like you're the only person who's ever had to face horrible things happening. You want to be treated like an adult but also indulged like a child, and those emotions conflict and try to outshine each other at every opportunity. It's not something you'll never be able to move past, but in the moment, she didn't know how else to react.'

Lissa has a load of little sisters, I'm going to have to trust her judgement on that one. 'Was she okay? When you went after her?'

'No,' Lissa says honestly. 'But she took the photocopied page and I promised I'd keep the rest for her. She's a lovely kid – I think she'll realise, in time, that it was the right thing to do.'

'I hope so.' And in the meantime, I can go back to missing them both, and actually being really annoyed with Ren over how he handled that on Sunday. Both of us have made mistakes this summer, but the one thing I'm certain of is that letting each other in was *not* one of them.

Lissa carries on trying to make me feel better. 'She loves you. She basically *is* you in smaller, louder, more excitable form. I've never seen such a Mini Me. You'll get past this.'

'It's not that simple. Even if Ava does forgive me, Ren never will. He is *not* the kind of man to let himself make the same mistake twice, and I'm not sure I'm the kind of woman to forgive someone for such cruel words so easily, for that matter.'

'No one calls my best friend a mistake. He'll be lucky if I don't punch him in the nose when I see him next.' She makes an 'I'm watching you' gesture towards the door, even though Ren is not likely to see it, and she manages to make me laugh again, even though laughing is the last thing I feel like doing.

'That's the spirit. And talking of spirits and lifting them, it's the second of September and Cleo's got an early-autumn special on pumpkin spice lattes, are you in?'

'Aren't you supposed to be working?'

'The museum can manage itself for a while. I've left my

Lumière statue in charge, he's great at covering for me.' She waves a nonchalant hand and then laughs and heads for the door. 'I closed up, Mick. It was so quiet this morning and hanging out with you seemed more important.'

'One day we'll get to fight a cause for you and pay you back for all this cheerleading you do,' I call after her.

Lissa is the most supportive person on Ever After Street and always the first to help anyone in need of assistance and the first to stand up for any injustice, and I'm proud to call her my best friend.

* * *

The days of the week pass like wading through treacle. I hadn't realised how much of my time had been occupied by Ren and Ava, and the diary. We've all spent so much time reading it, researching it, hunting for clues, searching the shop for other things that might've come from the same house clearance, and now all those questions are answered, and I'm left wondering how I filled my hours before that day, six weeks ago, when that grouchy man and his cheerful daughter walked into my shop.

And it's not just time, but headspace too. I've spent so many weeks with them. If not with them, then thinking about them. Thinking of things to do with them. Things to show them. Things to tell one or both of them. Ava had sent me social media memes every day, and links to websites she'd found about mermaid sightings in Britain. I *miss* her.

And then there's Ren. Not the grouchy, angry Ren, but the soft, gentle, tipsy Ren who was the most gorgeous man I'd ever seen, the best kisser I've ever kissed, and the best hugger I've ever hugged. I didn't know it was possible to grow so close to someone in only a few weeks, but when someone lets you in after shutting everyone out for years, it's been impossible not to let him in too, and open myself up to a relationship when I thought I'd be closed off in that department until the end of time itself. I didn't expect it to end so sharply and with such cutting, undeserved comments.

Lissa's been spending extra time with me, but she's got her own business to run, and the fairytale artefacts in the Colours of the Wind museum don't look after themselves. And even though my shop has been busier than ever since the antiques fair, the only thing it feels without Ren and Ava is dull and empty.

I haven't bothered doing my hair or putting on any sea-punned T-shirts. The only thing that remains of my Ariel costume is Ursula's shell necklace, mainly because Lissa had it made for me and she'd be upset if I stopped wearing it for no good reason.

Since the weekend, curiosity collectors and antiques hunters have been coming and going with regularity. The shop is much better organised now, and Witt, bless his soul, made sure that all the publicity surrounding the Philip Teasdale Antiques Fair mentioned The Mermaid's Treasure Trove, and so many new customers have now added it to their regular round of antiquing that I can barely keep up with the comings and goings, never mind the sales and ringing money into the till. I even had a queue last week. I'd never had a queue before, and I'm so grateful to Ren for his sharp, blunt honesty, because without him being a catalyst, I'd probably still be buried under masses of junk with no customers and Victorian-style birdcages that leap forth and attack unsuspecting passersby.

I look up as a man comes in and looks around.

'Can I help you with anything specific?' I ask, because some customers want to know if you've got certain collectibles, and others just want to browse and see what they find.

He seems like one of the latter as he takes in the wide paths through sensibly positioned furniture, displaying trinkets with plenty of space around them to fully showcase their qualities, rather than a hundred things all rammed together, hoping someone would rescue them. For a moment, he looks like he's going to ask for something, and then changes his mind. 'I'm looking for... Well, I think this is the kind of place where I'll know it when I see it.'

Amazingly, he's not the only customer browsing, and I lose track of him as I serve a lady buying a tulip-shaped candle holder, and a few minutes later, from the second half of the shop, there's an exclamation of, 'Ah, this is it! Exactly the thing that I've needed all my life without ever knowing I needed it!'

He makes some grunting noises as it sounds like he's attempting to pick up whatever it is he's found, but he refuses my offer when I call out to ask if he needs any help, and soon enough he reappears, carrying... the dragon fruit table. I clamp the inside of my cheek between my teeth in an attempt to stop the tears that instantly make my vision blurry. I desperately *need* to tell Ren and the fact that I *can't* tell Ren makes my heart break all over again when it was already shattered into enough pieces this week.

'You want to buy *that*?' My voice is hoarse and sandpapery, and I try to cover it by taking a drink from my water bottle, but it has nothing to do with being dry-mouthed and everything to do with it being the dragon fruit table that Ren was so sure would never sell. The dragon fruit table that he singled out because he didn't want to admit how much he liked it really.

'Oh, absolutely. What a delightfully quirky piece. Do you know if there's a story behind it?'

I go to tell him the story I told Ren all those weeks ago, about the man who carved it for his dragon fruit-loving wife, but no words come out, and I end up shaking my head mutely. 'There isn't one.'

'What a shame.' He digs some notes out of his wallet without attempting to haggle. 'It looks like the sort of piece that would have a story behind it.'

'It does, doesn't it?' I murmur as I hand him his receipt, and he shoves it in his pocket and lifts the table again.

'Charming shop you've got here. See you again, I hope.'

I thank him and watch as he leaves, and it feels significant. That stupid table had become important for no real reason, and watching the man walk off down the street with it is like saying goodbye to the last piece of everything good that happened this summer, and I hope that no one else comes in for a while because I'll never be able to explain why I'm crying over a resin table made in the likeness of a fruit I've never eaten.

21

In the course of a few days, summer has turned to autumn. Schools started back this week and as I watch streams of uniformed children clutching brand new bags and trotting to school with their hands clutched by harried parents, I can't help thinking of Ren and Ava. They both must be back in school now. My summer holiday visions of Ava coming here every afternoon when school finishes and Ren coming to pick her up and spending lazy autumnal evenings together have wilted like The Beast's enchanted rose petals, but unlike a Disney fairytale, there's no magical enchantress coming to cast a spell and undo all the damage that's been done.

It's suspiciously quiet on Ever After Street as I walk to work on Saturday morning. It's always quiet in the lull between summer holidays and the rush of Christmas shoppers starting towards the end of next month. My shop is a few doors down from the bookshop and I wave to Marnie as I pass because she's in her window, rearranging a display around her cat, and then I wave to Cleo and Bram, who are both in their windows, putting cakes out to tempt customers in. Oddly, Sadie is also in the window of The Cinderella Shop, putting a beautiful gown on a mannequin, and Franca and Raff have found something to fiddle with at the archway that separates Ever After Street from Christmas Ever After, and Imogen is standing at the doorway of the 1001 Nights restaurant, which doesn't open until late afternoon, chatting to Ali, who is *never* in work at this time of day...

I stop and turn around, looking back the way I've come, and I get the feeling of walking down the street during a zombie apocalypse. Everything is menacingly quiet, curtains twitch when I glance in their direction, and there isn't a customer in sight. The only thing that's missing is an upturned car, a Hollywood hero running around, and the sound of distant sirens.

'Hi.'

The scream I let out is so blood-curdling that it could definitely be associated with a zombie apocalypse, and I spin around in shock to see Ren waiting by the door of my shop... and on the street in front of him is the dragon fruit table.

There's a chair on either side of it, and on the tabletop is a book, and a dragon fruit. An actual dragon fruit, on a plate, with a knife. 'What the...?'

'I owe you an apology.' He glances behind him, and Ava appears from round the side of the shop, with Lissa behind her. '*We* owe you an apology.'

Ava waves nervously and I wave back at her, and then my eyes flick to Lissa. 'I thought you were going to punch him, not help him!'

'I am. He'll just never know when,' she says cheerily and makes that 'I'm watching you' gesture at him this time. 'In the meantime, maybe listen to what the man has to say. Come on, Ave, let's give them a bit of privacy. Cleo's going to open up early just for us. Anything you want is on the house.'

'So you *are* all in on this then?' I call after her as she leads Ava away, not expecting an answer because it's obvious. I've worked on this street for years – not once have I seen so many shop-keepers find something vital to do in their windows in such perfect sync.

Ava glances back over her shoulder and I give her what I hope is a reassuring smile. Whatever's going on here, I want her to know that everything that happened last weekend is water under the bridge, if she wants it to be too.

Cleo's waiting at the door of The Wonderland Teapot and I watch her open up and let them in, and then I watch all four of them pretend not to be looking at us, before I turn back to Ren. 'What are you doing here? What is *that* doing here? I sold it on Thursday!'

'You sold it to me. That was my mate from work. He's a teacher in the art department. He only did it on the condition that he can borrow it sometime as a still-life subject for his students to draw.'

'I *knew* there was something off about him! He said *exactly* what I said to you the first time you saw it!' I'm absolutely delighted to see it again, and totally shocked by how much trouble Ren has gone to.

'You didn't tell him the story.'

'There is no story,' I mutter, because it's long past time I stopped making up stories about the items in my shop and sold them as what they are, not what I want them to be.

'Yeah, there is, and that's what makes your shop so special. *You.* You make everything special because you *see* everything as special, and—'

'I thought I was a "mistake that should never have happened",' I interrupt by paraphrasing his words from last weekend, because hearing that is not something I can forget easily.

'You're not. Of course you're not, and I'm getting to that part, but I don't want you to stop believing in magic because I'm a creaky old curmudgeon who doesn't get it.'

'You get it, even if you pretend not to.' His suitably guilty look makes me smile to myself. 'I was *devastated* to see this table gone, and to sell it without being able to tell you, because I knew you secretly loved it.'

'I do. From the moment I saw it – not because of *it*, but because of you. Because of what you see in it. Ava cleared a space for it in our front hallway because I want to be reminded of your approach to life every day, but I couldn't just walk in and buy it after last weekend, I needed more time to put together a decent apology, hence the calling in of favours and a bit of hoop-jumping. Also, it's very hard to find an actual dragon fruit. I feel like I've been on a week-long tour of Britain's supermarkets.'

The thought makes me smile. Despite my love of the table and my curiosity about what a dragon fruit itself would taste like, it had never occurred to me to actually look for one, and I love that he's made such a simple gesture into something truly special.

'So what exactly is going on here?' I wave a finger towards the rest of Ever After Street behind me without turning around to look because I'm certain that *every* shopkeeper will have given up the pretence of fixing their windows and just be overtly watching by now. 'Why does everyone know?'

'I was looking for insider intelligence on how much you might hate me and how much of a chance I might have. I only spoke to Lissa and Cleo, but word has apparently spread.'

I hate to tell him that that's what words *do* on Ever After Street – they spread, because if this little community can find a way to help one of their own, they always do.

'But that's not the point.' He checks his watch. 'Right now, I figure I've got about ten minutes before customers start arriving, and there's something I want you to read. It's not as interesting nor as historically important as the first diary, but it's written by someone who is almost as incapable of saying the things he *should* say at the times he should say them, so I'm going to take a lesson from our mermaid – shut up and let written words speak where my spoken ones so often fail.'

He nudges the book on the table towards me. It's a leather-bound notebook with an old-fashioned look and a gorgeous smell of vintage paper to it.

I open the cover, and on the first page are the words:

Diary of a modern-day history teacher who wouldn't know a good thing if it smacked him in the face.

An unexpected giggle escapes and I look up at him, but he refuses to meet my eyes, and I can't quite believe what I'm seeing. 'You've written me a diary?'

Instead of nodding, he holds a hand out towards the chair, inviting me to sit down, and I realise that he's right about the time, and if customers are likely to come along shortly, this seems like something I would rather read *without* Mrs Moreno's cat's bladder issues coming into it.

Given the two chairs, I thought he might sit opposite me, but he paces, wringing his hands together. He was doing a good job of covering his nerves until now, but they're suddenly so tangible that it makes my heart pound faster as I sit down, wondering what on earth he could have written that would make him so nervous.

I start reading his account of this summer, the first two diary entries recounting the first days he and Ava came into the shop, a handwritten apology for his initial insults and rudeness, but I'm struggling to concentrate because he's pacing so much, but there's something else. While it's a nice gesture and a thoughtful throwback to the thing that brought us together, it feels a bit impersonal and cold too. 'Isn't this a bit... detached?'

He stops pacing to look at me. 'I thought it was a sentimental touch. You loved reading Mayme's diary.'

'Mayme isn't here to tell us her thoughts in person. *You* are. I know you aren't particularly good at dealing with feelings, but why do I want to read this on a page when you're standing right in front of me? If you have something to say, *say* it.'

'Not giving me the easy way out, huh?'

'No. Why should I? You were way out of line the other day. You said some really horrible things that were undeserved. I'm not sure why you've gone to all this trouble today, but if this *is* an apology, or an explanation, explain it to me.' I look up at him expectantly, trying not to show that I'm really touched by this gesture, even if I do think he needs to work a bit harder and get a bit more personal too.

'But that would mean ugly, messy feelings...'

'Yes, exactly. And exactly the example you should be setting for Ava. Sometimes feelings *are* messy and you can't keep them all in a nice, neat notebook, even if I do appreciate the displaced romance you were aiming for.'

'I knew you were going to do that.' He nods to me as I close the book. 'I knew you were going to *say* that.' He paces a few more times, and then finally slumps into the seat opposite me.

'What does it say?' I push him to elaborate when I start to get the feeling that we could sit here all week and he still wouldn't have found the right words for whatever it is that he's trying to say.

'The first one says I was an arse on the day we came into your shop.'

'I know, I read that part.'

He sighs. 'It says something changed in me when we hugged in the café. That hug untethered something inside of me and made me feel like a boat rocking on a stormy sea when I'd spent years trying to keep *every* water as calm as possible, and how I couldn't get you out of my head. And when I came to start decluttering, I felt lighter than I had in years. Talking to you was like a metaphorical weight being lifted off my shoulders. It's about how you can see right inside me, how I really wanted you to know why I'm like I am, and how long it had been since I wanted anyone to know *anything* about me, but you made everything feel different, and opening up to you was eas—' He hesitates. His eyes flick to mine and then he looks away again. 'Well, it wasn't *easy*, but it did feel natural and right, and it had been a long time since anything felt right in my life.'

He's twisting his fingers together and deliberately avoiding eye contact, and I stretch my leg until I can push at his boot with my toe, trying to prod him into carrying on. I know he's trying to apologise for the other day, and I'd be lying if I said I wasn't enjoying his discomfort just the teeniest little bit.

'It goes on to mention the argument we had and the night on the riverbank.' He pushes out a long breath and seems to steel himself. 'I fell in love with you that night.'

I don't even try to hide the intake of breath at the surprise of him saying it so openly. I didn't expect him to lay himself quite *this* bare, and he carries on quickly, like he's trying to make sure nothing derails his determination to get it all out there.

'You're the most affectionate and open person I've ever met. That night, you stroked my hair, kissed my cheek, gave me the best hug of my life, and I fell in love with you. My heart felt like it had increased in size. The next morning, I kept touching my cheek because I could still feel the imprint of your lips. I felt giddy and joyful and I ran away because I could *see* life being wonderful again, and I wasn't ready to really believe it yet.'

I can feel my own heart increasing in size because there's something truly special about hearing him candidly say what I thought was happening at the time, but was never sure if I was reading the situation quite right.

'...If it makes you cry, maybe it's not a good thing?'

I sniffle and swipe away tears that I hadn't realised were rolling down my cheeks. because I've been so consumed by his words that everything else has ceased to exist. It's so impactful to hear him say it so frankly, and to know that somewhere in this book I'm still caressing, he's written it in permanent ink on white paper. A fact. Something that will last forever, like Mayme's diary. What felt like an easy way out earlier has suddenly become by far the most thoughtful and heartfelt thing anyone's ever done for me. The idea he's taken inspiration from a diary he never believed in and used it to give me his perspective on the summer we've spent together is illuminating and moving. I want to get up and hug him, but I don't want to move a millimetre in case he clams up again.

'You must've known,' he says gently. 'Everything changed in me. I could suddenly believe in the impossible. By the time we went to Wales, I could barely keep my hands off you, and I know you knew I was holding back, trying to cling onto my sensible side, and then we kissed, and every doubt I'd had went up in flames. I didn't need to write that bit down, you already *know* it.'

'I thought I knew a lot of things... until last weekend.'

He lets out a low groan. 'The kind of weekend I would rather erase from my mind completely than put anything about it down on paper to be remembered for all eternity?'

'That's the one.'

'I'm so sorry.' He shakes his head. 'That doesn't even begin to cover it. I'm more than sorry. I wouldn't blame you for never wanting to see me again, and if that *is* the outcome today, that's fine, I deserve it. You did the right thing in returning the diary, of *course* you did, but Ava was so distraught and I was out of my depth in consoling her. She feels like no one is ever on her side. People forget how isolating it is to be a kid in a world of adults, even when they're nice adults who go out of their way to include you, you still feel like a different species. And I *had* to support her, especially when she was so worked up. I couldn't make her feel even more isolated, like even her own father doesn't care about her feelings. You understand that, right?' His index finger scratches at an invisible pattern on the table in front of him.

'Yeah, of course I do, but it shouldn't have been about taking sides. There were no sides *to* take. The three of us got that diary back to where it belonged, it should have been a moment to celebrate, even though it's always bittersweet to say goodbye to something that's brought you joy, the most important part is that someone was missing it and *we* helped them get it back.'

'It's easy to say that *now*, with hindsight, and without a teenager having a meltdown, but in that moment, I overreacted. I *should* have given us space and a chance to talk things through afterwards, but I'd been waiting for everything to go wrong between us – because that's what relationships always *do* in my life – and rather than fighting it, I accepted that the inevitable ending had come sooner rather than later. I did what I usually do – curled myself into a defensive ball and fired venom in your direction like an angry, hissing cobra.'

'Yes, you did.' I fold my arms, feeling uncomfortably prickly about last weekend. I *know* he was out of his depth and he overreacted, I know he does that, but it's not easy to forget being on the receiving end of that defensiveness.

'Mick, I'm so sorry. I said so many things I shouldn't have said.

I should never have called you a mistake when you are, quite literally, the best thing to ever happen to me. I'm embarrassed by how far below the belt I went. I was rude, cruel, and the worst version of myself I could have possibly been. You've changed our lives this summer, and you didn't deserve any of that from either of us. Ava's written an entry too.' He nods to the diary. 'At least read that one. It took her a long time to work out what to say and she knew it would probably come across better on paper than in words from a sulky, shouty teenager.'

I open the book and let my fingers trail across the pages until I find the one that changes from neat, uniform lettering in black ink to young handwriting in pink pen that's dotted with hearts and stars.

I'm so sorry, Mickey. I ruined everything. I didn't mean anything I said. I knew the diary didn't belong to us, not really, but I didn't expect its rightful owner to come and for it to just be gone. I thought I'd get to keep it and read it forever, and Dad says I needed time to adjust to the idea of letting it go, but it all happened so quickly.

The diary doesn't matter. This has been the best summer we've ever had, but it wasn't because of the diary – it was because we met you and spent so much time together. You've made me realise it's okay to be myself, and I hope you'll forgive me because I'm a real cow sometimes, and I'm sorry.

Dad's sooo sad without you. Please don't push him away because of me and make him go back to being miserable and mopey.

Oh, he's shouting. 'Ava, don't write that!'

The entry ends with a squiggle where it looks like the pen has been taken out of her hand, and I make a noise that's somewhere between a snort, a giggle, and a sob. The next entry changes back to Ren's handwriting and I go to start reading it, but he reaches over and gently closes the book.

His hand stays on my side of the table and he takes another deep breath and turns his palm up, inviting me to slip mine into it, and when I do, his shoulders physically drop in relief.

'When I walked into your shop in July, I was a tightly sprung angry ball, full of fear and frustration that was whirling around inside me and screaming to get out. You are the only person who's ever heard all of my fears without a word being spoken. You're the only person who's ever understood my frustration without me having to bungle an explanation. You're certainly the only one who's ever been able to start unravelling my thoughts by running your fingers through my hair, and you've changed me this summer. I shouldn't have acted like I did last weekend. I shouldn't have walked away just because Ava was upset. You are both the most important people in the world to me, you were *both* upset, and I should have found a way to navigate that rather than shutting down.'

He hesitates, like he's expecting me to chime in with an agreement, but I stay quiet because it takes a lot to be *this* honest, and he deserves a little credit for that, and for all the effort he's gone to today.

'Since July, I feel like a sailor enchanted by a mermaid's song, and I'm hoping you'll give me another chance because I am completely, hopelessly, and utterly in love with you. You once said that we never own anything in this world, nothing is truly ours, but I am the exception to that rule. You've owned a piece of my heart since the moment I saw you. And despite how much I've criticised you for it, now I'm hoping you might recognise Ava and me for the lost and unwanted things we are and see fit to help us find a place where we belong again.'

I'd managed to stem the flow of tears for a few minutes but they're falling freely again and he squeezes my hand tightly and wordlessly reaches over with his other hand and holds out a tissue, but instead of the tears of sorrow they've been for the rest of the week, this time, they're tears of happiness that we still have a chance.

I know what it takes for him to say that. To open himself up enough to share these feelings with me when he *knows* all too well how vulnerable you become when you let someone know you love them, and that he cared enough to make himself that vulnerable, for me.

Suddenly, holding his hand is nowhere near enough, no matter how many people are watching. I get up and pull him to his feet too, and reach up until I can slide my arms around his neck and pull him down for a hug.

He makes a noise of surprise and it takes a moment for him to realise what's happening, and then he lets out a sigh and curls around me, his body enveloping mine and holding on tightly. My hair is in a messy bun at the back of my head and his hand tangles in it and pulls me closer as he buries his face in my shoulder.

'I didn't expect that.' He sounds as exhausted by this week as I feel. The juxtaposition of missing him so much and being so hurt by his words last weekend has been like a physical weight pressing down on me, and this hug is making it start to lift.

'You're well within your rights to tell me to sod off. I said some awful things the other day and I'm sorry.'

'I'm sorry too. I've never witnessed a teenage meltdown before and I could definitely have handled it better.'

He pulls back and cups my face, brushing his thumb along my jaw. 'It's safe to say that all three of us could have handled last Sunday a lot better.'

I think he's going to lean down to kiss me. His eyes flick to my mouth and back again, but he pulls away before going through with it.

I slide my hand over his forearm and pull him back towards the chair he's just got out of, ones that I'm fairly sure he's borrowed from the Colours of the Wind museum, and I sit down again too. 'You really mean everything you just said?'

Instead of answering, he reaches across the table and squeezes my hand until I look up at him, and he holds my gaze, and I realise what he's doing. He's letting me *see* every feeling he's just spoken so openly about. Emotions blaze though his beautiful blue eyes, and I *know* he is absolutely laid bare and he's trusting me not to hurt him.

'Oh, Ren...' I murmur, squeezing his hand so tightly that it must be painful. 'And Ava? She's okay with this? With *us*?'

'You have no idea how angry she was at me when she realised I'd ended things because of her. She's been threatening me all week, and just so you know, thirteen-year-olds are really creative when it comes to the threats they can make. You have to wonder where they learn these things.'

'I blame the parents – or the teachers.'

He laughs and then jiggles my hand, making me look at him again. 'Ava is incredibly sorry too. I was tossing and turning that night and she came into my room in tears because of what she'd said to you. She wanted to come and apologise the next day but I got this stupid idea and made her let me run with it.'

'And what about going forwards? I can't do this if you're going to break up with me every time Ava and I disagree about something. She's a young woman with her own opinions and values – this is unlikely to be the last time we'll ever clash.'

'Well, let's face it, Ava's thirteen. Things are only going to get worse from here on out. But I can say one thing – I *never* want to feel like I've felt this week ever again. I feel like my heart has been ripped out and trodden into the gravel we were standing on the other day. I even had a, "What's wrong with you, sir?" in class the other day. With everything with my ex, I prided myself on never showing it, never sharing it with anyone, never letting it affect me externally, but with you… I can't stop thinking about you and replaying last weekend and how I should have reacted differently. I've been a wreck this week.'

'So have I. I sobbed over that damn table being sold.'

He smiles, even though he probably knows full well it's not the first item I've cried over and it probably won't be the last.

'I don't want you to just be my girlfriend. I want you to be part of me. You are not someone I can walk away from. You're not disposable. Ava understands that too. If we're in this, we're in it for the long haul, all three of us. There *will* be arguments, disagreements, an unreasonable amount of sulking and door-slamming… and I'm not sure what she'll do, but probably worse.'

I laugh, appreciating his attempt at lightening the mood.

'But the one thing I do know is that I want you beside me. You make me see things in a different way, and Ava needs that. You bring joy and magic and love back into our lives and we *both* need that. So let's toast to it with a dragon fruit, which seemed like the most appropriate choice. You said you'd never tried one and I haven't either, but someone obviously loves the things.' He presses the toe of his boot against the base of the table. 'So they must be pretty good. To trying new things.'

'To finding someone who makes trying new things exciting rather than terrifying.'

'Exactly.' He slices the dragon fruit into quarters and offers me one. We each peel the skin off and hold up the soft white flesh full of black seeds and we clink them together like the finest champagne glasses, and then take a bite.

'Wow, that's…' he says around a mouthful.

I can feel my face screwing up in revulsion. 'Is that ripe?'

'I don't know. I never thought to check how you find out. Surely it's not *meant* to taste like that?'

The street is filled with our noises of disgust. Thankfully he thought to bring napkins so we can both spit out the offending fruit and deposit it in the nearest bin.

'Well, the thought was there.' I brush my hands off, even though it will take more than that to get rid of that particular taste. 'The metaphor about trying new things was a good one, just maybe not an unripe dragon fruit next time…'

'Maybe people should just stick to making tables in their likeness. On the plus side, it does mean your story is definitively untrue, because no one, and I do mean *no one*, would like this thing so much that they'd require a table made in its likeness.'

I burst out laughing and it's such a huge laugh of relief and I feel the weight that I didn't realise I'd been carrying all week floating away like airy balloons.

Ren gets to his feet and holds out a hand to pull me up and slips an arm around my waist. 'I'm not sure if I should be asking your forgiveness for my behaviour last week or for making you eat that. That was truly offensive.'

'You know what, it wasn't the worst experience I've ever had.' I lean back in his arms and reach up and stroke his hair back and when his eyes drift closed, I push myself up on tiptoes until I can touch my lips to his cheek. 'Mainly because it was with you. You have a way of making everything better than it is.'

'Ditto.' His eyes spring open and a smile spreads slowly across his face, making the sexiest little lines crinkle up under his eyes, and his eyebrows quirk in a way that asks silent permission before lowering his lips to mine.

It's a pressing, crushing kiss this time, that releases all the anguish of the past week and explodes, like a firework bursting in the sky, and then it turns gentle, a kiss that represents a mutual sigh of relief as the pretty colours float back down to earth, and it takes a long, long time until I feel like my feet have touched the ground again.

In fact, the only thing that makes me remember where we are is the sound of whooping and cheering from the shops on Ever After Street.

There's a clatter as The Wonderland Teapot door bursts open and Ava comes dashing across to us and throws her arms around me with such force that it nearly knocks me over and the momentum sends us both crashing into Ren.

I return her hug with just as much enthusiasm, thrilled to bits that she's okay and willing to move on after last week.

'I'm so sorry, Mickey, I was so horrible to you. I didn't mean anything I said.'

'It's okay.' I squeeze her even tighter. 'It was an uncharted situation and we both could've done better at it. Friends?'

I pull back and offer her my hand to shake, which she does and then pulls me into another hug. Her hair colour is fading already and I think we might have a battle on our hands to persuade Ren to let her get it done again during term time.

'I saw you k-i-s-s-i-n-g,' she sing-songs when she pulls back. 'You two are *sooooo* in love!'

'You know this doesn't change anything, right?' I say, because *this* is uncharted territory to me and I'm not sure how to handle it. 'I'm not going to try to be your mum or anything.'

'I don't want a new mum, I've got more than enough parental challenges to handle with my dad, but I *have* always wanted a really cool older sister...' She motions for me to come closer so she can whisper to me. 'Can you persuade him to let me get a puppy?'

'I heard that!' Ren says with an indignant laugh.

He looks so blissfully happy and as intoxicated as if the single bite of dragon fruit had been half a bottle of wine, and I'm filled with a rush of love. 'To be honest, he owes me for that dragon fruit, we could probably go for a puppy *and* a pony right now.'

He's laughing as he holds my gaze. 'It's a good job I love you.'

'I love you.' I stand back upright as I realise what I've said. It's the first time in so many years that I've said those words in a romantic way, but it feels so very, very right, and the butterflies that burst into existence when he clonked his head on a Victorian birdcage all those weeks ago are still alive and well and living their best life inside me.

'I love you too, Mickey. And you, Dad, even though you're my history teacher and you're *sooooo* embarrassing. Apart from today. Today you did good because you got Mickey back for us.'

I'm wiping tears from my eyes while giggling at the same time. 'How am I supposed to work after this? I'm an emotional wreck!'

'We can help, right, Dad? This means I can come and help *every* day, right?' Ava dances over to touch the blue scales of the mermaid's tail statue outside my shop window. 'I'm sorry the diary wasn't written by a real mermaid. I wish she really had been.'

'Me too, but it's okay. The diary brought us together, and maybe that was its real purpose. We've still got plenty of time to find proof that mermaids may once have existed.'

'Oh, *nooo*,' Ren groans jokingly, but in a probably-*not*-joking way.

'Maybe mermaids live not just in stories, but in the hearts of every person who stands on the shore and looks out at the ocean, wondering what might be out there, and that's all they were ever meant to be.' I grin at them both. 'And who knows, maybe one day, we *will* find proof that those stories are real.'

Ava squeals her agreement, and Ren puts his arms around us both and turns his head to murmur the words against my hair. 'I love this place.'

I'm not sure if he means Ever After Street or being between the two of us, but I agree on both counts. I love my place on this fairytale little street and I love these two gorgeous humans I'm lucky enough to call my own.

They say mermaids sing songs to find love, and somehow I managed to find it with a little help from a lighthouse keeper of so many years ago, who proves that, no matter how unlikely, sometimes your happy ending can burst into your life when you least expect it.

* * *

MORE FROM JAIMIE ADMANS

Another book from Jaimie Admans, *The Ginger Bread House in Mistletoe Gardens*, is available to order now here:

https://mybook.to/MisteltoeGardenBackAd

ACKNOWLEDGEMENTS

Thank you, Mum. Always my first and most important reader! I'm eternally grateful for your constant patience, support, encouragement, and belief in me. Thank you for always being there for me – I don't know what I'd do without you. Love you lots!

Marie Landry, my best friend, my absolute favourite spectacular nut and esteemed fellow house goblin! What a year, my friend, what a year. Thank you for still being the most caring, supportive, and loving friend, even while going through the worst time of your own. I love you, I'm *so* proud of you, and so honoured to wave the flag for the Welsh branch of Team Landry! Your mum would be so incredibly proud of you too, and *I'm* so proud to adopt her title of your #1 fan and supporter! Just remember – the horrors persist, but so do we!

Thank you to Bill, Toby, Cathie, and Bev for your continued love and enthusiasm. Thank you to Jayne Lloyd and Charlotte McFall for being such wonderful friends, and an extra special thank you to Becky Summer for the continual support and whole-hearted cheerleading, always!

I want to say a massive thank you to everyone who I chat to on social media, who I've connected with thanks to books, and to all of you who show me so much support and kindness on a daily basis. A big shoutout to some Facebook groups who support me tirelessly and are an absolute pleasure to be part of. A huge and heartfelt thank you to all the members and admins of Vintage Vibes and Riveting Reads, especially you, Sue Baker. All the bonkers ladies who try to keep The Friendly Book Community in line. Fiona Jenkins at the PMDD/Severe PMS Support & Information Group, and all the admins of Chick Lit and Prosecco, Book Swap Central, and Fiction Addicts at Socially Distanced Book Club. If you're a booklover looking for somewhere to brighten your day, lift your spirits, and make you feel like you've found a group of people who understand why we always buy more books even though we need scaffolding to hold up our current to-read pile, please find your way to these groups! You will be glad you did – although your to-read list may not!

Thank you to my fantastic agent, Amanda Preston, and my brilliant editor Emily Ruston, along with the rest of the wonderful and hardworking Boldwood team and the lovely Boldwood authors! It's a total joy to belong to Team Boldwood!

And finally, thank *you* for reading! I hope you enjoyed getting lost in this magical curiosity shop with Mickey and Ren, and hopefully got swept away in diary pages from days gone by! There's just one more book to go in the Ever After Street series, and I hope you'll join me as this journey comes to an end with Lissa in the Colours of the Wind fairytale museum! There are always many more happily ever afters to come!

ABOUT THE AUTHOR

Jaimie Admans is the bestselling author of several romantic comedies. She lives in South Wales.

Sign up to Jaimie Adman's mailing list for news, competitions and updates on future books.

Visit Jaimie's website: https://jaimieadmans.com/

Follow Jaimie on social media:

X x.com/be_the_spark
facebook.com/jaimieadmansbooks
instagram.com/jaimieadmans1

ALSO BY JAIMIE ADMANS

Standalone Novels

The Gingerbread House in Mistletoe Gardens

The Ever After Street Series

A Midnight Kiss on Ever After Street

An Enchanted Moment on Ever After Street

A Wonderland Wish on Ever After Street

Christmas Ever After

Finding Love at the Magical Curiosity Shop

BECOME A MEMBER OF

THE SHELF CARE CLUB

The home of Boldwood's
book club reads.

Find uplifting reads,
sunny escapes, cosy romances,
family dramas and more!

Sign up to the newsletter
https://bit.ly/theshelfcareclub

Boldw∞d

Boldwood Books is an award-winning fiction
publishing company seeking out the best
stories from around the world.

Find out more at www.boldwoodbooks.com

Join our reader community for brilliant books,
competitions and offers!

Follow us
@BoldwoodBooks
@TheBoldBookClub

Sign up to our weekly
deals newsletter

https://bit.ly/BoldwoodBNewsletter

Printed in Dunstable, United Kingdom

66683820R00170